Leeds to Christmas

For Kirkpatrick Dobie

Leeds to Christmas

John Cunningham

Polygon
EDINBURGH

© John Cunningham 1990
Polygon
22 George Square, Edinburgh

Set in Linotron Sabon
by Koinonia, Bury
Printed and bound in
Great Britain by
Redwood Press Ltd, Melksham, Wiltshire

British Library Cataloguing in
Publication Data
Cunningham, John
    Leeds to Christmas
    I. Title
    823.914 [F]

ISBN 0 7486 6086 0

The publisher acknowledges subsidy
from the Scottish Arts Council
towards the publication of this
volume.

That time in Leeds was my first away. On the train going home I recognised mountains and hills I'd never thought about, and was surprised to know their shapes. The voices on the station platform had been going on all the time . . .

It was four miles to our village. I had made that journey to school for years and knew every tree and gatepost. Mum's faded anorak showed through the garden hedge as the bus passed. I got off and walked back. She was busy at a flowerbed and I knew without seeing that she'd be putting weeds in a battered bucket, and wearing the suede shoes that weren't fit to be seen in. She stared with her mouth pulled in when I walked through the gate, as if it was a stranger. We met at the edge of the grass. Then she stood back smiling, and looked at my suitcase. I kissed her again.

'Come away in!' She glanced at the other houses, pulled off her rubber gloves and bustled to the door; her hobbling walk in the thick stockings was like any old woman. In Leeds I'd seen more people than ever before and some of her wasn't only her any more; looked at one way, she was an old woman with a hobbly walk and thick stockings. 'Tea?' She asked as if I might not still like it.

I sat in the old chair and heard the pop of the tea-caddy lid; and then, water gurgling into the brown pot. 'We'll let it infuse a minute' – this had been going on too. 'And tell me why we have this unexpected pleasure?' She talks in this comforting and irritating way. It was easy telling her, drinking tea and eating biscuits, as if we'd both quit the job.

I said I was going to look for work in Gledhill. She knew I

meant I would stay there too, though it's only an hour's bus ride; and perhaps she'd have liked to have me stay at home, but she was pleased I'd have something to tell Dad.

We met in the garage when he got back from school. He thought I was home for a weekend, but I explained the whole thing without letting him interrupt, including that I was going to Gledhill, and soon he was saying, 'Excellent, excellent!' He was relieved that I wouldn't be at home for long.

Mum talked while she cooked. And I ate a lot – their big son – it assured them I was alright. We sat at the fire and Dad played his fiddle. Probably he didn't play much now Helen and I were away, I thought that it hadn't been out for a bit, and this was an occasion.

We went to his study. I'd often come home in the evening from Mark's house and seen him through the window, leaning over his desk, the anglepoise lamp and the red bar fire shining. On the door and skirting were swirls of wood-imitation varnish. The usual pile of essays, bits with different writing sticking out, was corrected in his small, red writing.

'I'll look for something in the selling line,' I said.

'Would you be good at it?'

'I don't see why not.'

He closed his eyes. 'What would you sell?' He opened them. 'Anything. A rep.'

'What though? Machinery? Cosmetics?'

'Doesn't matter.'

'You should make a choice.' He closed his eyes again.

'I've no qualifications.'

'Hmph. See what you mean.' A pause. 'I suppose starting as a rep's the way to understand a business from top to bottom.' A flick of the eyebrow and quick smile. 'From bottom to top. Unless you start off making the tea.' I had seen the serious look in his eyes, though he went on smiling and talking in a light voice. 'It'll be interesting, selling. You've a brain. You never know, you *might* be a commercial genius!'

We were away in the clouds. He was cheering himself up after my failing the Business Course at the Tech and quitting in Leeds.

'I know most of the high heid yins, one way and another,' he said. 'Doubt if any of *them* had an education – what we'd call

2

one. You're well qualified for business!' He smiled, his eyes closed and he opened them at once, serious. 'Have to work though.'

I found digs in a three storey terraced house. Mr Fulton, short, fat, bald though not old, was at home. We went to the back of the house where the steep narrow stair, painted yellow including the handrail, rises to the small landing and this room (there is only this room up here, once for a maid). The glass pane over the landing leads into a loft, the true skylight in the roof letting the light down to this frosted lower pane where bluebottles crawled around the day Jack showed me the room.

'Come on downstairs,' he said and we went into the kitchen. 'Are you working?'

I told him I'd come to Gledhill to look for work.

'You'll be alright,' he said. This was generous. The other places I had tried wouldn't let a room to the unemployed.

'What do you do?' I asked.

'I'm a watchmaker.' He burst out laughing. 'I'm Jack.' We shook hands. I was swamped by his life pouring from his brown eyes. 'I often shut the shop and come home for a rest in the afternoon. I'm a lazy bugger.' I said I hoped I hadn't woken him and he said no he didn't sleep but read a book or watched the racing. He'd put the kettle on the big Aga stove and asked if I'd like a cup of tea. 'Toast?'

'Yes please.' While he was at the toaster he said in an offhand way what the room would cost. It seemed a lot, but included hot water and having my washing done; and later, though I didn't know at the time, my tea.

We took the tea and toast into a room where the TV was on: racing from Chepstow. He forgot me, staring at the horses and nodding at the comments of the TV guys. Nothing much happened, the horses lobbed round getting ready to start or waiting till it was time or something, but he said nothing, pushing the plate with the second slice of toast toward me with only a glance away from the screen. He sat back in his chair with his feet crossed in foreign leather shoes turned up at the toes, thick soles, walker's shoes, which gave him a prosperous

3

look. He wasn't the walking type, must have bought the shoes because he liked them.

The race started and the horses went along in the mist, rising over the fences at intervals always in the same order; the toast, a couple of bites from it, dangling in his fingers; they came round the last bend and began to go and the crowd shouted. At the finish he shot his arms in the air, toast waving. 'Wheee!'

'Did you have money on?'

'No! But I like to see them go! Great, great!' He flopped back as the winner, darkened with sweat and red of nostril, was led through the crowd and unsaddled, steaming.

'Right!' he said, leaning forward to switch off. 'To work! I'll give you a key for the back door Michael. You can come and go as you please.' He crammed the toast into his mouth as I followed him to the kitchen. 'I'll be seeing you,' he said and bounced away on the narrow flagstoned path round the house.

I went back to the room. It had a double gas ring and an electric kettle, a few plates and mugs and so on under the sink. I ran to the nearest shop, the general store, where the man looked at me, buying matches, coffee, bread, marg and tins of beans, knowing I'd be moved in somewhere, but he didn't ask.

I drank the coffee black because I'd forgotten milk, and ate some bread. That day I needed to eat in the room, to get to know it, though I wasn't hungry. The ceiling followed the shape of the roof, not as far as the apex, the middle being filled in at a lower level. The slope came down so that I couldn't stand upright near the walls. At a point halfway out from the wall I could bump the edge of my skull on the ceiling, standing upright. The ceiling and walls weren't original or ancient. They rang hollow and were only plasterboard but I'd never had a room like it.

I sat on the bed looking at the walls, the dusty floorboards and the threadbare Indian rug; the tall brass light at the bed-side which was tarnished and from which a plaited flex crept over the edge of the table. I couldn't believe my luck. At the back the gardens were separated by high brick walls. Next door a tree had been lopped of its branches leaving stumps, like the dead trees in the cages at the zoo where the eagles live. There was a lane at the end of the gardens, dividing us from similar gardens and rough stone house-backs with tatty windows.

I was going out, but heard the glassy shudder of the front door, and then soft footfalls on a tile floor, a woman's step, it must be Mrs Fulton. So I stayed where I was because she might not know I was in the house. Likely she wouldn't, and the longer I waited the more difficult it would be to break my silence. She was in the kitchen below; if a board creaked I'd have to start coughing and humming and clattering downstairs as if I hadn't been standing like a statue and not breathing. She left the kitchen and went to the front of the house.

I could creep down and let myself out the back door with my key. Or go down noisily and unlock the door slowly as if I didn't know she was in the house.

She went into the bathroom and I waited till she came out; then waited till the cistern had filled, because I wouldn't have been able to hear her and she wouldn't have heard me.

Then I walked down the stair and was facing the back door. Hearing nothing I went along the passage to the left past the kitchen and bathroom, to the entrance hall. It was quite dark, I'd been sitting up there a long time, and I didn't want to go further without putting on a light. In the room with the TV the screen glimmered in the light from outside, there were tall windows and dark curtains pulled aside, a piano, plants in pots on the floor, a big dark picture. I could see all this without moving. I felt her watching me, from another doorway.

'I heard you,' I said.

She didn't answer for maybe several seconds.

'Here we both are creeping about!' She walked forward and held out her hand. 'I'm Barbara. I knew you were here – he actually phoned me this time.' She gave a small laugh and stood close to me holding my hand and it seemed natural because it was quite dark and we couldn't have seen each other otherwise. Her face was pale. She had green-brown eyes but maybe I knew that later. 'Come through.' She let go my hand and put on the light in the kitchen. 'I suppose you're Michael,' she said, mocking, joking as if it should have been my turn. 'Can I make you a coffee?' There was a slight accent, from the films, from outside ordinary life, but I didn't hear it again that day and everything was as ordinary as it could be. We sat at the table. She swung her foot, an ordinary foot in a flat shoe, then

5

her ankle and calf in black tights of a heavy, winter, no-nonsense kind.

'No thanks,' I said when she offered sugar. 'It's good coffee.'

'Neescaff.'

She told me later that she said it that way because she'd heard it mispronounced in a grocer's shop and thought it very funny. That was like her, taking up a joke, and not a good one, and keeping on with it in a kind of sneering way, chewing it long after the taste had gone.

'I like the room,' I said.

She smiled. 'The best room in the house. The rest are square and ordinary.'

'Have you lived here long?'

'Since we were married. Fourteen years. William's thirteen.' She sighed at her cup, her face hanging over it.

'I'm looking for work.'

'I hope you find it quicker than the last two yobbos. A pair of deadbeats, one after the other.'

'In the room?'

She nodded and continued to stare gloomily downwards, her face heavy, as if pressed down by the weight of her hair, the colour of rhubarb-and-ginger jam; as she breathed it glinted in the light from above. She looked up and smiled, a change she seemed to manage easily. 'What sort of work?'

'I don't know.'

'I'm a teacher,' she said. 'That's where I was. I teach disadvantaged children. Part-time. It brings in a bit of lolly.' She was putting on indifference. 'He phoned the school. Good of him. That's how I knew you were here – might be here.' She looked at me steadily.

The back door opened and two children rushed into the kitchen. A thin nervous-looking boy and a girl with a pigtail and large ears.

'This is William and Stephanie,' Barbara said, 'and Michael, our new lodger.' They both said how-do-you-do and I wondered if they went to a private school.

Barbara's eyes seemed to be greener as she looked at them.

'It was rotten, Mum,' the boy said. They were picking biscuits out of a tin and the girl had gone to the fridge for a carton of orange juice. Glowering at her brother she filled a mug with juice, grabbed a couple of biscuits and I heard the thump of her feet on the main stair. He soon followed, Barbara calling after him, stretching towards the door, that tea would be ready at half past six.

'Will you have tea with us?'

'No thanks,' I said – and that I was going to meet a friend. I noticed while telling her this lie that her ears were quite large too but because of her hair they didn't stand out like her daughter's from that pale freckled face.

'They aren't usually as late as this. They stay for music on Thursday.'

After a bit I asked, 'Do you play the piano – yourself?' She twitched her mouth. 'Used to.'

'The piano's for Stephanie,' I said.

'William. Steph plays the cello.'

I hitched my knee against the table edge. I'd run out of conversation. I wanted a biscuit but didn't ask or take one from the tin on the table.

'What will you do about food? Can you cook?'

'Yes.'

Bella stepped back and let me into the room where George had been last time. He wasn't there.

'He's through in the kitchen.' She went round me, where I stood at the door, to the fire, and turned her back to it as if she was cold, standing right up against it. Lines round her mouth showed through the powder when she licked her red lips, and her hair was fluffy and soft; she seemed to be waiting, but not for me. Since George's brother, her husband, had died, and George had come to stay with her, she'd been looking for a man. He'd told me before I went away that he should have stayed on his own but it was too late because he'd sold his house. She seemed much too old and it was disgusting. 'Go on through,' she said, tapping a long ash from her cigarette over the fireplace tiles.

The kitchen's pale-green walls and fading light through the net curtain gave it an underwater look. There was no-one there. On the table was a partly eaten plate of pie, beans and chips. He'd be in the toilet or the garden – but there was a cough.

He'd been hidden by the dresser, tucked between it and a cabinet, his feet up on the rail of the chair, hands folded on his stomach, and wearing his jacket and cap.

'George!'

'Michael. How're ye?'

'I'm back. Living in Gledhill.'

'Job no work out?'

'No.' He was ill, knackered, and there was no reason to say it, but I added, 'I'm looking for a job here.' I put my hand on his arm, not keeping all the annoyance out of my voice: 'You're not so well?'

'Aye. No.'

I leant on the table. It slid away and I pulled it back. Some of the pie had been eaten and the fork beside the plate had pastry on the prongs. I looked at the plate and at him but he ignored it. 'I'll show you out the back,' he said, unhitching his feet from the rail and gripping the furniture either side for support. He didn't want to be helped off the chair.

He stopped in the doorway holding the jambs; then stepped carefully down three concrete steps. There was a square of grass where Bella hung the washing, and the vegetables. We went along a path between swelling sprouts and dark earth where tatties had been lifted. I wondered if she'd had the doctor to him.

'Nephew does it . . . comes twice a week.' He paused, and belched.

'If you want a hand . . . '

'Worst thing's the fucking cats. Shoot the buggers.'

'Like you used to!' When we did the gardens he'd bring an airgun and pot at them for sport as well as to scare them off from digging up the gardens, and I'd get annoyed, specially if we were in our village and I knew the cats.

He pushed back his cap. Beads of sweat sprinkled his white forehead. 'Gave them a scare just.' He stared at the rows of vegetables, far more than they could eat, and he might have been anywhere for all he saw of them or me. He was not thinking about cats.

8

I moved to stand in front of him and flicked a dandelion root off the path with the side of my shoe. 'Is your nephew taking over? Your round, I mean, the gardens?'

'Eh! . . . he drives for the Co-op, Chrissake.'

'I thought maybe –'

'The gardening job was part-time, man, for a retired fellow. No worth him giving up a good job driving!' He looked at me as if I was mad.

'I'm looking for something. Maybe I could work it up.'

'You wouldna could do it boy.' He said that because he was ill, because he couldn't take a hand, because of the trouble in his stomach – but it was bad all the same.

'Er – has he got your van?'

'Sold it.' George's mouth clapped shut suddenly, with the trouble in his stomach.

I had been happy when I came over the bridge from the centre of Gledhill. I'd found somewhere to stay and all I had to do was see old George and get work. And though I'd said selling to Dad, and liked the idea myself, it seemed easier to take up the gardening again for a start. That seemed obvious. I'd stopped on the bridge for a while, leaning over the parapet still warm from the sun, to see the water lying low, between white-rimmed banks; out from them hung branches and rags of grass, the height of the last flood. I'd watched for a shadow or stone to turn into a trout lying in the current, but nothing had moved in the brown water that looked shallow from up there except a shoal of minnows spreading and clustering over a patch of sand, so I'd left the warm stone, and gone through new schemes to the old one, where the houses are all behind the same green hedges and have roses in their gardens. George's had a row of parsley against the house. I hadn't thought what to say. He'd be glad of help and he was getting old. I was going to get a job with him alright, that's what I'd thought.

'Passed my test,' I told him.

'First time was it?'

'Second.' I nodded. With no van to drive, I'd only told him because it had been in my head when I came.

He nodded too. He was giving in to this illness. He was going to die.

We looked at the vegetables silently. He'd have flipped open a packet of cigarettes and watched the woman next door stretch to unpeg her washing in the old days.

When I hadn't known him long and we were eating our sandwiches, when I was younger, he'd said, 'There's one, eh?' and I'd looked across the road and seen Mrs Harris. They came to our house sometimes, Mr and Mrs Harris and the daughter whose name I'd forgotten at that moment in front of George's sprouts. We were friendly with them. But Mrs Harris was different this time, sauntering in a shiny open mac, high heels, and turning her head about, making her sleek hair move on her shoulders. 'She gets about, that one!' George said, and slapped my knee. 'She'd learn you, that one!' Then he'd said, 'Aye but – she's got a daughter, wee fizzer, home from school in Edinburgh, Michael, you'd do alright with her Michael. One apiece, eh? What do you say, eh? Harris is away making his millions.' He drove down the street and parked at her house. We went round the back and he knocked. She'd taken off the mac and was in the clothes she'd have worn to tea at our house, but still different; she nodded to George, and it seemed normal for him to be at her door, and said, 'Hallo, Michael.' Another world. I was meeting her in another world.

'Me and the boy. We're in the area,' George said.

Her face was like his in some way. She stood at her half-open door, resting her weight on one leg and swaying, maybe not swaying.

'No thanks, George,' she said after this long time, and shut the door.

He whistled as we went away. 'Had a man in there for Chrissake. How does she manage it!'

'Eh?'

'Saw his foot round the door, man, sitting at the kitchen table there.' He looked up and down the street. 'No car. Crafty bugger's parked out of sight.'

'Maybe a friend?'

'Pffft! That'll be right!' He strode to the van, and I gazed into space, meaning to be cooler next time.

'She's no for boys!' he'd said with a grin, contradicting himself. Was he just winding me up? Surely not Mrs Harris. The daughter, Emma her name was, was maybe still at school.

I'd cut the lawn very straight at the next place, my head whirling. From then on our village hadn't been the same. She wouldn't like him now, Mrs Harris, the bitch.

'Shoot the buggers,' he said again. 'See, that's their pad.' He pointed to part of the garden fence. 'Through where that broken stick is, the buggers,' he slurred. They were too much for him, the cats.

'I'll need to go soon,' I said, moving towards the house. I touched his arm and in this way, my hand on his arm but not round it, we got a few yards along the path. It was not right, leaving him in the garden.

'I'm fine here.' He turned from my hand.

I went round the house, avoiding Bella, and away.

A Joiner and Builder had advertised a driving job on a card in the window of the paper shop.

Their yard was on the edge of town beside a railway and a big neat fellow was there, cap on his grey hair, ears small and close to his head. He wore a boilersuit and brown boots – the boss, Mr Crawford. Had I a clean driving licence? The job was part-time – a bit of driving one day, maybe more in a while, then none of course when the regular man who was sick came back. His manner was easy-going.

I said that was okay.

'Not want to know how much you'll be paid?'

I shrugged to let him know it was alright, and he told me a sum. Then he kept me and asked where I was from, what my Dad did, what my 'career' was. That happens, everyone's nosey here; our village is thirty miles from Gledhill and the guy wanted to know it all till he'd placed me in the web of others he knew, and knew about. He named people and asked if I knew them. I'd gone to Leeds to get away from this and here I was back in it. In the end he went to his office, coming out a moment later with a line and telling me to go to a certain yard.

We were standing by the truck and I hoped he'd go away before I had to drive out of the narrow space in the yard. He went in again. He trusted me with his truck and hadn't seen me drive – it seemed to be a test. He seemed to interest himself in me.

At the builders' merchant I handed over my line. I was given

11

a typed order for Harry in the yard. A man resting on a heap of pipes told me to back up to a loading ramp. As I went to the truck he was whistling and had begun trundling stuff with a sack barrow and stacking it at the ramp.

I found the reverse gear and curved in first time not knowing where I was relative to obstacles but hitting nothing. With no time to think I piled everything on as he brought it. He was wheeling forward drums of Snowcem on the silent rubber-tyred barrow and he said, 'You've still your pipes.'

'I'll have to come back for them.'

'No. Here.' He got onto the truck. 'Shift that forward. Put your Snowcem along the edge.' I rearranged the load while he watched. 'Right now. Draw your motor over there and I'll give you up the pipes.' These short pipes for some kind of drainage were slippery. 'Here,' Harry said, heaving himself slowly up again. He stacked them. When that was done he took papers out of his top pocket, handed me a green one, stuffed the yellow back in and swung to the ground.

'Show me how to tie the rope!' I called. My reputation here was zero anyway and I didn't want the load sliding off in the middle of the town.

He waited for me to get the coils of rope from the cab. The drivers in Leeds had roped their loads in a secretive way and I'd never seen how they did it. He looped it the same quick way, untied the hitch he'd made and handed me the straight rope. I twisted it about hoping to hit on the right combination of loops, but it fell apart when I pulled; so he guided my hands till I'd made a proper hitch and tightened a rope over the front of the load.

I moved to the back and made a hitch on my own. 'Thanks Harry.'

'Dennis,' he said, pointing at himself and grinning.

I was afraid he'd pulled a trick and the ropes would come loose in the town, but the load was steady as I reached the slope up to Crawford's, and I saw that he wouldn't have done that.

The yard stretched along the railway embankment, surrounded by a high wire fence like a secret government place. Inside the double gates, on the left, was the office, a Nissen hut with a door in the middle of its long side where a white board

12

stuck out with 'Office' written in black. The hut itself was painted grey and rust showed through. On the right were stacks of pipes, paving stones and building material, and straight ahead with its back to the railway stretched a long wooden building of different styles, like a row of shacks joined together. I swung left at the end of the Nissen hut to where the truck had been parked before.

There was no-one in the yard. A van that had been there was gone. The silence meant it was tea-break. I hadn't brought anything, and stayed in the cab. I didn't have to think because I was temporary, entitled to wait till someone told me what to do next.

The end of the yard behind the Nissen hut, where it narrowed as the road slanted toward the railway, had a row of concrete pens against the embankment, with sand and gravel and other stuff in them. One was stacked with logs three or four feet long and another with railway sleepers. A fork-lift truck the same as I'd used in Leeds stood beside the pens, and behind them the railway embankment was covered with willowherb leaning over and gone to seed, the fluffy white seeds floating and stuck in the wire-mesh fence.

A tap on the passenger window suddenly. An old man. I leant over and wound down the window.

'Over to the ramp, son.' He crossed the yard and climbed some steps onto a stage in front of the long wooden building. I drove to it, swaying at the potholes.

We unloaded without saying who we were, just remarks about the drums of Snowcem and so on. He pointed to a stack of pipes similar to mine and I moved the truck; we unloaded them and some concrete things, and that was the truck empty.

'You better go and see Annie,' he said, coiling the rope and putting it in the cab, and as he'd nodded towards the office, that's where I went.

Inside, two more doors, one with chinks of light showing. I opened it and faced a wooden counter. A large woman sat behind it holding a biro, her arm lying on the counter – a fat pink arm with the flesh tied in at her wrists and elbows like a baby's.

'I'm Michael. What will I do now?' I said, looking past her. Behind her hills of shoulders and black hair the place was bare

13

and light blue. On the brick end there was a school-type clock, above a chair and desk. There were windows in the curving tin sides and under one of them a bench with a kettle and cups on it.

'He says you've to help Peter,' she said in a timid voice. She hadn't moved.

The heat was stifling, an electric fire was burning. I leant on my side of the counter. She had not been writing, at least there was no paper to have written on. Close up she was not so big, but very broad. There were blue channels and cross-grain lines and circles scored in the counter with the biro. She saw me looking and frowned.

'I'll go back out then,' I said.

We were filling a honeycomb of boxes up the wall in the long wooden building with nails of various sizes from the packages I'd delivered.

'Are you Peter?'

'Aye.' He seemed pleased, he smiled and looked even healthier, a blue-eyed, red face over a tartan lumberjack shirt. He'd rolled up his sleeves and there were a few short hairs on his hard forearms as if the rest had been worn off. I asked had he worked at the yard long. He'd worked here all his days, and now he was retired and still working here. He pulled out a watch and frowned at it in his hard palm – seeing it was five to twelve he put it in his pocket, pulled the sticky tape off another packet of nails, and we worked the five minutes.

I ran to a shop and bought rolls and a can of coke.

Through the other door in the Nissen hut a passage ran against the edge of the hut so that I walked curved to the left. Half-way along, another door in the hardboard wall; sellotaped on, a big calendar several years old of a girl in a bikini crouching beside a tin of paint, big tits hanging over it as she held the brush. The frostproof store and the toilet were in there, I found out later. At the end of the passage a door was marked tearoom, freehand in white with an inch brush, the green door showing through the letters. Peter sat with his elbows on the table. There was another bench at the side.

'That you back?' He was probably deaf and hadn't heard me in the passage. I sat with my knees sideways as they wouldn't fit under the bench. 'Aye,' Peter said, bringing out a tobacco tin and laying it on the table. He rolled a cigarette

14

while I ate, and he glanced at the coke. 'Want a cup of tea? She gives me plenty.' He grinned and brought a huge flask up from a bag on the floor, filled the two cups and handed one across. It was strong, milked and sugared.

He rolled another cigarette and made a slight gesture with the tin before he shut it, in case I was a smoker. He stowed it in his pocket. Near the end of the cigarette he scratched the back of his grey hair making a bristly sound and drew on the butt as if it was delaying him, but smoked it down till it glowed on his stained fingernails. The watch came out. He was looking out of the window, a small high one in the end wall from where you just saw sky. The truck was out there but the window was too high to see it. I finished my tea quickly and we went out at five to one.

Old Peter was pathetic with the boss who'd come across to where we were working. He did this imitation of a busy man even though he was busy. But a real job came – a wagon rolled in at four o'clock loaded with breezeblocks; for some reason they weren't palleted and we had to hump them off. I put on the rubber gloves Peter gave me, to please him, but was soon glad of them, the way the blocks scraped above the glove. We were taking them from the driver and building them into a stack. About chest high Peter winced at each lift.

'You get on and build. I'll throw them up,' I said. He climbed the stack dourly and I began throwing them up, swinging them up good style in a steady rhythm, using the weight to fly them up. The boss was going back and forward between the office and the workshop and his many trips could have been to watch us.

Peter brought out the watch when we finished and seemed satisfied. I offered to hand him down from the high stack.

'I'll get down myself,' he said, seeming to not want to touch my hand.

He came down backwards with his skinny old bum stuck out while I was taking the driver's line to the office. I was sweating heavily.

'You've been working!' Annie said, jokey and different with the boss there. The boss wrote and figured with quick flicks of his big hands and I imagined his figures.

'That's it finished. Anything for tomorrow?' I asked.

15

He looked at me as if the question, my asking it, was interesting. He held up his finger to me to wait, lifted the old black phone on the desk under the clock and talked into it about things that meant nothing to me. Annie was sorting through a drawer as if to have something to do. Something was going on, whatever it was, being decided bit by bit, about me.

'I want you to pick up some timber at Bond's tomorrow. Mrs Curran'll give you the line.'

Collecting the timber was followed by other work. I parked the truck each evening at the end of the Nissen hut, over the black stained ground, checked its oil and water and wiped the wing mirrors. And there was a pay packet at the end of the week. The boss was away and Annie, Mrs Curran, told me to come back on Monday.

Milkmen and postmen and paperboys and people going to work were in the streets of Gledhill, and I was one of them.

In the yard they were loading their vans. An old joiner and two younger ones sometimes made things in the workshop but today they were setting out on a job. A brickie and a slater – I'd delivered bricks and stuff to where they were working – threw bags of cement in the back of a pick-up and drove off. 'Give Peter a hand,' the boss shouted, diving into the office.

Peter was revving the forklift with a pallet of bricks hoisted. He had one pallet onto the truck, with its corner hanging over the edge. His face was all bunched up and he stopped and climbed off when he saw me, leaving the engine roaring.

'I canna work the bugger!' he shouted.

I could work these things, I'd done it in Leeds, no bother. I shut down the engine and found a line stuck in the dash and finished the load with more of the pallets of bricks bound with metal bands. 'Well done boy!' Peter shouted.

I went to the office and the boss was away again. 'Where does he want me to take it?' I asked, not liking to call her Annie. She gave me an address. Then I'd taken a couple more loads after that. In between whiles, when I'd come back to the yard, Peter was sweeping up round the stacks of material, and I wondered if he'd been asked to do this. It seemed totally

16

useless, and was more likely his mania for keeping busy. I
didn't want to upset his routine. From parts of the yard you
could see Annie seated at her counter, against the light from
the opposite window. A majestic flowing shape, a small bump
of a nose, a buddha. From that end of the hut a stovepipe
poked up from the roof, no stove below it, with its squint tin
hat to keep out the rain. Possibly she was a fortune-teller.

She would certainly know secrets, but she was pretending to
be ordinary when I went in. 'He wasn't expecting you till
dinnertime. He's not back,' she said. It was eleven o'clock.

'I'll go for something to eat.'

She flowed sideways, her hand went below the counter and
brought up a black bag. It was on her lap and she rummaged
in it. 'Here son,' she said, holding over the counter a slice of
cherry cake.

I didn't take it right away and she reached further over, to
put it in my hand which had moved forward. While she did this
she looked aside with her head slightly down, level with her
raised hand, as if giving the cake was everything.

I thanked her and took it out in the sun and sat on a pile of
railway sleepers, giving off a smell of creosote, summery
although it was autumn, and the cherries melted the cake
around them with their sweetness. My hands and face were
sticky after I'd eaten them. No reason to help Peter because I
was the stop-gap truck driver, at the moment without instruc-
tions. I could only wait. The man I replaced hadn't been
mentioned. Perhaps nobody liked him or he was so well
known for being off that it wasn't worth a remark. It could be
years since he'd been fit to work and there had been a string of
temporary drivers.

The boss was going to tell me the job was finished. That was
maybe the funny atmosphere in the office at the end of the
week. I didn't do anything except wait; it was a time to wait,
if he gave me the boot there was cash for a while. I'd have liked
to do gardens but I didn't know what was going to happen
about George, and there was no chance of starting on my own
without tools or money; and he'd sold the old van.

The boss drove into the yard. I stayed on the sleepers. I
couldn't decide if it should be Mr Crawford or Andy. He
stepped smartly out of his van in his boilersuit, as if he made a

thing of physical fitness. He was in good shape compared with Dad's bent and bony frame. They'd be around the same age. He strode toward me in such a way as to pin me down. I stayed where I was. I wasn't going to argue.

'Finished?'

'Yes.'

'Um . . . '

I had to walk about the yard with him, both of us looking for a way to dismiss me; for the words, and a place where they'd come naturally.

'Uh – ' he started, resting his hand carelessly on paving stones. 'You like the work here?'

'It's alright.'

'Haven't thought you were wasting yourself?'

I shrugged.

He took a grip on the pavers and looked solemn. 'I'm going to offer you a job. A good one.' His voice came out low as if he was choking. 'Taking over from me, in a sense.' He paused a long while.

What! A trap! Like Mark, into the bookshop from school for life . . . that was probably better than straight on the dole; lying in bed; drunk on giro-day; vanishing. But this! Not for all the tea in China, Dad's words I was never going to say . . . 'I prefer driving.'

'Come on, you can do better for yourself! Look, I'll tell you what the situation is.' His voice was level and friendly now he was started. (I thrilled at being talked to in this way in spite of myself.) 'I'm going to take things easier, a bit easier' – he widened his eyes – 'expanding my interests and so on, and I need someone in the office here. You've a head on your shoulders and the job's straightforward. I like the way you go about things' – a shrug – 'it's just ordering, seeing you don't run out, knowing what we're going to need, that kind of thing. Main thing's not to be held up on a job because you haven't got the stuff. A child could do it! No no, I didn't mean that!' He laughed for a while. 'You'll make mistakes at first, but – '

'Is the other driver coming back, or what?'

'Eh? No, no. No. I'm not needing him. You can drive when it's needed. There'll not be much of it.' He looked at me as if I should understand.

18

'I don't want an office job.'

'You'll be out as much as in! Peter's not up to much now.'

I don't want it, Mr Crawford.'

'Call me Andy, eh, mhmm. You'll be getting a wage I may tell you. A clonking good one. More than it should be, but the job'll grow to it.' I'd no idea what he meant. I asked how much. '£150 a week.'

An enormous sum. My God. My head spun, I was at £200 in my mind already, rich rich rich – wanting it more than anything, the money.

'Will I show you what to do, then?'

'Ach, I dunno.'

'The way it's worked out, you've been lucky.' He made it seem nothing to do with him.

I couldn't refuse, and followed him to the office; I hadn't decided yet. (The money wasn't as good as the thought of it, I found after a week or two.) I felt wonderfully greedy. Why was it so bad with money? It could have been chocolate, quite okay.

Anyway, following him to the office, there was Peter between the stacks. He'd been listening. He was beside a coil of yellow pipe and staring alertly into the distance, except that the railway embankment was right across his vision; a listening look was all over him. The old guy was slightly uncanny. The boss – Andy! – had picked the wrong square in the chessboard, Peter was cunning, he knew the place like his home.

'I've told Annie about this,' the boss said. 'She's away for her lunch.' The room was different, looking from his desk. A calendar hung out from the wall above the cups at an odd angle, because of the curve. 'I'll get you a desk. You can sit here meantime,' he was saying. He might have upped the wage a bit because I was reluctant, and I gave myself credit for bargaining, in this way easing myself into the position of accepting the job.

A light-coloured path with round footshapes had been worn in the dark wood floor, from the flap that lifted in the counter to Annie's chair. I listened for where I had to put in a yes or a no; there was nothing to it, the job; I'd not be hooked on it like Mark, loving his books in a nasty old man way, I'd walk out, anytime, anytime. It was difficult to believe it, the job, The Job!

The records he showed me were simple, how would I fill the day? And Annie; us sitting with our backs to each other. I asked what she did and how it fitted my, ah, what I'd be doing.

'You'll get on grand. She won't bother you. She does the accounts and pay and answers the phone – done it for years, she'll keep you right.'

'Yes but . . . will you be here at all?'

'I'll be here quite often. Yes. Any time you want me. But I'm not going to be tied down you understand.' He rubbed his chin and frowned. 'There's not a lot of work on at this moment in time, you might think Annie could do it. But it'll get more – and I'll tell you what – needs a man! She wouldn't want it, she's got her bit. And as I said you'll soon have enough to do. You'll soon have enough.'

He described the rest of the work. There was a file for each firm we dealt with in a filing cabinet beside us, and the stock lists as well, and bundles of paper, brown at the edges.

He drew forward a pad and calculator: 'Here we need roofing washers . . . we need rhone bolts . . . we need glass. Imagine it's you. You go and check in the store that it tallies with what's here – we'll assume you've done that – then work out how many more of whatever it is you want. So, just at random . . .' He wrote, perfectly formed figures and letters – I'd expected them to be awkward. 'Now total the quantities.' He prodded the calculator as if it worked mechanically. 'And get on the blower. Here's the phone numbers. I'll write at each number who you've to speak to. Monday morning off you go. Okay?'

'You want me to start, then?'

'Yes!'

'Would it be okay if it was a trial period?'

'I suppose so.'

'And, er, when um, if I'm writing a letter or something, does . . . do I get Annie to type it or what? Do I dictate to her?' I laughed.

'Oh no. No, she – just do it out in pencil, I mean – or tell her what you want. She knows the letters.' He stretched, blowing out his cheeks. 'Come and I'll show you over there.'

He ran up the steps of the wooden ramp. 'Railway sleepers,' he said, stamping on the scarred boards. 'Been here twenty-five years. Twenty-five. We got them when they closed the line. Do

20

another twenty-five.' The building took advantage of a slope so that it was dug into the bank behind and level with the ramp in front. The first part was concreted, with machinery bolted to the floor. 'Drew and me built this in 1963. Just the sawbench then, the same one.' He touched the dark blade and it turned slowly, rippling the reflection of the floor. 'Whenever I bought a new machine, we set it up. Then concreted the whole thing. Much better. Same old roof.'

'Did you build it all yourselves?'

'Aye, of course!'

I'd forgotten they were joiners. It was well made, you could see how it all fitted together, and there was a band-saw, a lathe, and a planing machine as he explained – I didn't know what they were – and other light-green machines shining dully under the high cobwebbed roof, light coming through clear sheets that had gone yellow. From the machines grey jointed tubes led to the control boxes with red and green buttons. I ran my hand over the steel surface of the planing machine. These machines had all been used a lot, like in an old, busy kitchen where everything was used. I looked at the band-saw's vertical ribbon of toothed steel. 'She's deadly,' he said, 'but efficient. Better than the old buzz-saw.' He went back to it, and spun one of the wooden rollers.

I knew the place like somewhere I used to live; as if I'd got into his life through a warp and it was mine too.

'This is not the part for you, I'm just showing it you!' He laughed.

In the store: 'Second-hand,' he said, 'we had to do it on the cheap. The windows are out of a village hall and the roof's off the old prisoner-of-war camp.' The windows stretched along the front, with a workbench underneath. The back wall had been patched with boards. 'Prefab floors.' The boarded-over holes were toilets, wastepipes, fireplaces.

The wall had been painted with the shapes of axes, shovels, saws, hammers and other tools; the nails were there to hang them on, but no tools. 'Fine when it was Drew and me, but when we took on the young boys . . . '

I was looking at the painted shapes.

'That was me. Now here's the stuff you need to know about.' It was the honeycomb of boxes I'd filled with Peter. When we'd done that he explained a big rack of different sizes

21

of timber, each section inked-in on the cross strap with what it contained. And there were rolls of roofing felt, netting and many other things on the floor. Really he didn't need to tell me. I'd taken it in at a glance and knew where everything was. The last building in the line was for bigger items, such as corrugated iron near the sliding door and a rack of glass and a felt-covered table. 'Cutting table,' he said.

The job had changed from just figures in the office. I saw myself coming in here and cutting glass, or making things in the workshop in the smell of sawdust and shavings – a moment I go back to, when it appeared I could have done those things.

I did two deliveries with the truck that afternoon.

Switching off, I heard the scrape of Peter's brush and found him sweeping an alley between the stacks. Sritt, sritt, sritt. In the earth between the stones weeds were only temporarily flattened. I'd watched him already. The debris would be swept onto his wide shovel in a clean whoosh of the brush, taken to the dump; useless work. But what was he thinking of my job!

'What do you think, Peter?' I asked.

He gazed into the distance, somewhere about my chest. He looked down. 'Uh-hu,' he said, and brushed the bare-clean ground a couple of times; turning from down there, to face the tearoom: 'Aye, it'll be yon time likely.' He started in its direction, whistling. I leant forward there with a grin a fool.

The corridors had a lot of glass like the hospitals on TV. I'd expected the Gledhill one to be old-fashioned and another thing was the heat. The last fresh air had been outside and I was on the third floor. I asked a nurse where Ward 9 was. She had green eyes and pale skin and I realised she was the same one I'd asked when I came in, but she gave no sign of recognition. She must have come up a different way.

Inside Ward 9 were four, two- and one-bedded rooms. I peered at the unrecognisable figures, wondering if one was him, but knew him at once. He was in a room by himself.

'George, it's Michael. How are you?'

He was sitting against the pillows in blue-striped pyjamas, and his eyes looked the same except bluer and that's what made me think at first he might recover. The rest of his face was yellow instead of red. His ears had turned into big, joke-shop, rubber ears. The great yellow nose that used to be boozy and red as a strawberry seemed to keep from rotting by being bathed with the spirit that smelt everywhere. He had a plastic band on his wrist.

The chair was awkward, my face close to the rough sheet and twisted sideways to look at him. I shifted to sit on his high bed, almost standing. His smile was shy, him of all people. I started yakking. 'It was temporary to begin with but now it's permanent,' I said. 'Kind of yard manager.'

'For Andy Crawford?' George raised his eyebrows.

I went on, 'I've been driving, getting the hang of the town, delivering to their building sites. I was past your garden, it looked fine. Your carrots are lifted – will Bella want a hand at all? I'll call in.' I couldn't stop.

He mumbled and was turning to the bedside locker. I went round and he said again and this time I caught it, 'They have these bloody . . . ' He was pawing, his hand useless, at the stuff on top of the locker. I shuffled through papers and magazines, he meant the hospital menu. 'Aye, that bloody thing. I want mince and tatties.' He looked really sad about it.

On the hospital lawns were beds of fleshy red and pink roses. Over them the sky was grey, a mild Saturday afternoon. The clouds seemed to carry the smell of damp earth in the rose beds and I was mad to get out there. The air of the hospital, compared to out there, was dry and horrible. Next to the grounds a field with tufty grass and cows was edged by houses whose long back gardens stretched into it. I'd been to the nearest house. I remembered the tree in the garden vividly.

'Hey George! That house out there.' His eyes turned to me but he didn't move his head to look out of the window. I tapped his arm through the sheet to make him turn, but he continued to look at me. 'I used to play there when I was a kid,' I told him loudly. 'Friends of Mum or something.' I recognised the glass door to the garden which I'd not expected to see again and certainly not from here because we'd thought it was some kind of office block although people called it the hospital – recognised it and knew it didn't interest him, I should have kept my mouth shut. 'We were climbing that big pear tree in the corner, and the boy shouted not to knock the pears off. I'd climbed highest and he was fed up. They were some kids we didn't know. We just went there because Mum knew their Mum. We stood under the tree wondering what to play next, me and Mark and my sister and him and his sister. She jumped and swung on a branch.' The top of the tree was all that showed over the garden fence. 'She was looking at us all the time. She swung up her legs and hooked her feet round the branch, wriggled her legs up to get a good grip, brown legs she had. Then she let go with her hands, very slow as if she was swimming – she hung by her feet, her skirt came right down and she was wearing nothing! There was her bum!'

I hadn't beaten the hospital, the bed, the ward, the pyjamas and the name-tag; his dark eyes were living somewhere; my story had certainly not touched the place, even with its exaggeration – she'd worn blue knickers – but to us the mystery was the whole performance, the slowness and twining of her legs, her black hair hanging down and her eyes looking coolly at us upside down past the hem of her skirt, and that was what I wanted to tell George. He was dying on me.

I could have put him in a wheelchair; imagined I *had* and was wheeling him to the beds of roses. I laughed. They're red and pink you know, the tall ones. Is it floribunda you call them? You'd know their names. You'd prod your finger at them and say their names as if you were answering in school, a bit ashamed of knowing every one of them. I jumped off the bed. 'If I took you out there,' I said aloud. I crouched and put my head beside his to see from the pillow. The roses were a red blur or he didn't see them at all. 'Do you see them, George, eh?' He hadn't even leaned toward the window and I shook his arm. It was flabby and heavy. He belched but not in the old way, it just came out of him. He put down his head, creeping back into himself and I felt like punching him under the ear at the corner of the jawbone that jutted out because his head was turned away. My knuckle would stun him back to life, stop him fooling at being a corpse.

I was walking outside, in the gusts of a breeze that was working itself up into a wind. I looked at the one I thought was his window, one without flowers, and it seemed locked into itself, as if I hadn't been there. The best thing was to forget it till next time, and anyway out in the street the wind was blowing.

Mum hadn't come to the church. It seemed none of the ones he'd worked for in the village had come, till I saw Mrs Harris in a seat on the other side. I'd come late and sat near the back. Most of the people in front were men, with red and brown necks and black suits, like he'd have been. I'd seen him dressed for a funeral once. Was that how he was in the coffin? Had Bella put the suit on him, or the undertakers? She'd flown to her daughter in Canada the day before, a flight booked in advance, a man told me later in the cemetery.

The singing started and the man next to me held the book forward, his spade-shaped thumbnail squashing the crease between the thin pages. A deep humming like bees rose in front of us. I blushed. Sweat pricked under my collar. The hymn went on for ages, sad, nothing to do with George. The pew-ends, going along there in an overlapping line, were picked out by the sun; and the sun made window-shapes on the wall, a sign maybe, since the sun-shapes had appeared when the hymn started. We were all getting a peep as the door opened to let him in, and he'd float away in the golden haze like a big chrysalis.

The service went by fast in its slow way; no time to think what it was like in the coffin. At Aunt Liz's, in the crematorium, the coffin had sunk down under the purple cloth in a horrible caving-in process; we knew she was going to be burnt and that would be the end of her.

I hadn't thought he was dead, from the moment I'd phoned Bella to ask if she was going to the hospital and heard that he was. I hadn't believed there was anything behind the words though I'd believed her words as far as she was concerned.

The minister was telling us to stand and sit, he'd have seen that some might not know. Then they were carrying out the coffin. They passed close with the box and I held back a smile.

The people from the front went out first. Their rubber and metal heels struck the diamond-patterned tiles softly. The slow walking and the organ music and the silence gave the sensation of having had a good meal.

I didn't know if you should speak to people and what you would say; anyway I didn't expect to know any. Mrs Harris had left, pale and covered like a nun, gone away as if there was no-one in her clothes.

I saw Andy Crawford. I hadn't seen him in the church. He came over, and I said I didn't know he'd known George; that was stupid because they were both from Gledhill. Andy, in a dark-blue suit, just smiled, and the two of us together with another man set off for the cemetery. Most people from the church went that way, in dark suits but some like me in ordinary clothes with a black tie, and one with a black armband on his raincoat. People watched from their doors. They'd get a lot of this on the road from the church to the cemetery.

There was a mound of yellow earth at the end of the shiny stones and clear gold lettering and flowers. It looked too much to have come out of a hole for one man. Round the hole they'd put green plastic mats like grass. I didn't go up close and look in.

The cemetery sloped from a wood and leaves floated down to lie among the graves and on the heap of earth. People had broken into groups and lit cigarettes, one man a pipe. Andy and his pal discussed the price of ready-mix and the others would all have been talking about the same kind of things, their voices slightly different from usual, as they leant on the tall stones across the red-chip path from the new graves and the hole. They could have been at the Cross where there were always people in fine weather, or at the cattle mart where I'd been for a job, and looked into the ring on the way to the office, and they'd been talking and leaning, in the sawdust smell, same way, same people.

We waited a long time. It was hot. The good smell of the pipe smoke was around. It would be alright to be put in a hole and covered over when the time came.

The hearse arrived and they were sliding the box out. It would be his nephew that helped with the garden standing at the hole, and he was the only one to look upset after the box was lowered. His face was twisted and red. That was fair enough, but how did the rest feel, did they feel like me? I felt pretty good. The minister at the end of the hole was impressive, as if he believed in God. I'd seen him in the street once or twice, padding along like everyone else; I could see him tucking into a plate of chicken soup afterwards.

The grave-digger held forward a shovelful of earth ceremoniously, he reminded me of a waiter offering cheese over a customer's spaghetti. The sprinkled earth sounded far away as it landed on the lid. It was alright, him and the minister doing their jobs right.

After that people broke away. The nephew and the minister shook hands and the grave-digger rested on his shovel. I'd have waited till he started shovelling properly and he'd filled it all in, but everyone was going, even the minister. I wanted to hear the earth thudding on the box and be there when it was finished, but because everyone else was leaving I went too, saying to myself I'd come back later.

The people were spread out on their way to the gates, walking on the grass between the headstones, smoking. Andy was waiting at the corner outside the gates.

'Coming for a pint, Michael?' He tilted his head, looking at me through the lower half of his glasses. The other fellow stood slightly behind as if we were picking teams and he'd been chosen.

It hadn't occurred to me you could go for a drink after.

If you had the afternoon off for a funeral . . . and then the farmers and retired men, there they were. Groups split off to pubs. It was strange that it was not strange. Andy pushed ahead and I stood back to let the other fellow in before me. The door with glass panels swung behind us, shutting out fresh air. I stood there a moment. Andy said 'C'mon,' and we went to a table.

'Michael' he said to the man, and to me, 'Maxwell.' We shook hands. 'Maxwell's in the building trade, among other things.'

Maxwell's hand was like Dad's with its veins and red knuckles. He drew it back and my hand brushed against his stomach as he looked up at me from his bent-down head, from his red face the texture of orange-peel with eyes sunk away in. He was a wreck, a big belly, flabby legs, breath I avoided after

27

a whiff. 'You're the schoolmaster's boy,' he grunted.

'Yes.'

'And what are you going to do with your life?' He gave me a fraction of a look.

'I might go to Canada!' Surely he knew Andy had given me the job! What did he mean? The way he'd put it . . . hard to answer with Andy there. But I went on, 'We've friends out there. On the prairie.' They were far-out friends of Dad, these prairie farmers. It was theoretically possible.

'Whereabouts?'

'Eh? Ah, Minnesota.'

No-one said anything for a while.

'Not following your father's profession,' Maxwell's deep voice said, and he looked at me to make it a question. 'You could do worse than work for this man!' He glanced at Andy and jiggled up and down laughing wheezily and poked me in the ribs; with the movement of his elbow I smelt his layers of clothes. Andy smiled. Was Maxwell taking the piss? Were they both?

The fuzzy brown curtains of the bay window were looped from a rail halfway up so people couldn't look in. Through the join they could be seen passing, sometimes a whole person if I moved the curtain with the back of my head and looked sideways. A woman leaned over a push-chair and adjusted something; beyond her was the road to the cemetery.

There were people in the pub from the funeral and some I must have met with George. A crowd of them were getting down to it near us, coats and caps on the backs of chairs, their elbows spread on the table, pints and whiskies in the middle. A thin man was hanging the raincoat with the black armband on a hatstand at the door.

'Good crowd,' Andy remarked to Maxwell.

'This is just the second funeral I've been to,' I said. 'The first was a cremation. I'd rather be buried any day!'

'Is that so?' Maxwell looked at me; he wasn't interested in the comparison of funerals, but in me saying it, the schoolmaster's son. I was going to tell them about Aunt Liz's cremation, but he started hitching forward to pull himself to his feet by the edge of the table, and went off to the bar, where after a word he veered to the toilets.

28

'Does he know my Dad?'

'Eh? Maxwell knows everyone. He's on the Council. Aye, I told him who you were.'

I eventually asked, 'How do you know?'

'You get to know things. I found out.'

'What for?'

He just kind of waved off that subject. 'I was interested in what you said about funerals,' he said. 'We used to be under-takers you know. Most joiners used to be. But we had to take on a couple of extra hands, hire the car and that, it wasn't worth it. Luckily the Co-op put us out of business.' He leant forward grinning. 'The stink made you boak. For all they camouflaged it, you got a whiff – and the thing rummling in the box when you carried it.' He'd said this in a different voice, then changed to his usual: 'It was me and Drew in those days.'

'Did you make coffins?'

'Drew. He did.' Andy said to Maxwell who'd appeared, 'Where's the drinks, man?'

'The lassie's bringing them.'

They grinned on each side of me as if they'd had a good day or something. Andy's face was pale, solid and round, and his hard workman's hands pale too. He and Maxwell continued to sit grinning. Whatever it was made them grin could be heard in the laughs and talk of everybody, the way they looked and the way they sat – it was a kind of getting away with something or winning on the horses feeling. Maybe because we were all alive, none of us was dead, or something else from the funeral. I was grinning too.

The girl from the bar came over with three pints on a tray.

'How're you, Bridie?' Maxwell asked, putting his hand on her wrist.

She moved away. 'Fine.'

Andy had leant forward. 'Mind after Willy Craig's funeral, Bridie?'

She gathered the empty glasses and rested the tray on her hip. 'Aye, I do! You lot were disgusting.'

'I'll tell you about it,' Andy said, 'you'll not know who we're talking about.'

'He's not saying much,' she said.

'He's young.'

29

'So I see.'

'Hey!' Maxwell shouted after her, but she didn't turn.

'We had a meal after – after his funeral – in here, up the stair,' Andy said. My pint was cold and gassy but warm inside, in fact I was smiling while Andy told his story, thinking I'd keep up with this pair of boozers, I felt so good. The story was complicated and I grinned; I saw my hand holding the edge of the table and wondered would I usually put my hand on the table in such a way, gripping with thumb uppermost, the side of my thumb seeming enormous. I tried the fingers on top and the thumb underneath the thickness of the table; the hand was perfectly steady. I had an endless capacity to go on with this session, a big diesel engine I was, chugging away, taking in fuel and chugging on.

I looked round while keeping my face to Andy. There was a man behind the bar, and the girl Bridie. A string of coloured Christmas tree lights hung along a carved wooden canopy over the bar like the furniture in old peoples' houses, Granny's for instance; curly and showing the grain of the wood and solid. The man in the red tee-shirt was at the beer taps, filling pints and handing them out and putting money in the till which he could reach by turning round. Bridie bobbed smoothly, from the gantry to the bottles and crisps on the shelves below, coming up with a toss of her head. She handed change with a smile, gave a smaller smile to the next customer. She scooted out to collect empties, nipping between the men.

Some were leaning back with their arms hooked over the chairs, hanging down – a big hand twitched ash off a cigarette by itself – and some were close over the tables, their faces together. The hatstand was hidden under coats.

'That was them at the doctor!'

I'd missed the punchline but laughed, it was no effort, I wanted to laugh. Andy and I leant to each other with big smiles and for a moment I saw his eye, a grey pebble.

'Three pints please,' I said to Bridie and stood back, not to stare at her directly. As one hand held the tap and the other the glasses one by one she looked round to see what was next and was rubbing the back of her ankle with the other foot, I knew by the way she was jiggling very slightly. When she'd put down the third pint I asked for three whiskies. 'And something for

30

yourself?' She said no, including me in the general smile.

'Ah!' cried Maxwell when he saw the whisky. 'Some fellow this, eh! Your very good health!' He raised his glass and tried to remember my name, drank and shook the last drops into his beer. 'Canada, eh? Chances for a young man there!'

'I work for Andy.'

'I know that, son.'

I'd thought I would raise my glass and say 'here's to George' or something like that, but the old boy had drunk his too quick. I peeped through the chink in the curtains. Daylight was going, the streetlights were on, I was hungry.

I'd have a poke of chips, and I saw myself eating them; it was a long time since I'd said hullo to myself; there was a route through the tables I'd take when this pint was done.

They were talking about a Housing Association in the town. I listened in favour of it and suddenly remembered George was dead. The hole would be filled and the grass mats removed – they'd have kept soil off the real grass, as well as being clean for the clean black shoes. Now the real grass would be round and over a hump, the turf squares stretched apart by the rise. Going there was out of the question. The hump in the moon- light covered with the terrible wreaths. He'd come to an end; nothing could be done. I could smash Maxwell's head in but what was the point.

I went to find the toilet: a narrow damp passage and across a small yard with a step down into it, another wooden door with a row of holes along the top. Inside, a dim light, smell of piss, green copper pipes and imitation marble speckled like catfood. I got back to myself there, then went back inside.

Maxwell had gone and there were two new pints on the table.

'He's away home,' Andy said. 'Not good for the old tum. The doctor put him off spirits. He's not supposed to drink, except beer.'

'But he took it quick enough!'

'He likes it! One'll do him no harm.'

'What was that about Canada?'

'It was you said Canada. He was having a bit of fun.'

I shrugged.

'I've a son. You didn't know maybe. They get on at me

31

because he's not come into the business.' Andy sipped from his beer. 'You've not to worry. They're kidding on I'm going to get him back, but I won't.' He wiped his lips. 'Fancy a wee half with that?' He signalled for Bridie's attention with his big hand. 'Anything in it? Ice, water, lemonade, soda?'

'The way it is thanks.'

Bridie brought them and he waved away the change.

'Why were you finding out about Dad? It seems weird.'

'You like to know who you're employing,' Andy said.

'It's me, not Dad.'

He rubbed his eyes, the specs riding up and down on his fingers. He settled them on his nose. 'And how did you know Geordie, by the way? You asked the afternoon off for a funeral. I thought it was a ploy,' he said.

'Mum got to know him. He did the gardens at the Trust and she worked there too. Then she fixed him up with work in the village when he retired.'

'She helped him, eh?'

It would have been better if he hadn't asked these questions, but I kept on answering. 'They both like gardening.' I explained myself in a hurry. 'I started helping him, I used our mower, he didn't have one you see. Dad hired it to me.'

'What? He hired it to you?'

'So much an hour. And I bought the fuel. It was okay.'

'Your Dad!'

'Yes.'

I went to the bar and bought a packet of peanuts. The beer in my glass was chestnut coloured, bubbles rising . . .

Andy's solid back at the bar in his dark suit. 'There you go,' he said, coming back and setting down beer.

An old man sang 'Bonny Gallowa' with one hand on his chest and the other held out. His voice trembled. Then someone told jokes. Was it not terrible just after he'd died? These drunken sods and the guy hypnotising them with his swinging finger and his eyes and lips swaying about. His tongue licked along the soft lower lip, a pink fillet from the butcher moving along another. The men started to grin before the punchline, then the terrible laughing.

Coming from the toilet my foot caught on a chair and I saved myself from falling with a hand on the table where the

32

old fellow had been singing. I'd knocked over a glass and a roar went up. I was saying something and then when I could be heard found it difficult to speak the words. 'I just tripped, my foot caught on something.' In the middle of it I stuck, hypnotised by their eyes. 'I'll buy you another.'

'Give us a song!' someone shouted and then all.

'Ach no. No, I –' I was quite steady, supporting myself with the fingertips on the table. I was just looking at them, in the end with a faint smile.

'A song,' a voice said, dying away. I mumbled and set out over the dark red carpet.

'Alright?' Andy jerked his head in their direction, grinning. After a while they'd closed over the table, busy with the next thing.

I was parched. I signalled Bridie. They shouted when she came over, about the whisky I was to buy. I couldn't get the words out to tell her to take one to that table, wondering if I was supposed to buy the whole table a round.

'Don't bother with them. They're pals of Geordie's,' Andy said.

The others near us would be George's pals too. He'd have been following the stories too, his eyes big and boiled behind the glasses. I didn't know him at all – these were the ones he'd gone around with. His pals! I didn't like this. 'He'd have been there right in amongst them! This is what he'd have wanted us to do! See him down there in the hole with the earth coming down round about ' – I pointed at the wall, past which a long way there was the cemetery, I was shouting something like, 'Looking up! The earth all coming down on him like blankets! He can see us! Hullo George, here!' I held up the glass. 'Go on boys!' And I raised it to them.

'Aye, you're right there.' Andy had moved in front of me. I wasn't mistaken in his expression, he was angry and pretending he was calm. He'd stayed sober and let me get drunk. Hell mend him! Bridie held my arm and I couldn't put it round her and I told her several times I was alright.

Thinking couldn't be done till I'd had a piss. It escaped from the bladder and poured out as I fiddled with the zip.

The liquid drained from the top of my head leaving it shrunken. Leaning against the wall in rising steam. A look down caused swirling. I was in a lane between the backs of houses, this was where I was, off the street, some street . . . it was the middle of the night. Somewhere about then . . .

Could be the lane behind my house – a calm place all the same, old brick wall capped with a semi-circular glazed bit. This was actually a doorway; the cool side-stones pointed neatly, this side, the top, down the other side, a good bit of pointing. The brown door with a black handle and keyhole, thick muddy brown – I fell with my hand on the sharp road and the other on dandelions at the wall, and threw up. To lie down. If not for the mess under me I would put my head on the grass. But I stood up. Leant on the wall and shut my eyes. Was I upright or lying down. Must be lying, beside George. All we could do was lie there. It was hard to say where we were, the effort had made tears run down my face. There was a calculation to be made, which way the tears ran would show what way up I was, and – but I wouldn't be shifted. Slowly we made some kind of living quarters under there, only something was wrong – we both did it, busy in this underground cavern: what we were doing, walking, pushing low dark furniture or logs against the wall, always in a green light and always the same room, though we saw into the next one, with a dull light, like an aquarium. I never moved, always pushed the same dark thing against the same bit of wall, curved in and made of stones and dry earth. The only thing, I didn't see him, his face. My back was to him. When I keeked round, he was turned away. It was too much.

I opened my eyes at someone coming down the lane, my head a volcano. Some distance he was and hadn't seen me maybe. There was time to get away, out the end and away through the streets.

So bad. The torments of the damned. I did not think about George though it was one of the things to be done like getting up, washing etc. They'd have heard me. Hardly moving my eyes I saw the twisted clothes I'd got out of.

Next time I woke warmth coursed through me. The benefits! Super-warmth can only be got by getting drunk and lying-in next morning.

11 a.m. Down below, the house would be empty except for Barbara. I began the process. There was a sink. After running the tap for a minute hot water rose from the kitchen.

Washed and dressed I looked alright – I hope I didn't disturb you last night, I said to the mirror. Was I yobbo number three? But if I'd crept in without a sound there was no point her guessing I'd been legless.

'Hope I didn't wake you,' I said between door and table, the kitchen strip-light glaring down.

'We weren't in bed at ten o'clock!' She leant back on the sink. She wasn't angry, a bit angry, but programmed for disapproval I stumbled on with my apologies; my breath smelt hellish. In fact all over I probably smelt hellish.

'I came to help you but you'd gone up,' she said.

'We went to the pub after the funeral. George, the man I worked with.'

She turned to the board where she'd been chopping carrots. At the point where her neck joined her shoulders there was a fat white crease. Then her loose black tracksuit and pink socks, shoes worn at the heels. 'Like a hair of the dog?' She asked.

I was sick from looking at that fat neck and those scuffed shoes. 'Eh?' I'd heard the expression about the dog and didn't know what it meant.

'A drink!' She pulled a can of beer from the fridge and then she'd turned round again, evidently she was finishing the carrots; and I sat at the table with the beer. I felt better after a swallow of it.

'Was I drunk?'

'Drunk? Hah! You were paralytic boy!'

'Sorry.'

'That's alright.'

'Was I sick?'

'You had been.' Facing me she added, 'I don't mind – okay?' She sat down. 'I don't mind once in a while. It's every fucking night I can't stand.'

Her deliberate, educated voice was followed by silence. I was a bit stunned. I went onto Jack's side. She was making a big problem of coming home at night; she'd never be pleased.

She looked up with a clear, loving smile. 'You won't get like

35

that, will you?'

We hadn't anything like this at home.

The start of my £150-a-week job: I was at the office early. Annie ran her pen down columns of figures in a thick book. She could be looking for a particular item, or checking the addition, or only finding her place from last week; getting herself into position. The fire glowed behind her and a mug of coffee sat on the top of the sloping counter.

I leant on it beside her, carefully not looking at her book. 'What will Andy be doing when he's not here?'

'Huff! He wouldna tell me!' The phone rang. 'Hullo, Crawford. He's no in yet.' She listened, and put the receiver down. I realised that she'd spoken to me in a warm voice compared to her telephone one. She wore a thin wedding ring on her small hand which disappeared, and reappeared with a square of chocolate that she popped into her mouth. She tucked it away somewhere and I couldn't tell which of the bulges it was. Inside her mouth would be sticky and brown and warm. She frowned at her figures and hesitated with the pen.

I was jiggling my leg, and the counter. 'Sorry.' I stood up, and at that moment heard a car and went out.

Here was Andy yet again, after his boilersuit and dark funeral suit. It was a tweed jacket, light blue it was, with an oily smell, and new, thick grey trousers with a crease and turn-ups, below which his usual boots.

We were looking at the car and he was telling me that it was a Triumph-something he'd bought secondhand, trading in the van; I noticed his white shirt and a tie. There was a cap lying on the passenger seat and it was new too, a shiny mushroom-coloured lining.

He showed off the engine and the size of the boot and condition of the upholstery. It was about three years old. As we walked towards the office he was like someone who's just won an election, walking towards the cameras.

Annie's eyes were as big as grapes when she saw him, so this must be a new Andy. She didn't move however, or show any other expression. 'Mr Somerville phoned.'

'Right, Annie, I'm going there anyway. Here,' he said to me, 'I'll show you what to do – small day to start with.' On the list of phone numbers pinned to the wall he'd added beside each number the name of the person I should speak to, as he'd said he would. 'Are you with me?' He grasped the edges of the desk with both big hands, the jacket wrinkling across his shoulders. 'Drew'll be in for timber, you can help Peter with it, they'll be in a hurry.' He seemed to be repeating this. 'And here's the people I want you to phone.' He pressed out the creases of a folded piece of paper. 'Alright? After today you can work them out for yourself.'

I was glad to have something to do and started phoning as soon as he'd gone, sitting at his desk and using his phone.

My only problem was a man in Irvine who couldn't supply concrete lintels till Friday. I told him we'd need them before that and he asked to speak to Mr Crawford. I said I was sorry he wasn't in, and I had to buy these things and might have to try elsewhere. When could he speak to Mr Crawford? Early next morning. He put down the phone.

Annie had swivelled her chair to stare at me but she didn't say anything and handed over the Yellow Pages. I found and rang a builders' merchant who would deliver that afternoon, cheaper.

'He always deals with them in Irvine,' she said.

At coffee time we ate Twix bars from her bag. She was friendly but unavailable, engaged deep inside her mind in sending and decoding messages in a language I didn't understand, while I made do with her visible person. That was reasonable because I was an outsider.

I thought about Barbara – the crease at the back of her neck, the mystery of her accent, her whole life that was a mystery to me. I went out to Peter with the timber list and we assembled it on the loading ramp. He would hardly speak to me, and this would be because from what he'd overheard I was one of the bosses.

This was ridiculous. I wondered why he bothered working now he was retired – maybe admiration of Andy; he seemed to think he was some kind of god. Now and then he'd say, Andrew Crawford, Esquire, in connection with nothing, not to me, it just came out of him into the air as if he said it inside all the time and sometimes it came out. It was fair enough for him to worry about the changes, Andy in his new suit and car, me in his place and so on.

'What's he doing? They're saying he's buying up places.'
Peter had been nerving himself to ask and he stared at me
frowning, waiting.

'I don't know, Peter.'

'Aye, I doubt . . . '

'I've only been here a few weeks. I don't know what goes
on.'

'Aye . . . ' He shook his head grinning. 'What's he supposed
to be buying then?' I asked. 'Ach, you'll ken better as me.'

'I don't know!'

He turned his shoulder.

We finished laying out the timber and sat on the ramp. Peter
rolled and lit a cigarette. How would I work with him now that
I was some kind of boss. He was right in that. He was old, I
couldn't be telling him to do things. Very nasty. And the
money. Poor old guy. He finished his cigarette and I clapped
my hands to my knees. 'Let's move the sand!'

No hurry to move it, but this way I didn't have to tell him to
do it on his own. We got shovels and started. It was spread
over one of the bays and we piled it on one side to make room
for some other stuff; it might be more sand; what was the
point? I worked faster than him – as if there was a hurry –
making him go more than his natural pace. I was worried
about what we'd do next.

A ring came from the rusty bell on the end of the Nissen hut.
I went in to the phone. Andy: 'McCrirrick's been on to me!
What are you playing at?'

'Eh?' (McCrirrick? – man from Irvine).

'What kind of answer's that!'

'He said he couldn't get his lintels here till Friday and you
said you wanted them before that.'

'Well?' (This wasn't the man who'd left so cheerily – what
had happened?) 'Well?'

'I thought you wanted them quick. They'll be here this
afternoon.'

A pause. 'Look, em . . . Michael. Take things easy, eh. You
don't have to be so bloody sharp.'

'These are cheaper.'

'What the fuck do you know about it! Just play it straight,
eh?'

'Right.'

'You've upset McCrirrick. He's a touchy swine. He'll take years to get over it. Annie'll keep you right, eh. Take it easy. I won't be back for a day or two. I told McCrirrick to send as usual by the way.'

Annie said, 'I tellt you he wouldna be pleased.'

'Huh. It's sorted out. How would that guy contact him?'

'At Wallaces, likely. They're old buddies.'

'Wallaces, what's that?'

'The builders.' She picked her teeth with her forefinger which I'd seen her doing before. It made her look like a rabbit. 'The one he's bought,' she said.

'He never told me!'

'Nor me neither. My cousin works there. But everyone knows.'

'Huh!'

'Aye.'

'What's going to happen?'

'Aye – that's what we want to know,' she said, going red. She too thought I knew something that I was hiding; but said nothing straight out about it. 'If that bugger Somerville . . .' she went on.

'Who's he?'

'The fellow over there.'

'Oh, I see. Have you not asked Andy what's going to happen?'

'Couldn't ask him that!'

'Why not?'

She was still picking at her teeth. 'You don't know what he's like. They say he'll close this place down. You've only to look at it.'

I was surprised at her. I thought she really liked the office, or something; she seemed part of it.

Our truck came for the timber, and then another vehicle, as I got back to the office, a big enclosed van. Peter seemed to have an argument with the driver who climbed out of the cab and came across with the paper he'd been showing Peter.

He smoothed and held it out. 'Desk for Crawford, Station Yard.'

I took the paper. While I held it without speaking I could

send him away or tell him to unload. The three of them waited for me, a pleasant feeling, like money. 'Bring it in,' I said.

When he'd backed up we took an end each. It was the desk Andy had mentioned. 'Alright here?' I asked, pushing it against the counter. I'd sit beside and behind her, not seeing her writing, but in arm's length of the phone. 'Is that alright?' I asked. It was her phone after all.

'It's okay.'

I thought I could handle her. I thought she liked me and maybe she did in a way.

The desk was scruffy, with a torn, faded red-leather top. The drawers should have been filled with what had been in a house, but I had nothing to put in it. It should be in a house like Barbara's, polished and ready to be written at whenever she wanted to, its drawers full of paper, family stuff, photo albums. And here it was in the office making me think about getting out of the place I was just settling down in.

Andy bounced out of his car on Thursday in the clothes as neat as before, but he was not grinning so much. It was Annie's half-day. He switched on the electric fire and kettle and dumped coffee powder into the mugs, as if it had to be thought about. He sat at his desk when the coffee was made and motioned me to sit opposite.

'Right. I've bought the builders, Wallace. Negotiations have gone on bloody ages, but it's clinched.' He sipped coffee which spilt down the side of the mug. 'Willy Wallace retired last year there. His manager's been a chap Somerville. I've taken him on. He's got his head screwed on.' He pinched the bridge of his nose, closing his eyes, then raised his eyebrows and the glasses fell back into place. 'It's what I've needed to go with this, you know, to complete it, to give me a full service to offer the public. Just being a joiner's no use any more. You can see how we've kind of half-expanded. I couldn't tell you this when I took you on you understand, it was in progress.' He sighed. 'They're bigger than us, but never mind, it's done. Now I can do the job from start to finish, build a house from start to finish without creeping to any of these builders, see? You'll have heard rumours, that's what you get even when nothing's happening. But I signed this morning, so that's it!' He slapped the desk.

'Is this what you meant about expanding interests?'

'More or less.'

'How about – will you keep this place going? Annie and me were talking about it. She seems to be worried.'

'Aaaah she's an old worryguts! We might use their workshop, but we'll keep this on. Couldn't do away with this!' he said as if I'd suggested it.

'You'll need us then?'

'Annie? Aye, and old Peter of course. He likes to be doing something. But you, I was thinking of moving you sideways as you might say. See that building out there?' It was locked, tarred like an old boat, with a rusty iron roof, a Noah's Ark in the sea of wild grass stretching beyond it to the big road. 'Used to be the church hall and before that God knows what. Anyway, I've bought it. I'm going to make it a secondhand furniture place. I want you to run it. Martin Somerville'll be keeping an eye on this place, instead of me; I'm taking a back seat.' He gave an embarrassed smile and went on. 'You'll be needed here of course, but there won't be quite so much to do. I was thinking you could manage both jobs.' Turning his head sideways he made a face and scratched his neck. 'I think so.' I was hardly listening. It was all moving quickly behind the scenes and that's what I was trying to latch onto while he talked: 'I've had enough of busting my pan. I'm going to take it easy. Martin can run the business, ha, he'll be glad to have me out the way! I'll dodge about the country buying furniture – your desk, I've started already and I'll get in a lot of fishing. You a fisherman? Never mind. There's places down in the north of England, the hills you know, the wild country. Very wild down there, you're miles from anywhere, never think . . . and burns full of trout, man . . . course I'll pick up furniture there, too, I've made a start . . .' He stretched his arms. 'Time to think, eh?'

'What'll I be doing exactly?'

'I'll show you.'

We went out, onto the road, along to the shed. Worn steps led to a double door under the small porch. He undid a padlock and pushed the doors. They swung heavily as if the whole shed was really solid.

41

'See here,' he said, sticking his penknife into the doorpost, 'best of stuff. This is imported timber, pre-war. Sound as a bell. Only thing's the roof – needs half a dozen clear sheets for light and that could be dodgy – the old tin's ripe. I'll put in strip-lighting too.'

It was dark and dusty. By the light of the single bulb the walls were narrow-boarded to the roof; up there some hardboard nailed under the rafters had come down in places. 'I'll rip that off,' he said (meaning I would). A smell of burning dust came from the lightbulb. There was a balcony at the end of the building with a stair leading to it.

'Look at that! A feature, eh? Pity it's not a bit wider and we could have had another floor up there.'

'Are you going to buy enough furniture to fill this place?'

'I could fill it in a week! D'you like the job – once it gets going?'

'Yes,' I said. I thought he was away with the fairies. A daft look, too happy. He was including me in it, so I left it at that.

'Sure?'

'You want me to be here and over there at the same time?'

'We'll put a gate in the fence.' He laughed, well back into his cheery mood. 'Well, first of all I'd like you to clean it! Could be a bit dirty. I'll get someone to help. We should open before Christmas. All that time I think you can dodge back and for-wards' – he raised his eyebrows – 'do both jobs. And maybe for a while after we're opened. Then I might get you an assistant.'

'You won't be here?'

'I'll be out buying.'

He was smiling at the wall and out the dirty window and seemed to have forgotten me. 'I've bought some already, I told you that. The desk's part of it. The fellow's storing all the rest till we get this place ready. So!' – jolly, like Dad – 'We must get on with it!'

He'd put off the light and was locking the doors.

'Do you know a lot about furniture?' I asked, meaning how did he learn, meaning to ask him to teach me or something like that.

'I do.' His mouth snapped shut.

'Will it be antiques and silver and stuff?'

'Antiques! God no! Plain honest furniture. Well, there might be a bit of that stuff.'

'You'll keep me right, then.'

'Sure thing.'

I looked at the shed that evening on the way home, and imagined it lit up, full of furniture except for a space at the door where I talked to customers, leaning forward, laughing, making notes in my book, wearing a suit.

I got up during the night. The glow of the street lamp fell on the lopped tree. The garden below was a black hole. I'd been dreaming about Peter or maybe been half awake. At any rate I couldn't get it out of my head. Look here! I grabbed my head and stared at the close darkness outside. This is terrible! Over and over had gone the story about Peter – he was at the door of one of the cottages in the row that had been engulfed by the town, it was his home and in it his quiet wife with her best friends, her sisters. They sat whispering and chattering, these sisters, among the china ornaments. Then he was out the back washing his car. His wife filled the enormous flask and gave him too many sandwiches and too little tobacco money. Always this scrimping on tobacco and throwing away tea and crusts. Then Andy told him there wasn't a job for him and he killed himself out in the back garden. I didn't see what he did, only his scrubbed pink face, still and shiny like a gnome's. Annie: she took the bus to a house with rusty steamed-up metal-framed windows next to a dungheap, and there at night a thin farmworker, her husband, beat her when he was drunk and she ate sweets and cakes because she was hungry, hungry. She was left to stare at the dungheap all day when Andy told her there was no more work for her. And she ate all the time.

Oh dear! Second sight! But when I saw them at the yard next morning they were grumbling as usual, complete and solid, and I felt guilty of trying to get them out of their jobs by supernatural means.

There was nothing to do, but Peter's hand was on the doorlatch. He seemed to be going in the next second. That was his way.

'What did I tell you?' Annie said, 'It's Wallaces. Michael here had it from his nibs yesterday. And he's bought the old church hall,' she added, nodding her head at him.

'What's he wanting with it?'

43

Annie looked at me. 'A furniture store or something.'

I didn't say anything.

'Wouldna mind seeing it. We used to go to whists there,' Peter said.

'It's filthy and the roof's falling in.' I shouldn't have told Annie about the shed and the furniture. 'I'll be ages sweeping it out. You can give me a hand,' I said to Peter.

'I'm bad with my asthma.'

'Yon place used to be full of bowling boards,' Annie said. 'They had it every week. As well as the whists. I don't suppose they're there now.'

'No, Drew has them.'

'Our Drew?' I asked.

'Aye. Our Drew.'

'He'll have flogged them,' Annie said.

My pal Mark had stayed for sixth year and gone straight into a bookshop. What a life. He meant to stay in it for ever. I could have seen him any day after work, but now I wanted to let him see my freedom and tell him about my new job.

He immediately got keen about my 'prospects' and put me off. I hadn't thought of them in the excitement of my new job in the furniture shed; I'd been thinking perhaps no-one would come; I'd thought of schemes to advertise and draw crowds. I hadn't thought of after.

'If you do well you'll get offers. You'll have a track record,' he was saying.

At that time it was easy to get a job if you were of a certain sort – if your father was a teacher or a doctor, if you were middle class in fact, even if you'd failed most of your exams; as long as you spoke well and you were clean and not long-haired you were alright for a job. Mark was clever enough to have gone to university and to annoy him I asked again why he hadn't.

He answered some stuff about earning a living and getting on in the real world; I suppose he thought as he'd brought himself down to our level – not that a bookshop would have had me – he should still be doing better because of all his

44

Highers; yet here I might be getting ahead. 'You'll probably be the leading antique shop owner and I'll own the biggest bookshop! We'll both be Councillors!' he joked, watching the traffic through the window behind me. To keep him from being silent and going away, as he used to when he was upset, I bought two more teas. The café was along from his bookshop and he parked the car behind it every day, he said; they knew him; the girl who brought our tea smiled at him. He lived with his parents.

'Second-hand Marina,' he was saying. 'Good nick, not a spot of rust on her.'

'How many miles to a gallon?'

'Thirty-five. More on a long trip. MOT next year, she'll sail through.'

I didn't know any more questions to ask about cars. 'See Jill much now?'

'Eh? No, not much.' He looked at me and said after a bit, 'She lives in town now, you know.'

Jill had been in our year and gone to university in Edinburgh so it seemed strange that she was living in Gledhill. She came from the same village as Mark where her father, old Pellegrini, had a big house, and Mark used to fancy her but she never paid much attention to him. She was thin and nippy, more adult in her ways and looks than the rest of us, which I put down to her Italian father. More interested in men than boys. 'Is she not at university?' I asked. Being away on that job in Leeds I'd lost touch.

'She dropped out in first year,' he explained as if he didn't want to part with the information.

'Oh yeah,' I said. The café was emptying of the Gledhill sixth-years with their bogus adult look, and the girl who'd smiled at Mark was clearing up their cups and ashtrays, picking up biscuit wrappers with a flick of her wrist and coming back to wipe the tables. I nodded at her and smiled to Mark. I rehearsed some more things in my mind about the job, but didn't say them; we talked a different language about it; I told him about the digs just to stir him up, exaggerated: ceiling lower and steeper, the straight stair twisted – spiral gesture – my cooking on the double burner elaborate, pretty elaborate actually, things I picked up when I was away, curries and so on, the impression was that someone else was there to eat them – I made Steph out to be stunning, Jack a character, and mentioned Barbara in an offhand voice that sounded wrong. Mark understood alright but he wasn't the type to shove open any gap you'd opened into yourself. He didn't make any jokes about the landlady. 'Wasn't that the old guy you used to work for that died the other day?' he asked.

I hadn't thought of George for days. I saw the people leaning on the gravestones again, and George inside the box in his usual scrubbed, red face morning state, small blue eyes roving behind the glasses. 'Yes, that was old George.'

Mark was buttoning his coat. 'I'll need to be away.'

'Be late for tea will you?'

'I'm going out.'

'With Jill?'

'Wouldn't tell *you* if I was.' He gave me a peculiar look as he was putting on his check scarf. After he was gone I was impressed by his appearance. He wore a long dark overcoat over his suit. It was the start he'd got on me when I was away. I didn't care about those kind of clothes, of course, but he'd left school far behind.

Barbara must have been waiting for me. I'd made no noise coming downstairs in my bare feet.

'Have tea with us tonight? There's plenty.'

I held the towel round my waist. 'Yes, thanks.' Under the shower I remembered that I'd been going for a pint with Jack, but I'd forgotten about it and gone to the café instead. I shouldn't have forgotten.

She gave me a handful of knives and forks to lay the table, and she'd shouted the children and started to put out macaroni cheese and spinach while I was doing this. I'd expected her to be slow and not like cooking; chaos, I'd expected, and rotten food. It surprised me that she liked cooking; I knew by the way she spooned out the macaroni. Her face was rosy from the stove and I watched her mouth as she ate, appearing to be keeping to myself, invisible, the lodger. I wondered if the yobbos and those before had come down to tea, and if they'd come every day, and what they'd been like and how they'd got on with her. At last I had to speak to the children.

'You at the big school too?' I asked Steph.

'Yes.' She shot a glance at her mother.

'First term? Got there young eh?'

'I'm nearly thirteen.' She blushed over her blue and white tie, kind of unformed about the mouth as if she was still in primary, but she got angry and dark looks shot out.

'What's it like?'

'Not bad . . . '

We couldn't carry on because of the powerful feeling of being listened to.

'You alright?' I asked William.

'Okay. I'm doing O levels next year.' He'd taken off his tie and had that patient expression of a clever bastard.

'My Dad's a teacher,' I said. 'I know what they're like. All the same. Trying to make you something you're not.' I remembered Barbara was some sort of teacher. 'He wanted me to be a teacher,' I added, God knows why.

William laughed, though it was not at Dad. I could see he liked teachers. He went on smiling and looking at a corner of the kitchen. 'I'd hate to be one. I'm hoping to be a doctor,' he said.

Barbara sighed and looked at the empty place. She'd given me five sets of knives and forks so I had set them all out, one for Jack. Steph was giving her looks of solidarity and we were being divided into two camps, her and Steph, me and Jack, and William neutral. Should I say he was waiting for me at the pub?

We heard him, and then he stuck his head round the door and grinned. He raised his eyebrows at me; they'd think he was surprised I was having tea in the kitchen.

'Yours is in the oven,' Barbara said.

'He hasn't eaten it, then!' Jack was enjoying the situation. He'd had a drink. He leant back on the Aga warming himself, watching us; the children looked down.

Barbara had her back to him anyway, but she knew what he was doing. He began to footer about, looked into pans and hunted for the oven glove. 'Oh, sit down, Jack!'

'Macaroni cheese!' he exclaimed as she put it in front of him, in some way making a joke of it, referring to a thing I didn't know about, but I was the only one who laughed. Steph left the room and I was glad that Barbara had scraped the dish of macaroni onto my plate without asking if I wanted more –

a continuation of our bond before Jack came in. 'How've you been doing?' he asked me.

I said okay, not wanting to go into a lot of explanations about the pub.

'Huh.' He was eating the macaroni in big sticky lumps. 'This is great – just how I like it.' It was unlikely from the look of the stuff and he was maybe being sarcastic.

'Who's Peter Henlein?' I asked.

'Oh!' He laughed.

I'd been round to his workshop one dinnertime and found this card hanging in the door, 'PETER HENLEIN'S BIRTHDAY. BACK IN HALF AN HOUR.' The workshop was a basement and I'd read the sign from above without going down the steps. 'He'll no be long till he's back,' a passer-by had told me, but I'd had no time to wait.

'I was away for my dinner for Christ's sake,' he said.

'Pig,' she answered.

'Old Peter's our patron saint in a way of speaking. He invented clocks, way back about 1500 in Nuremburg – the spring mechanism.' Jack rocked back in his chair and looked at me. 'I bet they've got a monument to him out there, you know what they're like the Gerries. Very respectful people. If he'd been a Gledhill man no bugger would have heard of him.'

'Was that his birthday?'

'Eh? Oh well, it might've been.'

Barbara and William had been whispering. He left the room and she asked, 'Do you two want tea?'

'Yes,' said Jack.

'Michael?'

'I'll be going, thanks.'

'I'm not surprised you don't like our company. This chauvinist' – she jerked her head at Jack and her hair shook – 'you know where he goes, I suppose?' She was suggesting I went there too. No she wasn't. I shook my head. 'To gawp at those go-go girls in that bloody pub.'

'It's alright. No secret about it,' Jack said.

'Half the District Council are there – bloody fascist –'

'Sit down Michael and have a cup of tea for God's sake. I don't know where she gets all this stuff, she'll cool off in a minute.'

48

I stayed quiet, not knowing what else to do. I'd covered the shock instantly like a cut I was pressing to stop the blood before I saw it. How did they live together?

Jack nodded at the kettle. 'Make the tea for Christ's sake, I'm parched. We'll go for a pint later.'

'Drink as much as you like for all I care,' she said as she got the tea.

'We will. Thanks very much.'

I listened to the fridge charging as if the sound had to be attended to and its stopping noted. He began reading the paper. William and Steph would have heard; they'd have heard often but they didn't like it, I knew from their faces.

Barbara brought the tea to the table and poured three cups. 'Is this really the kind of job you want? Driving a lorry?' she asked calmly as if there'd been no argument.

'I'm not driving now. Don't you remember I'm kind of – manager of the yard? But I'd rather be driving than stuck at a desk! Anyway, I was going to tell you, I've got a new job.'

'Who? What?'

I explained to her while Jack supped his tea.

'That's great!' she cried, smiling in an official way as if this triumph was a credit to something higher, beyond me – as if I'd reached . . . well, I'd moved up a class and would meet nicer people, was not any longer in danger of sinking. Almost without pause she added, 'Oh, while I think of it Michael, we're going for a picnic at the sea this weekend, would you like to come?'

'Bathing?' – it was October.

'No. Unless you want to! We go down often. The kids love it. Make a barbecue and climb on the rocks. Don't we Jack?'

He held out his cup. 'I've known it happen.'

'Well then,' she said, looking at me.

'Yes, I'll come.'

'Fine!' She paused. 'You don't seem very thrilled with your new job. What do you really want to do?'

'I haven't a clue.'

'Come on. What were you good at at school?'

'Nothing.' I hitched my legs into the table edge to balance on the back legs of the chair. 'Badminton and volleyball.'

'You must have been good at something.'

'Not really.'

'You passed some exams; some O levels. How old are you?'

'Nineteen.'

'Nineteen! You've got time. You could do courses. Oh, I'd like to be nineteen.'

'Leave him alone.'

'I liked driving the truck.'

'But you must do something with yourself!'

'How could anyone know what to do in this world,' Jack said. 'He's as well driving a truck as anything.'

'It's a waste of his education.'

'What education?'

'I've got three Os and Higher Geography. That's my education. What use is it to me?'

'Your brain's been trained, it doesn't matter – '

'Listen, I've got a highly trained brain, a performing flea in my skull and it mends watches,' Jack said.

The door flew open – it was on a ball-catch that only needed a push. 'Mum, can I have some money for coke?' Steph asked, standing on one leg in the doorway.

'Bring the jar over,' Barbara said. She fished out coins and handed them to the frowning Steph.

'Get us a box of matches, Steph,' Jack said when she was on her way. 'Got enough?'

She checked her money and nodded.

The door hadn't quite shut behind her. Jack stuck out his leg and pushed it to. He sighed, elbows on the table. Red lino with a cream border was under the table, and his chunky shoes.

'You could have been more than a watchmender,' Barbara said.

'What the hell. It's my trade. It's turned out to be my trade.' He hunched forward in his ragged pullover, holding his head, his cheeks wrinkled by his hands. 'I might have been a teacher.'

'You see how easy it is to get stuck in something. Look at him!' she said to me.

'Four months is the longest I've been in anything – since school.'

'Oh, of course, you're nineteen! Imagine being nineteen again!' A smile came on her face. She was looking at the table and I didn't know if she was being sarky.

'Let's go.' Jack stood up.
'The dishes?' I muttered.
'Go and drink beer if you're going.'

Later in the week I went to Jack's shop again. His bald dome was bent over a workbench in the window.

Down the green-stained steps, the door opened with a ting, into a smell – paraffin! The stove was in the middle of the room and a man stood there warming his back. And something about the place –floorboards ragged at the door, a sheet of lino at the workbench scuffed by Jack's feet – was the same as Mrs Clark's shop in the village. The bread wrapping smelt of paraffin and soapflakes when you got it home. Oh yes, and the way George had talked to her – I hadn't heard about him and women then, before Mrs Harris, but in the shop he couldn't stop it happening with him and Mrs Clark. I suppose I was about twelve and picked it up. She would drop her shopkeeper look that she kept for Mum who's a bit respectable and for nearly everyone else, well, when I was there. I thought she was a shopkeeper because she had that look on her face. He made her stop being Mrs Clark and it was okay her laughing, she never could laugh, or put her head on one side before. She'd always been made of dough. Her name was Chris. George would buy cigarettes and sweets and smile out this force that turned Mrs Clark into Chris. It was the first time I'd noticed I was with a person who knew things and could do things. And he'd ended up helpless.

This place of Jack's was a workshop more than a shop; the only things for sale were a few watches in display cases in the window. 'Hi Michael,' he said. He was poking in the back of a small watch and kept on with it. 'This lady's banged her watch . . . silly girl, eh? . . . shifted the hair-spring . . . must have hit him a hell of a belt . . . I told her she should hit him with something else.'

'Whose is that?' came loudly from behind.

'Chrissake Jim . . . I couldn't, oh but . . . professional secret . . . secret of the confessional . . . I'm not telling you . . . you wouldn't know her, respectable lady . . . drives a . . . one of

51

those . . . drives, you know . . . a Range Rover.' Jack stood up, took the glass out of his eye, wrinkled the other eye too, which gave a smiling effect but was only stretching the muscles – he straightened his face, wrinkled it and straightened it.

'She'd hit him a crack!' The man laughed loudly, sorting through Range Rovers in his mind.

I got a bad impression of Jack although he'd been funny. In fact I was sickened. I was on the side of the lady with the watch, horrified at them kicking her private life around this cellar. That was how I was; I liked Jack but not him giving way, he'd told the fellow whose watch it was. Perhaps it didn't matter . . . perhaps he'd made it up . . . It was bad though.

The other guy was standing at the stove and the smell – it would be warm jacket and trousers and sweaty bum, mixed with paraffin fumes. There were lots of these guys, and there'd always be one at least in the shop trading news and warming his bum.

'They say Macdonald's wife's going with another fellow, you wouldna ken him – new doctor at the funny farm – young fellow – they should keel that woman, eh! Put a big red mark on her arse to see where she's been. Be some red faces then Jack. Red pricks rather. It's hellish!'

'Alastair said it was him in the paper shop.'

'No. Definite. Someone saw them in a car.'

'Hers?'

'Aye.'

'Poor old Mac,' Jack said. 'Aye.'

'Nothing else fresh.' The man scratched, turned round and held his hands over the vent of the stove. His jacket was rucked up and a fold of shirt came out of the top of his trousers. 'Bit of a ruckus going on at Wallaces I hear. New manager making them skip now he's got a free hand. Crawford'll not be the man to stop him.'

'Michael here works for Andy.'

'Ha!' The fellow jerked round to look at me, stuck up his chin and stared along his nose, over his moustache; I couldn't see his eyes because of the angle of his specs.

'I'm at the other bit.'

'Just so,' he said. 'And how do you get on with Andy? Fine, eh? Fine?'

I just looked at him.

'Aye, nothing wrong with Andy. And straight!' He straightened his arm and looked severely along it. 'You're lucky there.'

He was familiar – not the joke shop nose-moustache-specs; it was the way he moved while he talked, and the way his head was set on his neck, seeming to show his fixed ideas, and the way he stood back after he'd spoken, and sometimes before he spoke, and while Jack was talking – the way he stood really, like Andy. But only this chance likeness. Perhaps a common feature in Gledhill that I hadn't yet noticed, people of the same race or just chance, nothing in it. They weren't related or he'd have said something else than Crawford, they couldn't all be related. They might be.

I said, 'I'll be away, Jack. Looked in to say hullo.'

'There!' He'd been doing more work inside the watch and had pressed the back of it into place with his thumbs; he gave it a long easy wind, keeping his thumb on the winder, running it back. He checked the time. 'Another satisfied customer.'

'I'll just be off.'

The other guy was looking away. The back of his neck was pock-marked. The inside of his mouth would stink; the thought of his breath made me shudder. With these people you had to wait till they died, they wouldn't change. These dinosaurs. He swung around. 'Pleased to have met you . . . Michael, was it?' He didn't like being glowered at. 'Good luck to you.'

It was lucky he was repulsive. I'd have thought Andy like him in personality otherwise. But this fellow, when you considered him, didn't have one. He was anonymous. He'd grown the moustache to help out, but it hadn't – others had done that too! I tried to pretend that I worked for him, see how it felt, it couldn't be done. The difference would be clear if Andy was here too. I imagined his voice. What would he say? Would he back up to the stove too? Say the same things?

Ting! went the bell and I headed back to the yard. Wait for them to die, right enough. In a minute he'd have my surname, age, weight, what I had for breakfast.

Jack might tell him about Barbara. Why I thought he'd tell

stories about his wife, search me. And I don't know if he did.

It had started at the picnic she'd asked me to go on, to the sea which was only a short drive away. We – my family – had sometimes gone to a nearby bay when I was small, and I was keen to see the sea again, even though I'd left home to avoid family life.

The sea was out of sight. 'No chance of a swim,' Jack said. I didn't know if it was a joke. I didn't have my trunks.

We carried our stuff across grass and through bracken to the dunes. There seemed to be a circle of stones and ashes in every hollow, but no-one else was there. We chose one next to the beach.

William and Steph took off their shoes and socks, ran down to the sand and splashed through shallow puddles. I suppose they were warm because they were shallow and it was a nice day. They went further out and round rocks into the next bay.

Barbara had wandered back to the car for something. Jack moved the blackened stones into a regular shape and set down a paper bag of charcoal.

'I'd use wood, but these other sods have cleaned up every stick. Come on, we'll find something to start it.' He was wading through the coarse dune grass, picking up things. I came on a few shavings. How had they got there? I found a wet, charred lump of wood that had already been in a fire. Jack was holding a handful of twigs the size of bird bones and scraps of yellowed newspaper. He made a pyramid Scout fire. Away it went, crackling and sending up smoke with a good smell. It was red in a few seconds and he built charcoal over it. 'I worked in the woods, before this watch caper.' He handed me a can and we sat on the sandy grass among rabbit droppings. 'Life-a-Riley. We made our own time you know.' He grinned at the joke. 'Work like a bastard from when you get up. Get the fire going at dinnertime, lie around drinking billy tea and smoking. No-one to bother you. For as long as you feel like. Then an afternoon session with the saw till you're knackered. I'd like to get back to it.' He delicately moved the charcoal with my charred stick and motioned me to put more on. 'I doubt I'm too old. My back wouldn't stand the chainsaw. I'm lazy too.'

He got more cans out of the straw basket.

54

Barbara climbed over the dune and sat down near the fire. We said hullo and then we sat there for a while in silence. You could hear some birds squawking in the trees where we'd left the car. Barbara lay down with a sigh and closed her eyes. The sun was so bright it was hard to see the charcoal glowing.

Jack put more on and then got a square of wire mesh from the stuff we'd brought and laid it over the stones.

'When the charcoal goes white it's ready.' He opened parcels of meat but left them in the basket. He looked at me sharply. Then he looked up at the sky, and over the bay, and seemed to make an effort to be easy. He lay with his hands clasped behind his head. 'Great smell in the woods all the time,' he said through a grass he was chewing. 'Your clothes smelt of smoke and sawdust and roset.'

'Resin?'

'Roset! Call yourself a Scotsman?' He had a sharp look in his eye.

I said after a while: 'The sea goes a hell of a way out here.' I was thinking of walking out across the sands.

'They say it comes in faster than a galloping horse. Load of bollocks.'

'I'll risk it.' I took off my shoes and pushed the socks into them, stood up and saw Steph running towards us.

'Oh-oh,' said Jack. 'What's up?'

She was soon at the dunes, but stayed on the sand and beckoned Jack, biting her finger and frowning.

'Come Dad! William's stuck.'

'Don't put the meat on till I get back,' Jack said to me.

They walked quickly across the sand and then jogged to disappear round the rocks. William would be not far up, on a ledge half the width of his foot, and his legs shaking. He'd be pressing to the rock, fingers in a wee crack at face level, the rock seeming to bulge against him to throw him off. And probably he'd fall off, graze his knees on the red granite on the way down, land in the sand with a bump and pick himself up before they got there. He'd have been after a botanical specimen, not just climbing, that's how it would be. They'd soon be back.

Barbara had slept on. Heat shimmering from the charcoal now rippled her upper half. She lay on her side facing me, head on her arm, hair like water splashing over it. Clear of the distorting fire was the bulge of her hip, vertical from her waist like artistic licence, a trick of my eye surely; it couldn't really be like that, but it must, because she was asleep, it was her real shape. The pant line showed under the stretched black trousers on her hip, then it vanished into her crotch and I stared at this area, wondering what it was really like in there, really like. I stood up cautiously and went round behind. The fact of her lying there made me dizzy. I looked in the basket and found some buttered rolls and started to eat one. I opened a can of beer gently with a hiss instead of a pop. The meat parcels had fallen open showing grease stains on the paper and sweating oily bits of chicken. It was really hot now. There was no shade for the basket.

I had a right to watch her breathing because she was asleep and there was no-one else. My face was inches from the strip of skin between her shirt and trousers, my head turned so that my breath didn't tickle this strip of skin, covered by a thin film of moisture that became minute drops in the groove of her spine. My head almost touched it. I went to the other side of the fire, in a place where I could see without the heat interfering. Here I sat with the half-drunk can. Her dull red shirt's rise and fall suggested the weight of her breasts. Her face was still on her arm and the lower cheek bulged a little, the upper was slightly flattened. She moved her lips and sighed, the breath trembling the underside of her sleeve in the shadow.

My eyes smarted from the heat of the charcoal and the beach was glaring white, sand and sea and sky the same. They only separated if I screwed up my eyes. A group of seagulls all facing the same way along the beach stood on a sandbar among the puddles left by the tide and had no legs; they floated on the haze as if it was water. I looked away, and back at them, both ways along the beach (remembering the others when I saw the rocks), at the sky, the thin grass on the dune . . . quickly sideways – her eyes had been open.

I didn't watch now, in case she needed me to stare seawards while she pretended to wake . . . I looked again, bit by bit . . . she seemed asleep, but I felt the force coming from her the same as when I'd been looking at the gulls. The force was something between us, not a look or a thought, something like a bubble we both used, and she was putting in, 'I know you were looking at me' and I was saying 'I know you know', and there she was, asleep. The sunlight was like darkness – when you know someone's looking at you in the dark.

Get away before she wakes. We won't know what to say. I crept doubled-over to the narrow sand channel through the dune down to the soft sand; walked towards the rocks and halfway out began breathing normally, then running, not to get away from her or to them – a curve out to sea over hard ribbed and soft flat sand, puddles, channels and wormcasts and the dirty edge of the sea. I turned back to them at the foot of the cliffs. The scene came into focus: William lay on the sand. He sat up and Jack started lifting him. Steph was holding him too, and I was a few yards from them.

'There you are, Michael. Take his other side.'

I bent my knees for William to put his arm round my shoulder, and my left arm went round his waist over Jack's. Our heads were close together and William shivered, staring ahead.

'Let's go,' Jack said. 'Where's Barbara?'

I said she'd been asleep.

'Run on and tell her, Steph. Say William's hurt his leg. Go!' He gave her a pat on the bottom. 'Start getting things into the car!' he called as she ran off, thin legs drifting out below the knee and her black pigtail bouncing.

'Is it broken?'

Jack didn't answer. William was holding his leg next to me off the sand. 'It better not be,' he said shakily. 'It better not be!' He strained to hold it off the sand and we hirpled along, me with knees bent to keep to the level of these midgets, Jack talking. It didn't sound like keeping William's spirits up – the adult voice that thinks you're a child. Here I was equating myself with William. Jack talked as if we were strolling normally, though he wouldn't have if we had been, about plants, gulls' eggs, flatfish and salmon and worms dug for bait. He knew a lot and he wouldn't normally tell you this stuff.

William hissed when his leg touched the sand.

'I'll give you a piggyback!' I crouched and he got on. The sore bit was below the knee and I held him under his skinny thighs and strode along.

The car was being driven over the field to our picnic place as we

57

rounded the rocks – Barbara had made the farmer unlock the gate. She drove to the edge of the dunes and half-ran half-walked across the sand.

'Willy, what happened?' she cried, putting her arm round him as we continued.

'He came off. Lucky he didn't fall all the way,' Jack said.

'This one?'

William nodded and a tear landed on my neck. She kept her hand on his back while we moved, the warmth of her side on my arm.

Steph was putting stuff into the car boot. I lowered William to the front seat and Barbara tucked him in with the tartan rug she'd lain on.

Jack had grabbed all the rest. 'Fire's out,' he said as we piled in, Barbara next to me in the back. She looked forward during my glance, in which the side of her face filled my sight as if it was half the world.

'A ship at sea!' Jack groaned, the car plunging through sandy holes in the grass track. William gripped the rug with hands like birds' claws. They relaxed their grip and looked cramped and old lying loose on the rug when we were on the road.

'We'll get it X-rayed,' Jack said.

I was telling them about my work at the yard, Peter and Annie, the first day driving the truck – made more interesting; I made out Andy a wise fellow I admired, I don't know why. It wasn't what I really thought – a game we were all playing – they were listening. Jack said he didn't know him, but knew of him. I told about the Nissen hut, and just before we went under the railway bridge I could see its chimney and the top of the roof, but it had passed too quickly for anyone else.

At the hospital Barbara and Jack went with William to the X-ray. Steph was looking at a magazine she'd picked up from the dog-eared pile on the table in the middle of the room. I asked if she'd like anything from the dispenser. She said orange juice. I brought it and a coffee to our seats.

'What are you reading?'

She turned away and muttered, 'Something or other.'

I very much wanted her to like me, but everything I'd said made it worse. And then this business that she wouldn't look at me. I would not do anything ambitious like starting a conversation or even telling her more about the yard – she thought I was stupid whatever I said.

I finished the coffee – she tensed, expecting me to ask if she wanted another orange – and selected an old Sunday supplement, ignoring her. We sat side by side reading. She was beginning to tolerate me when Jack came from the X-ray room. He came over and for a moment we were held close by this phrase of his, 'It's broken.' We faced inward, a three-way glance, as if William had broken his leg for this moment.

Barbara appeared. Feeling uneasy about being with the three of them I said I'd walk home instead of waiting while the leg was plastered. She thanked me for carrying him across the beach and I got out quickly, an outsider with the three of them. There was no way I could connect to that kind of family-team. Jack and Steph and me had been fine. Barbara and Steph, Barbara and Jack or William, any two-combination, but as it was, better out and along the front of the hospital, past the garden with a few tattered roses. I could have looked up and seen George's window but I was busy, in a hurry to do something great, I didn't know what.

Next day William was sitting pale and starey-eyed in the kitchen with the big white leg and a pair of crutches. I felt sorry for him and gave him a game of chess.

Barbara came in, with the bright smile for us. I'd thought she was putting it on and sometimes she might have been, but not now for instance. She was pleased and it shone without her trying – not everyone has a spontaneous smile – and it was alright with me. She was pleased to see us at the table with the board between us.

She made sandwiches and that was when my game went to pieces, I watched her make sandwiches. We had a little party, the chess-board to one side, the piled plate in the middle and our mugs of coffee. We signed William's plaster and discussed broken limbs in a general way that kept off his leg in particular.

'Have you ever broken anything, Michael?' she asked, looking at me from close range with intense, black-centred eyes. I nearly fainted.

I'd been sweeping the shed and was covered in grime when I

met Barbara in the passage.

'You better give me those clothes right away!' she said. It seemed I couldn't go a step further into her house with them on. She didn't move to let me up to my room; I turned that way and she stood between me and the stair. 'Come on.' I stripped off jersey, shirt and trousers. She held the filthy clothes over her arm, amused. A breeze cooled my legs and I found myself looking at her, wearing her usual black tracksuit type of thing. It was tighter than a tracksuit, I saw the shape of her legs: from where I was looking, a downward perspective; the stretchy black woollen material had a sheen – I looked down bum, thigh and calf, marked out by the sheen. What they showed on the adverts was real here, a real woman; not a picture, not a girl. A tremendous smell. I don't know if there was a smell but there was the sensation of one. The top of her thigh bulged and I wanted to put my hands round it, one each side. I must have moved up to her. 'Go on, you're filthy,' she said and brushed right against me on her way to the kitchen. I vaguely registered that the passage was wide enough for her to have passed without touching.

I hung about while Annie took her thick blue coat from the hook on the back of the office door, a hook I wanted to replace with a stronger one before it tore out. She heaved into the coat and said goodnight in a significant voice (it seemed to me), warning me to lock the door when I left, and meaning what did I think I was at – usually we left together and she locked up with her key.

I stayed anyway; I had a key which I used in the morning when I arrived before her. My brain was busy with many things: the line of Barbara's thigh, the coffin in the bottom of the hole and the thud thud of earth once they got to shovelling in earnest; I thought of going to some place like Italy; reorganising the yard and this crummy office. I was really balanced, poised. I waited for Annie to come back under some pretence if she was going to; then when I knew she must have been turning onto the main road I felt under the counter for the key to her drawer, fitted it into the big worn keyhole and pulled out the drawer by its stained brass handle. It was loose in its runners. I moved back and looked down. From outside it would seem as if I was standing behind the counter thinking. The drawer was full of rubbish at first sight, books and books of carbons of delivery notes, stuff from the Government about wages and tax, a large book-keeping book that I recognised from the course at the Tech. I opened it – a mass of her small rounded writing, less easy to make out than the figures. She used a thick-ended biro that smudged and the smudges across the writing seemed still wet. Double-entry; I could master it in half an hour though I hadn't bothered at the Tech.

There was a wages book too in her drawer. Wages seemed to be a big part of her job – for the nine or ten of us! And that counted the two self-employed brickies! I didn't recognise M. Bell at first. I earned more than her or Peter. Seeing it in writing was bad. Of course Peter was on a part-time retired wage, but it wasn't right, in his case even. I'd only just arrived! And Annie had known this. She must hate me. The sooner I started the new job the better. I hadn't opened the drawer for this, but because I was in that balanced, inquisitive mood . . . I thought: I could run this place without her and I'd know where everything was and it wouldn't take all my time . . . I flew through the job at such a rate in my mind that I was looking for the next one, perhaps manager of a big sawmill; it was the smell of wood I liked best in this place . . .

Car headlights shone through the window. I locked the drawer moving my arm as little as possible and returned the key to its hook as I walked slowly along the counter, and round the end where the flap was raised and then casually to the door. Annie wouldn't have come back in a car. It was amazing I hadn't heard it.

I recognised Andy's number plate and was confused between 'of course it would be him' and 'what's he creeping up for at this time of night?' as he hurried forward banging his knuckle on the wing mirror.

'It's you Michael! Glad I caught you!' – but his face was anxious, and I saw how it would have been for him as he drove up, a light in the office and wondering if it was a break-in.

'Yes, I was finishing off a bit of work.'

'No, no,' he said, 'it's just handy I caught you. Come back in. You're not in a hurry?' He rushed into the office and fell in the chair. There was sweat on his forehead and behind his glasses. 'I've a load of furniture coming. You can give me a hand with it.'

'The shed's filthy yet.'

'We'll bring it in here, in here!' He laughed. 'Sit down. He'll be here in a few minutes. I'll tell you what I've got. I've had a great day.' He was licking his lips. The furniture was probably rubbish, and he got excited like this! I couldn't see Dad doing it. I was supposed to get excited too, but I thought of it as a matter of politeness, until I understood that it was because I was to be the furniture man! I hadn't been excited at all and was caught out: I was assumed to be keen on it and hadn't even thought it was anything to do with me! And I'd assumed I'd be keen myself, as well as Andy. 'I went down to this auction today, just to have a look you know, but there were some rare bargains.' He'd jerked his head in a direction, but it was from him saying 'down' that I guessed it was south, England. For north, he'd have said 'up'. 'I bought – well, you'll see them. Think you'll be pleased! A chest of drawers specially! Then I got a tip-off. There are some decent fellows down there.' His lip-licking look reappeared, he meant they thought he was a decent fellow. 'Aye, an old couple moving out, the lorry driver told me, too much stuff for the wee sheltered house they were going to so I took a good lot off them. Kept him right, of course. The driver. And before that in a village in the sticks I got this grandfather clock off an old woman.'

'We won't get much in here.'

'It's not all coming. The auctioneers are keeping some.'

'Just from the old couple then, and the clock?'

He grunted.

The wagon rolled in with an English name and phone number on the side. It was a cattle truck cleaned out. He probably went back to that next day, there was a strong smell.

Everything still on board was for us. The clock was tied to the side with old scarves and pairs of tights and between it and the side was a sleeping bag to cushion the jolts.

We carried in a bookcase, armchairs, a standard lamp, a table, various wooden chairs, the chest of drawers and the clock, which stood with its head against the curve of the Nissen hut; all these jammed behind the counter left hardly room to move.

Andy had gone out with the lorryman. There might have been a settle-up to do. The chest of drawers looked ordinary, the other things too. But what did I know about them. There was the clock though, a dingy looking affair, possibly an antique.

'That fellow followed me in his wagon, you know, down all the back roads. We chucked the stuff in straightaway.'

'Oh. Ah. The clock too? Does it go?'

'The clock? Aye! She wound it, the woman, and it gave a few ticks. Fellow had to stop it to move it.' He frowned.

I remembered the inside of Granny's clock. I opened the front of this one. The pendulum . . . the haggis-like weights that lay in the bottom not connected to the wires, but it would be all that was needed; put them on and whatever it was you did, wind it up. There'd be a key somewhere. 'Will we start it?'

'No. Not now.'

'How much did you give for it?'

'Tenner.' His back to me.

'And it works!'

'Needs doing up. I'll get a clockmender to overhaul it. If the case needs a clean, Drew can do that.'

'How much will you get for it?'

'Couple of hundred' – a quiet, throwaway voice, as if it might be more.

'She can't have known what it was worth!'

'She was well paid. It was no use to her.'

What did he mean? Maybe it hadn't been working? But that wasn't the present question. I hadn't meant he'd done the old woman, he'd picked me up wrong there. I'd meant to compliment him on his, well, not skill but luck, but maybe a bit of skill too in going through with it, not giving way to sympathy, regarding the old woman as his opponent in the deal, which she was . . .

'I meant, I meant –' No way of explaining. 'Business is business,' I said.

. . . which she was except that the poor old soul had never thought of selling her clock till these two men appeared at the door with a lorry just about when it was getting dark, a lorrydriver and the kindly grey-haired one – you trusted him and felt at home with him at once. If he said the clock was only worth scrap but he'd give you ten pounds just because he had a liking for them himself and he'd get it out of your way . . . he was doing you a favour really, it was too old to be worth anything, just an ordinary clock not the antiques you heard about going for fancy prices. She saw he had the money with him. And a fine open face. And she'd seen his car, it wasn't as if he'd come in the lorry cab like a scrappie, and well-dressed, well-spoken, a family man. He'd like a cup of tea but would have to say no because he had to get on. They carried the clock out one at each end, like a coffin.

'Everyone for himself. I'd like to come with you one time when I'm into the business. Learn to pick the bargains. I can see you've got to –'

His expression was what it must have been like to the old woman. The difference between me and her was that I knew this honest face was a con, at the same time being willing to be conned – maybe she had been too, perhaps she'd kidded herself she didn't know the clock was worth more because she wanted those pound notes she'd seen in his hand. Andy and me, we co-operated in silence, nodding slightly.

Maybe I had him confused, convinced that I was a hardened wee shite. And I could be: I had no trouble thinking of the deal with the old woman in that light, if I stuck to the buyer's side and made her an old scrooge.

He was ashamed of the deal with the old woman and did not want me saying any more about it. 'I got a bargain at the sale today, a bow-fronted chest. Mahogany. You'll see when it comes. This other guy was after it, this big dealer from the south – chatting to someone just for a second – he was too late – I got it at £200.'

There was something wrong, the chest, the big dealer, the price. I didn't know a bow-fronted chest, mahogany. I wasn't sure he did, the quick way he'd said it. Definitely something amiss, but I shook my head in amazement.

He described that after leaving the cottage of the old woman he'd followed the wagon along more back roads to a house on its own where he spoke to the couple – who'd been promised by the driver, it seemed, an honest dealer (how had he chosen Andy, I wondered, probably coming to a different conclusion than he would have) and the couple gave him the run of the house and never argued prices. It could have been a house near our village, with two people in it I knew, average old people, and he was buggering them about, him and the driver carrying warm furniture down the stair and dumping it in the metal body of the wagon, past the nervous old people. I tried not to listen to him. The two of them, him and the driver, gutted the house, and the couple, close together outside the door, watched the lorry disappear.

I thought how to learn about furniture, how to talk about bow-fronted mahoganies, how to see if Andy was as ignorant as he sounded, with that quick slippery way of talking as if he didn't know how to pronounce the words: I'd ask Barbara.

Jack hadn't come in and the kids were upstairs. She was beside the fire in the living room, and pointed to the other chair. 'Sit down.' In front of the fire was a carpet; I'd never thought about them but knew these patterns were Persian or Indian, from thereabouts: I had sympathy for these objects. She knelt down with lazy movements, striking a match as if it exhausted her and lighting the gas, blue and yellow flames above the imitation lumps of coal which soon glowed red. She had slid back to her chair. The rest of the room was darker because of the fire.

I looked round at the piano, the various bits of furniture. 'You must be an expert. Could you teach me about it?'

'Phoo! I'm no expert!' Her eyes shone in the gaslight and there was a glint of the edges of teeth. She waited for me to say something.

The plants in pots on the floor looked black not green in the gloom. I'd been up brought up not to like those big house-plants and here I was suddenly seeing their goodness, essential goodness in a room.

'You know more than me! You must know about the things in here.'

'Is this because of your job?' she asked looking at the fire.

'Yes.'

Leaning back in the chair she smiled slightly, no longer looking at me she shrugged. 'There's nothing much here. A few pieces I inherited. We've bought the rest when we could afford it, in one antique shop or another – what call themselves antique shops. They're often reproductions. The little chest of drawers beside you is reproduction.'

What a word. I looked at the chest sideways. It could have been any wood. 'Does it mean not real wood?'

'No, it means the style. Reproduction of a style. That's Queen Anne. As to real wood –' she came over and picked an edge of the top with her fingernail. 'Yes that's real wood, I thought it was veneer. Couldn't remember. But not like the old, real thing, not so heavy and strong.' She passed back across the fire to the chair.

'Can they reproduce anything?'

'I'm sure they can.' She fiddled with the piping on the chair cover. 'Hasn't your boss told you anything?'

'I don't think he knows. He might not.'

She raised an eyebrow. 'Some person to run an antique shop!'

'Not antiques, just furniture.'

She sighed, blowing out her lips. 'Alright, the piano, let's start there. It's a Broadwood, quite a good make. Remember the name if you're looking at pianos.' She paused. 'You know this could be interesting!' She twisted sideways and pulled her legs up onto the chair.

'What do you mean?'

'If your boss . . . ?'

'Andy.'

'If Andy doesn't know what he's up to it'll depend on you, won't it? Not to let anything slip through your fingers?'

'I'm not saying he doesn't.'

'You did!'

'It's the impression I got just.'

She found that funny, or at least smiled. 'Well anyway – you want to know, don't you? I've got some books, but I'll tell you about what's here, such as it is.' She moved her hand as if it was not much. And I made a face and movements to deny that.

I didn't take in what she said. She went into I suppose her teacher style and explained logically, at least to herself. I was listening to the foreign tang in her voice again and the movements of her body. On a section of skin between trouser and sock the bones showed through whiter. She stroked the hollow behind her ankle bone as she talked, the finger seeming independent of the voice and going on with its conversation, the one I listened to; the voice finished with the room and went on to tables and bureaux that she'd once had, or maybe it was her parents. The fat, squashy armchair accommodated her movements. In her pauses in speaking I looked at the fire. Keeping my eyes in neutral as she talked I saw her white neck, the collarbone and the dark entrance between her breasts.

'Are you listening?' She gave her hair a flick at the ear and me a wide smile.

'I wondered – I thought you had a sort of foreign accent.'

'Did you!' She laughed. 'That's from my mother, she was half-French. My grandma was Breton.'

'Oh.'

'From Brittany. Have you been in France?'

'No.'

'The north-western corner – of course you'd know that, doing geography. You ought to go there. Do you speak French? Well, that's a pity. Reach behind you to the light switch.'

The centre light came on. She gave a down-turned smile and seemed to listen. I wondered if it was one of the others but couldn't hear anything. Keep talking. 'What's that big picture?'

'It's a landscape,' she coached, 'mostly a loch, as you can see. Painted by a man called Noble. Like it?'

'I dunno.' Two men stood beside a boat at one side, in the shallow water; there was a wide stretch of grey water and misty hills; in the foreground again, the man's name was a scrawl in the bushes in the brown scum on the picture.

'It's valuable now, but I would never sell it. I love its greyness. Don't you?'

'Yes I do. Is it a . . . a family picture?' I noted the name, Noble.

'Well, I got it from my parents,' she said. 'Do you like pictures?'

'Yes.' I quickly added, 'Our first delivery of furniture's come. There's a grandfather clock, I think a good one.' I nodded. 'He picked it up. Was going, I think, but these weights, you know' – these heavy bollocks, oh the weight! – I eased to a wider position on the chair, 'they're lying in the bottom. They've been taken off.'

'Grandfather clocks are hard to find, good ones.'

The story of the old woman appeared in my head and I was confident of telling it in order. But I didn't; it might be a wrong done to Andy. Instinct stopped me and I was quiet when I should have been speaking in this pause, in this pause I saw it would have been bad badder worst to have done it but I nearly had – was I to be trusted? 'The clock's face is decorated,' I said.

'That's nice. What's the maker's name?'

I shook my head. 'Flowers and things, birds maybe. The flowers were in the corners, I can't remember.'

'Not the maker's name?'

'We've only had it a day.'

'Well, my budding antique dealer, these are the things you must notice! I'll come and see it.'

The thought of her coming to the office where the clock was standing with its head against the ceiling, and her arty-farty manner getting right up Annie's nose – this couldn't happen!

Feet on the stairs. We were smiling at each other and already I was looking back on our talk as if it had been a week ago – enjoying its sugary taste, the looking back.

I knew where everything was kept in the kitchen through having my tea there and I'd learnt to do various jobs, one being unblocking the waste pipe. Barbara peeled carrots, potatoes and so on into the sink; she dumped tea-leaves and swirled them away with continuously running taps; she poked remains of vegetable soup down the plughole with her finger – the U-bend blocked regularly. She ought to have had one of those chewing machines below the hole. Not having one, how could she block the thing again and again, a woman like her?

I lay on my side on the floor to reach between two shelves, unscrewed the old brass fitting that showed through its cream paint because it had been undone often, and let the brown water with its stringy bits and lumps of grease slabber into a plastic bowl; the drain smell not too bad, the peelings and tea-leaves hers. I liked the gunge they'd turned into, and the smell of pots, cardboard, plastic bottles of cleansers, soap powder, floorcloths. Under my elbow the worn lino with the cream edging strip, which seemed the only kind of lino in the world; beside my head, a unique wooden shelf. Sometimes she stood beside me and continued her cutting up or whatever it was on the work surface. Her shins were giant's legs and I smelt her own unique smell, of her skin and her perfume and her sweat, and moved to hide my erection.

I was handy about the place, filling the stove with egg-shaped coal, riddling it, the jobs Jack had done, and he watched with a bit of a grin. When I'd nothing to do while she made tea I lay on the couch. Steph would appear now and then with a frosty look. I wished she liked me. She seemed to have come for nothing in particular, or to say to Barbara something she couldn't say with me there. William never came till he was shouted. One day over corned beef and cabbage Jack talked about the tattie holiday, where they'd go and so on. It was my second year without one and I didn't mind – it was for school kids and surely they needed it poor sods – but it seemed I should be there all the same, the smell of heather, wet peat and peat smoke up the west coast where we'd always gone. Maybe the weather, the daylight shortening, brought it on and I'd have remembered Kintyre even if they hadn't been discussing their trip. They weren't going there, though. East Lothian seemed to be their place. Jack was making jokes about William and Steph really picking tatties. They had huge fields over there apparently. His head could look like a tattie as well as an egg – I saw him as a talking spud, little arms coming out where the ears should have been. Steph frowned and smiled, almost believing. William scowled. It was important for him to have the holiday he'd planned, even joking nibbled it away.

Barbara looked at each as they spoke, smiling, waiting maybe to hear more than anyone would say. Maybe she liked remembering more than looking forward; she wouldn't get anything new, probably just smile that tantalising smile all through the holiday.

William went with Jack in the car to be dropped off at a rehearsal on Jack's way to the pub. Steph went to her room and I returned up the back stairs. A while later I heard the radio below in the kitchen.

Barbara was fixing hooks on the wall behind the work surface. 'I can't get these bloody things in,' she said.

'Let me do it.' I put my hand on hers still gripping the hook.

'If you like.' She let go.

I made the holes bigger with a bradawl and started putting in hooks. She made coffee, brought the mugs across and jumped up to sit on the work surface. I swayed and touched her leg. My arms went round her and I kissed her . . .

My guts dropped out and I floated. The blood in her lips hummed on mine. I think my eyes were shut, I saw sunshine; they were open as I pushed my nose into her hair, not hair but a warm forest of this edible stuff, now barley-sugar now chestnut, undergrowth of scalp and shampoo. I journeyed to her ear while her scalding mouth touched my cool neck; the tip of her tongue, inching between my lips.

We were clamped together with this electricity running between us. My legs shook, elbows came down each side of her, my head pressed into her breast, my eyes were shut by these soft black breasts and I breathed from a crack at the corner of my mouth . . . coming up for air, detaching from her heartbeat, I pulled her from the surface and hugged her, legs shaking more though snugly against hers. I was pushing her against the edge of the work surface, or was she pulling me, this older woman, her daughter upstairs, her hand down the front of my jeans.

The front door opened – footsteps – William.

She'd moved out away from me, pushed back her hair, was getting seated at the table, self-possessed. 'Your coffee's here, come and sit.'

'God that was terrible,' William said, bursting in and throwing himself into a chair, his elbows spread on the table and his head in his hands. His music case was on the floor, an old leather thing. I raised my eyes slowly from it.

'Coffee, love?' Barbara was asking.

'Yea. Thanks.' His voice came muffled from under his arm, his head sideways, breath damping the crook of his sleeve.

'Was it your leg?' I asked.

There was a pause. 'It aches like hell, Mum,' he said, wiping his nose.

She put his mug on the table. 'It's bound to. The doc said piano'd be a good way of getting it strong again, the pedalling.'

'I know. I was there.' He gave her a look, pushing back his hair like her.

We all laughed.

I told Annie I had the dentist that morning, but Barbara was busy. I said I'd be doing paperwork in my room but she was busy cleaning the house; then she was in the kitchen and I waited for her step on the stair. She was there ages, perhaps cleaning too.

Then she went out. I saw her from my window for a second on the path from the back door, and ran down the stair and up the main one into her and Jack's bedroom. She was walking along with a plastic shopping bag. I kept back but she didn't look up – became a rear view, stomping along with the bag, in her heavy overcoat, a scarf on her head. She must be thinking of what she'd buy in Presto, hard to pick out, the further away and the more mixed among other shoppers she became, all walking in a zombied way, remembering and checking over the stuff in their heads, making themselves look alike. Maybe she was not different; would a time come when I wouldn't recognise her?

Oh, never! But strange to see that she looked like other people; it had happened too quickly – a mutation, something in the genes, irreversible. She *could* be like other people. A glowing woman had gone out and become another housewife – if only the change had taken its time! I looked round the bedroom, myself an invader in the mirror, smelt the sheets, rubbed a fold of her nightie between my fingers. The room was chilly and I'd have liked to jump into bed and pull up the duvet.

I went back to my room, spread out the files I'd lifted in the office and looked out, tapping my pencil on the windowsill. Tap, tap . . . tap-a-tap tap . . . I left the window and walked from the cooker in the recess at one end of the room to the head of the bed at the other where a small picture hung on the wall, a mountain or something. Four strides from one end to the other, look left out the window, turn, look right out the window. I crushed her in my arms, felt her cheek on mine, saw her hand slip into my jeans, felt the thickness with her fingers. I wanted to laugh and shout. When I passed the window in the cooker direction I keeked to see if she was back – I saw a section of the path; but I would hear the door when she came in. I forgot the shopping trip and thought of her lips, tongue, cheek, hair, ear.

The door opened and shut and parcels were dumped on the kitchen table. The stuff to be put away – tins of beans and tomatoes, bloody great bags of potatoes, litres of milk, healthy margarine and biscuits, yoghurt, yoghurt, yoghurt. A wasted morning. Jack would be home for dinner.

Her footsteps going to the stove, the kettle and she called, 'You there, Michael?' Pause. 'You want coffee?' Her draggy voice made me shiver – her voice Jack winced at, his face solidified. The voice drove him to the pub. Perhaps he came back for it too. I ran down, sure she'd have thrown off her trudging-housewife aspect – and sure, she had, warm from lugging the stuff home, locks of hair over her face.

I helped put tins in cupboards. We talked all the time. She was flushed and seemed to give me secret looks at odds with our talk – the real meaning of chat about additives in peanut butter, organic honey, free range eggs; all had secret meanings, were sacred objects.

She didn't say Jack would be home any minute, but told me by the way she turned her back, paused, bustled, paused again, like birds act with each other in the garden. I'd never known what they were saying but Barbara was clear: Jack's coming. Don't stay for your dinner – you see I'm not asking you.

I went back to the yard and wondered if I'd made it up. On the way home I decided that my room was the place. The thing would be to give her a sign on the way up. I raised my eyebrow in shop windows.

Jack was not there for his tea and soon I was sitting alone with her! She was too normal for me to say anything. William came down about his French. He settled at the table to do it with her help. He had a whole story to read, so I left. She could have thought my screwed-up face was about William's home-work.

After a walk I got into bed. I looked at the empty dark sky wishing I had a cigarette but I hadn't carried them for years; it was only at times like this. The duvet weighed heavy. Finally I began to wind down hopes. It appeared to be late, the house was silent and my eyes continually opened drily, seeing the edge of the pillow, clothes on the chair, the wicker seat of the chair at one corner, the little mirror shining over the sink, the same things over and over again. I stared at the pillow, the

72

weave of the cotton close-up.

I must have been asleep. She was closing the door. The air was moving. I saw the white of her clothes but her face was shadow under her dark hair.

She came towards the bed, her feet reaching for obstacles, a slow gliding, but she moved at speed in the half-dark, moonlight coming in the window. The distance from door to bed was solid time, accounting for her speed.

I sat up, reached to her hand and her face, where she was now sitting on the bed. On the back of my hand I felt her hair roll and slide; I stroked her full jaw, kissed her lips. We weren't speaking. Why weren't we speaking? Not to wake anyone, of course, but we could have whispered. My throat was dry. Her dressing gown slid off and I was pulling the tapes at the neck of her nightie.

'Don't hurry,' she said in a low voice, not a whisper, getting into bed, half sitting up, leaning on the pillow. Side by side, drifting on a quiet river, me and Barbara. I didn't see the room past the shape of her mouth and face, huge, mine too, a pair of giant statues, nothing between us or around.

'Lie down,' I said with difficulty, pulling. Her shoulders were cold, but as I touched them they became warm; her breasts shoogled against me. She lay in my arms on the pillow as if I protected her.

'There's plenty time.' She wormed further down the bed and I felt her blunt pubic bone through the nightie, on my stomach; the nightie rucked, the bone scratched its wiry hair against me, and her mouth moved in concert with it; then she was talking or humming, talking in a sing-song voice, a song, maybe French humming.

I started to climb on top of her. She pushed me down and went on singing. I coughed when I tried to speak, but listened to her humming and singing; her liquid-seeming shape fitted mine. Saliva returned slowly to my throat.

'Put your hand here,' she said guiding it to her warm crack, pressing against my finger. 'There!' I was taller than her as if holding her up with her feet dangling off the ground. With her hair under my neck and our ears together, her toes touched my shin. Her big toe stroked the inside of the bone now and then like a thumb. 'Look at the moon.' A thin cloud approached the three-quarter moon that rode in the top left-hand pane of the window, and drifted across. I'd slipped into her skin without trying; she'd let me in. Was it our skins being close together? Through every bit of skin I knew her. Is it what those old guys in the Bible meant? She'd deliberately let me, by the way she lay and touched, let me into her skin or made us into one, though what were we like? It seemed nothing and didn't matter, we wandered in her country and her share was enough for me and my share was enough for her – it was me, a thing I couldn't imagine . . . ghostly and fragile, about to expire; bodyless, and happy to be light.

'Fancy being an astronaut?' I asked.

'No. I'm an earthling.'

'Be good if we were in a capsule up there, eh? We could go anywhere. Nothing but a bed in it.'

'You'd regret it. I'm not always sweet.' A smile of pure sweetness parted her lips close to mine.

'Too late. I'm not getting out.'

She looked at me thoughtfully, still smiling, eyes half closed, a glimmer of light catching a little of the dark pupils.

I felt weightless on her. But my bones were heavy, pressing down, sinking in, stamping my shape in her, fingers gripping her spine's slippery channel. I made myself heavier, sank my weight in, my voice was her quiet screams. Oh I'd never heard anything like these wails for a place we'd never reach, this high/low soft scream, such a scream could not be, the bed breaking, my ribs breaking! I hadn't known I was trying to get to that place, hadn't known I'd never reach it, till I heard our scream and had known all along.

I didn't breath under her; gone-over by a steam iron, damp, pliable. Red shapes and brown, familiar though strange, joined by flickering lines, on the inside of my eyelids, the inner surface of the skull.

We lay on our sides. Her breath dampened my neck and she seemed to be asleep, but when she opened her eyes they were bright. 'The roofs are lovely. And the chimneys and their shadows. And the aerials.' She raised up in bed and looked out, glowing beside me. I grabbed her down again.

Later we sat up and looked out again, at the moon-landing scene I had not looked at, when I'd been alone. A thick frost covered the slates and the moon lightened everything distinctly, a bluish colour. In front were the black shapes of the kettle and coffee jar.

I woke and she'd gone. I drank a glass of water. The moon had disappeared and the tree in the next garden was a bone glimmering. I was wide awake and fell asleep at once.

I met Martin Somerville the manager of Wallaces' next day. I was cleaning the shed on my own because of Peter's asthma; he might have refused; he might have refused to put on a mask, which was definitely needed. The kind supplied by Andy were a gauze pad over your mouth and nose, held on by an aluminium shape and an elastic band round the back of your head. Your mouth was an unbandaged wound when you took it off, coughed and snorted up black stuff in spite of the mask.

I was knocking cobwebs off the roof with a brush tied to a pole. In the dust and cobwebs on the floor were fat, squashy rolled up spiders that got up and ran when you weren't expecting it; I kept sweeping in case they ran up my legs. A man in a Wallaces' van passed along the road, his profile sharp through the chain-link fence. He stopped in the yard. Brown boots shinier than Andy's.

He'd looked twice at me leaning in the doorway – a severe glance so that I could get myself together, stand up, smile; and a resigned one. 'Michael? Martin Somerville. Pleased to meet you.' His eyes flicked and a slight rise of his cheeks did for a smile. 'I thought we should get acquainted.'

Pens in the top pocket of a green suit, a short haircut. Clean about the face and collar like a photo of Dad in the war. In the war, Martin Somerville's head sticking out of a filthy trench he was putting up with would be neat like this.

'Andy said to look in when I had time.' He brought a clipboard from under his arm.

'Mr Crawford – ' But what was the use. I allowed a pause and started again. 'Andy said you might come to check the stocks or something.' We went into the office. 'This is Mrs Curran,' I said. They nodded. 'Would you like a cup of tea?' I asked him. But the phone went, Annie answered in a funereal voice and held the receiver to him, crumbs pressed in the underneath of her arm.

I slipped through the piled furniture to the kettle for the tea, but he looked at me while he listened and shook his head, then leant stiffly across Annie to put down the phone. He had said no more into it than short, clipped-off yes and no. That was his style, I'd spoken to him on the phone.

'I'm pressed for time. Shall we go and look it over?'

'Stocksheets are here . . . somewhere.' I pretended not to know where they were. His shortness of time, the clipboard and flat voice, his eyes moving on before you'd finished speaking, as soon as you'd begun to answer even, made people dislike him; that and his Englishness – the peculiar flavour of it came back, the flavour of Leeds; his accent was less than Leeds, the Englishness the same. Most of them in Gledhill – there were quite a lot because we were near the border – glossed it over a bit, but he was really foreign. Oil and water.

He interested me. So it was okay going along with him, but not wanting Annie to know I made a face to her behind his back, and I kept a space between us as we went to the stacks. It was surprising he didn't tally the materials exactly, but sized each stack rapidly by eye, checked it with the lists, moved on. In the store, out of the wind, there could have been a pause but here he proceeded the same way through paint, rainware, roofing, bolts, hinges without quite stopping. His eyes flicked about. He counted the timber on the rack and rested his hand on it. 'Nice place.'

The workshop machines which I could see through the door were about the green colour of his suit. The stained roofsheets gave a thin green light – Bella's kitchen with George, and the partly eaten food on the table – and because of that I seemed to know Somerville. It was fine standing in the store with him.

'Andy built it himself,' I said.

Somerville went to the workshop door and stood with his fists on his hips, feet splayed out, looking at the machines and up at the roof. 'I'm a time-served joiner, you know,' he said quietly.

I was looking over his shoulder at the tarnished silky blade of the circular saw with the out-pointing teeth making a bright band edge-on. It had been sharpened by Drew the old joiner,

76

giving out a ringing under the file, and a similar ringing sounded when it ran idle. The great whirring thing, its teeth a soft blur . . . I often thought – probably a dream once – that Helen my sister, bound with ropes, was being run towards the blade on the wooden rollers, and then was cleanly sliced down the middle, no blood, the two halves of her riding past the blade.

At the same time I sensed things flicking through Somerville's brain, it was no effort to know what he was thinking. There was no way of checking, but the subject he might have in mind wasn't the point; the point was I expected to be familiar with his thoughts whatever they were; they flowed between us, we didn't have to speak.

Somerville turned and went out.

'Nice to have met you, Michael,' he said in his flat voice, Martin the time-served joiner who was bossy, cold, English, powerful, but it didn't matter.

I returned to the workshop later in the day. I'd come to find what had been there . . . Peter had swept shavings into a pine-smelling heap beside the planing-machine. I pressed the red Start button for the saw. The two hums, from the electric motor and the blade, were soon at full pitch . . .

'What did the fellow want?' Peter said from the doorway.

'He checked the stock.'

'What's he want to do that for! A bloody good look round likely!'

'He seemed okay.'

'What'd he want then?'

'He checked the stock, I told you.'

Peter looked at me suspiciously. Then at the tidy pile of shavings. He was carrying a plastic bag. 'I'm taking this for my hens' litter!'

I switched off the saw.

He began scooping shavings into the bag with shovel-like hands. The procedure with shavings was, they were bagged and sold to a livestock haulier when we'd accumulated enough. It wasn't normal for him to take them for his hens, or to dump the bag, grasp the loose at the neck and tie the string in this masterful style, as if he was at home and not looking over his shoulder for Andy. He threw it behind the door, slapped my shoulder and grinned. 'I'll lift it on my way home the night! There, Michael!' Away he went across the yard, gripping the brush near its head, banging the end of the shank on the ground at each step and quivering the red plastic bristles at his shoulder.

'You shouldn't have let him in there,' Annie said in the office.

'He's a right to count the stock. Andy told him to come over.'

'That's what he'll have told you. He's too smart for our Andy.' She turned round in her chair, her eyes black holes.

'He's a decent fellow!' I shouted. 'He's okay. Needs watching!' In the following silence she was writing. I laughed. Those English were all the same, those people in Leeds, they were like us, a bit slower.

My smile; I felt the power of it myself, and it convincing Annie; I put my hand on her hard smooth shoulder. 'We're going to have to work with him. He likes the yard okay, but he feels strange – he didn't say, but I sort of felt it. He can't help his voice, but it's terrible though!' I laughed, patted her shoulder and sat on the counter. 'This could be the main yard. Once we get the antiques going – the furniture I mean – and they smarten up your office, give you an assistant . . . ' I swung my legs, making her look and smile.

She had no get-out. She groped down to her bag, popped a chocolate in her mouth and held one out to me. 'Look at the state of you. You should get a wash.'

I went out after a while and called Peter to move the furniture to the shed, just to keep things going. We carried the small stuff, then hauled the big wardrobe out. It looked strange on the muddy gravel. I came too close to it with the fork-lift and struck the base; he'd tipped it back and I was going to blame him for moving it or something, but it was because of it's being furniture, out in the yard, a different thing from a stack of bricks; the mark from the fork-lift was only a scratch, but I was very careful after that. I eased the arms under and we put sacks where it would touch metal, and roped it on.

I raised it high to see forward below it, moving slowly. The carved top stood out against the sky; sun and wind on the shiny surface of the dark wood could only be for a short time, like a procession-object, brought out once a year. My wheel went into a pothole, tipped the load over left and terrible creaks came out as it tightened into the ropes. Then the side was nearly battered on the gatepost.

'Steady!' Peter yelled, jumping. He looked angry at his escape from being crushed. I grinned at him and landed the wardrobe in the doorway of the black shed and then we went back to the office.

'Your chair next, Annie!' I said as we were manoeuvring the last thing, the grandfather clock, through the counter.

'Try!' she giggled, sitting with her hands on her knees as if we were to try and get it from under her.

'No! Why not come over to the shed and have a look – come on, I won't pinch it!' I was blushing.

'Aaww! Won't you?'

Peter grinned widely, showing the rim of his denture.

'You'll have to drag me,' Annie said.

Peter had rested his end on the counter. 'Eh!' he grinned at me.

I went and put my arm round her. 'I'm not man enough,' I said stupidly, feeling the tremendous heat coming off her.

'You mind the whists over there, Peter?' she asked after a while.

'Uh-hu.'

'Old Sam ran them.'

'Aye.'

'You'll have plenty hankies yet?'

Peter gripped the clock. 'I gied them away mostly.'

I was looking from one to the other of them. Peter was lifting his end of the clock, wanting me to get going.

'Peter was always winning the gents' prize,' Annie said. 'That's how he's got so many boxes of hankies.'

Peter just lifted his end again so that I had to do something with mine to stop it falling. Apart from the hankies he was worried as usual that Andy might find him not working.

I couldn't help trying to keep him hanging about. And I needed to be saying something. 'Drew's not been around . . .' Drew had come to mind because of the talk about bowling boards the other day.

'Got his hands full with that Somerville, likely,' Annie

79

muttered.

Peter didn't say anything to that, and neither did I.

I took my side of the clock and we carried it out. We stood it against the back wall below the balcony, opposite the door.

'Are you going to start her?' He braced his legs and shoved back his cap.

'I don't know how to.'

He was forward into it immediately. I didn't see what he was doing. The weights of course, the reason for its being heavy on the way across. I saw one in his hand as he delved it up from the bottom of the case, and he fixed them to the wires or ropes but I didn't see how. He was opening the glass door of the face and sticking a small brass starting handle in one of the holes. He wound, making a steady ratchet noise. Then he looked at his pocket watch and moved the big hand of the clock with his index finger. He pushed the pendulum to one side, let it go. TICK! The heartbeat of the shed! Another tick, after what seemed too long for the thing to be alive. The pendulum's doddery movement just reached the edge of its swing. Peter pushed me out the way to shut the case. We stood back. The second hand in a small dial below the 12 o'clock hesitated too, in sprung, feeble motion.

'Away and get a spirit level. We should have levelled her.'

He had bits of cardboard in his hand when I got back, torn from a box on the heap of rubbish. I stuck pieces under the feet of the clock as he directed.

We stood back again to look at it and he was frowning to hide his pleasure. I was just as pleased. I'd get a tin of polish and shine it up. Some day in the future Barbara would come to see it.

I'd had no time to think and I went to a pub for a quiet drink on the way home. I was well inside when I saw Drew and another joiner, Kenny, at the bar in front of me. I seemed to have come in on purpose to find them. Of course that wasn't it, but I couldn't go out. The bar was U-shaped and they were standing at the bottom of the U at the door. Back at the end of each arm of the bar were quiet areas where I would have gone.

'Well, boys!' I said.

They looked at me and Drew made a slight movement of his head to the man behind the bar. With my being tall and him small I think he disliked me because of that. But Kenny was tall and he seemed alright as far as Drew was concerned. Maybe it was the way I stood. Maybe it was being skinny. Kenny was broad as well. I'd have liked to be as strong and quiet.

I was trying to speak to the barman in spite of having seen the signal and him now filling a pint. I pretended surprise when it was put up and mumbled thanks to Drew who'd lifted his hand from lying on the bar, just his hand, the wrist remaining there, and the barman took the folded note from between the fingers, a dirty limp note. 'Cheers. I'm on my way home. Usually go to Mailers.'

'Oh aye.'

We stood in a triangle. I'd reached between them for the beer. They remained against the bar and I an arm's length from it, my back to the door. I'd have liked to put my bag down at my feet as theirs were at the bar rail, but kept it on my shoulder, not to clutter the floor and have people falling over it. The door opened all the time letting in cold air along with people. I drank large gulps to catch up, to get my round in, remembering I had to have time, to make time somehow to think about Barbara, and so drinking quick to make time . . . 'Nice place,' I said.

'Liking your work in the old hall, then?' This was Drew.

'Yes,' I said, remembering he'd lifted the bowling boards. That was Peter's version and Peter didn't like Drew – it showed on my face, I thought. 'Peter was saying it had once been a hall.'

'Oh aye, old Peter.'

'They were talking about the whists and the bowling.'

'No-one was prepared to give their time.' Drew supped and swallowed in a neat movement. 'That's how it closed down.' He looked at Kenny and then away. Kenny was too young to confirm this.

He wouldn't have talked this way if he'd stolen the boards. Peter had made it sound like that without actually saying so. What was happening was that I was believing the person talking to me, that he'd be telling the truth, us being face to face. In this case Peter hadn't said Drew had stolen the boards

81

and Drew hadn't said he hadn't. But I believed he hadn't while talking to him. I sighed to show sorrow about the hall, and said, 'They're going to put clear sheets in the roof.'

'Those buggers.'

'You should come and see.'

'We're working on a house. Twenty-four hours a day, eh?'

'That's right,' Kenny said.

'When's your store opening?' Drew asked.

'Two or three weeks. Before Christmas.'

'Need a bloody miracle!' Drew's fuzz of grey round the bald patch seemed to stick out angrily.

Kenny moved his arm on the bar and smiled.

'Has he *got* furniture?' Drew asked.

I explained that it was in store in the auction rooms and wondered if it was. I'd been wondering about this.

'He's out of his head having a place up there. Should be in the town for fucksake. Who's going away up there?'

'People who live round about. It's going to be a warehouse. Like a bargain warehouse, not fancy stuff.'

'Does he think we're too poor to buy new furniture for ourselves or what?' He laughed. He was talking about Andy like someone he didn't know. His face now made a quick change, from angry to something else. 'He's maybe right!'

'Aye,' said Kenny.

'But we don't want manky secondhand stuff! Nobody here does!'– angry again.

'What's wrong with buying secondhand? And it won't be manky! People will come from other places too.'

'Oh them! Rich bloody hoors driving about looking for nice old fucking pieces! Bloody make you sick!'

I ordered a round of beer. While getting it a good number of people came in and we moved along, leaning on the bar, Drew in the middle.

'Aye, but what kind of place will it be, an auction room, like?' He looked at me. 'You an auctioneer?'

'No!'

'What then? You put money in? Your old man put money in?'

'He hasn't got any!'

Drew made a face, a sideways movement, setting that question aside for the moment. 'It's fucking incredible I mean.

Wallaces too, I mean. Somerville could be in it.' He looked at me hard, Kenny looked and moved closer. They could have brought me for questioning. But they hadn't – had I come here on purpose? They hadn't asked a question. We all knew the situation although it had just occurred.

Drew thought I was in league with Martin but wasn't sure. And the firm of A. Crawford, Joiners had once been him and Andy. 'Aye, we're not getting on too well with *Mr* Somerville,' he said.

'I just met him the other day.'

'Did you not know him before?'

'No.'

'I heard you'd been working down in England.'

'Well! – That doesn't mean I met him! Doesn't mean I met him!' I spoke on one tone and fast, staring at him. My heart thumped, pressure blocked my ears and I saw nothing but his face, the middle of his face.

'Aye but . . . ' He grinned, shook his head as if he thought I was lying.

'Are you saying I met him?'

There was quite a sag round his eyes, the lower lids sagged away from them, and there were the dark round centres – the blunt nose, dark stubbled chin – grey on the cheeks. 'Mebbe not.'

'Mebbe?'

'No. I'm not saying it.'

'Right. Because I didn't.' Still the fast-speak, blocked ears, when I'm someone else and hyper-alert. I felt a relaxing behind me. It was Kenny, he must have been ready to grab me or something. 'That's the first time I've seen him, when he came round the other day to the yard!' I said.

'Okay. For Christ's sake.'

'He knows his job.'

'See, Michael,' Drew took a cigarette from behind his ear, 'we've nothing against you . . . just, eh, you know?'

I saw us in the mirror behind the bar. Something was to be done, I didn't know what. I wished I was out of here. Kenny's hand was loose and still on the bar as if it had just happened to be lying there and the straight glass had dropped into it. He was smiling faintly and had turned sideways to face me over

83

Drew's head. The sharp beer-smell wafted from the sloptray and I turned my glass in my hand mechanically, the pads of my fingers sliding over the coldness, warming it. It was just that we were embarrassed. Kenny sorted it by calling for another round.

I had to keep on. In my head I sounded like Dad. 'You must have spoken to Martin,' I said to Drew.

'Martin, eh! When I had to!'

'Yes, *Martin*. He's okay, right?'

'Listen here, boy, it's our jobs are on the line.' He was tapping his black-nailed finger on the bar.

I nodded. 'He's not daft.'

'It's you's daft, boy.'

Three pints came. I saw my lips stretching for the rim of the glass in the mirror. 'He's a time-served joiner.'

Kenny raised up from leaning. 'Eh?'

'Don't give us that!'

'He is, he is.'

'That wee shite! Couldna bang in a nail!' Kenny shouted. His huge face screwed up. 'Who told you that, him? Aye, I thought that!' He touched his long fingers together, his forearms spread across the bar. The muscles stirred on them, a flush spread over his face, and he banged his fist: 'Wee cunt! What right's he –' he stared ahead and in towards us, a king's head in a regal rage – 'Why should he be over us! So that other bugger can go off . . . '

'Right enough,' Drew muttered, 'that was it, him going off, so he could get off – he got a pack of, hah, to stand in for him, so he could go off. Go off his rocker.'

'Christ,' Kenny said, seeming not to like being looked at, 'what's going on behind our backs, that's what I want to know.'

'That, we'll never know, eh Michael?' said Drew. 'Eh, Michael.' He edged along the bar. 'How're you doing in the old hall?'

'You asked me that.'

'Andy buying plenty stuff, is he?'

'Enough for a start. While we get the place ready.'

'When, eh?'

'I told you, before Christmas.' I paused. It was strange I was

84

calm. 'You'll maybe show me how to do restoring . . . French polishing and that. Andy said you were good at it. You might . . .'

'He said that?'

'Yes. I was hoping you'd . . . '

Pause. 'Think you'd pick it up easy?' asked Drew.

'Oh, yes.'

'I'll tell you son: I wouldn't touch a fucking stick of it if . . . who the fuck does he think – '

'Aye,' Kenny put in.

'I can't believe this.' Drew was shaking his head, looking down.

'He said you were good, that's all.'

'Fuck.'

'Unless he's meaning to show me himself.'

'Ah-ha, ah-ha, ha ha ha! That'll be the day!' Drew controlled himself. 'He's no tradesman! How come he was running about hunting orders while I was doing the work, eh? He couldn't do it! He never could! Folk complained – aye, but we were a team. He was a master at licking arses, I'll give him that. And still is!' He waved his hand in my face. 'I know him. Don't tell me what Andy says and doesn't say! I know him!'

'Canna bang in a nail,' Kenny said.

Drew darted a look. 'Aye he can, but that's it!'

I laughed.

'Don't you tell me!'

'Sorry.'

We were stuck in silence.

'It'll not last anyway,' Drew said. 'Borrowed up to here.'

I frowned at him. Kenny drew in, shielding us from the other drinkers.

'The moneylender. That fellow in Melville Street,' Drew said, looking nowhere as though not speaking.

'How do you know?'

'Everybody kens.'

'What'll happen?'

'Search me pal.'

Approaching the house my hand reached for the gatepost, lifted the lug of the latch which opened a jaw to let out the pin fixed to the wooden gate, and the gate swung open with its own weight. I pushed it shut with enough force to go into the latch and not jump out, and went along the path to the back door.

Steph came along the passage as I headed for the bathroom. Thinking she was going in there I swerved and put my hand on the stair rail as if going up, but she kept on for the door giving me a blip of the eyelids. The pure dislike in it may have been of my falling about clowning to get out of her way, or the smell of beer, or it may have been that she knew her mother slept with me last night. How could she? Dear Steph, it's alright, I wanted to say.

She went out without a word, presumably for something from the garden. I dived into the bathroom. Dear Steph, for heaven's sake. In the mirror was a face not ready to be looked at. I tried to change it: the funeral. The dead make you look serious. Even thinking the word my face changed, it looked as if it had sagged, the eyes blank. Earth, falling on the coffin; crumbs becoming heavy blankets, bedding, the covers, good earth for a gardener; what was it like down there, could he see, get out? In some way get out, wander, return to the snug bed? I'd buggered it now – the face had spread, fallen open, a small crack let out the sexual thought, what was this? Does thought . . . There it was though, a religious sexual thought. George down there. The calm faces of nuns; the faces at the funeral; their backs, clothes, everything – smelling of it! The crying of my mauve aunts, delirium! Crying, mourning, oh boy!

Steph passed the bathroom door, toward the kitchen, a child. Why hadn't they told me about funerals? – someone, an adult, if not Mum or Dad, then Andy who I'd been with at it and after it, in his black suit and black shoes hardly worn, still with the clearcut shapes of their leather soles and no doubt the pale instep showing from behind as he walked. And the pressure of a dead person as if more alive than before. Mrs Harris in the church, she couldn't help looking good in black. It wasn't spoken about, all those people going along in their black clothes for a thrill which . . . they knew about even if they didn't say, even to themselves. Geordie's funeral eh, Geordie's funeral, nudge, wink understood. The pressure of the dead and

86

the release of pressure. I could hardly believe this. It slipped out of sight and I wondered if I was sick, but it was there though out of sight. They'd conspired to keep it out of sight: adults, grandfathers and mothers, those further back in the old brown photos – the aunts at Auntie Liz's funeral, they never spoke to her, they couldn't stand her, came for the orgy and had it right there in front of me and I never saw.

This massive con, terrible. I made an exception for Mrs Harris, who'd gone quickly. I strode to the kitchen.

'Do the toast, Michael.'

I buttered the slices from the toaster, took them to Barbara. She doled out scrambled eggs from the pan on the stove. . . . a lump of a woman compared with Mrs Harris, arms and legs of marzipan.

'You and William,' she said to the plates dolloped with egg, her casualness nervousness (I thought).

'Two more bits?'

'For me and Steph please. Leave Jack's.'

I glanced from the toaster, past the litter on the work surface. Her arms were dull white and round her eyes dull white too. I hoped and feared she'd look at me when she put the egg on these bits of toast. Poor old Jack wasn't getting any egg – the pan was empty. She didn't look at me but the dimples at the corners of her mouth showed and from them her skin and person became glowing and springy. But I didn't get a look from her throughout the meal, and after I went upstairs.

William and Steph stayed in the kitchen all evening, being kept or of their own will. They went to bed and I was nerving myself to go down. Jack came in. Quiet words. Silences. I opened my door to be sure I heard him go to watch the TV, but he never went through there. They went up to bed.

I was at work before it was really light, I can't remember why, and Andy was already there. He came out of the workshop in his boilersuit with a board. He showed it to me – CRAWFORD in black letters on white. FURNITURE in smaller letters beneath. It was a square of ply, framed in half-round.

'Don't touch. The paint's wet. The black, see. Even the

white. I used quick-drying but it's still tacky.'

'Have you done it just now?'

'Yes! Early bird! Bring the ladder, we'll fix it.' He had tools in his hand. I got a ladder from the hooks in the workshop. The sun was lighting the smoke of the chimneys below us. From our hill we saw over the town.

'Right above the door.' He climbed the ladder and reached for the board with its sticky black paint. Placing it firmly, holding it with his left-hand fingers splayed between the letters, he holed the shed's boarding with a bradawl through holes he'd made in the corners of the notice, took screws from his lips – must have put them in his mouth before climbing up – and screwed them finger-tight before driving home with the screwdriver. Then he climbed down and the board was dead straight.

'Paint'll dry before it rains,' he said, and I knew he was pleased. The sun had risen to catch the angles of chimney-stacks and roofs. It looked like a painting of a town.

'How did you come to know old Geordie, by the way?' he asked suddenly. He had probably forgotten asking in the pub after the funeral.

'I used to work with him. I told you in Mailers, remember? He came out our way doing gardens.'

'So you did. More than gardens, the old bugger.'

'How do you mean?'

The town before us was becoming golden, not itself – an illusion before the light changed to ordinary daylight. 'He was a bad old boy.' Andy shifted and grinned. 'He had Mrs Maclean I know for a fact.'

I laughed – a cover-up – Mrs Harris bursting out of my head. I didn't want to know any of this, to admit I knew, tell him 'Mrs Harris'. I looked away . . . Mrs Maclean, what sort of depraved taste was that? Older than Mum. There was a pause – inside my head – calm, a distant heart-stopping sight of Mum naked, as I'd once seen her, unexpectedly smooth, white limbs; his veined face; his smoky voice, Marjorie.

'Did you ever get over there yourself, Andy?' I croaked. The first time I'd called him Andy.

'Come on! I'm a married man!'

'They're the worst, eh?' A married man, not Dad, Jack, or

Andy in his boilersuit here with the tools dangling in his hand, maybe Andy pouring milk in a cat's dish on a windowsill, leaving the house before the rest were up to drive hungrily about, a Married Man in a hatchback with room to lie down.

'We better get to work,' he said.

I moved towards the shed, wanting to show him the clock, but he didn't come with me. 'What about the gate in the fence?' I asked.

'I'll get it done this week. Some of the chaps from the other place'll be over. And the electrician.' He nodded, trudged to the workshop while I opened the office, and soon he came out in his proper clothes, tweed jacket and pressed grey trousers.

Later I saw the boilersuit, faded across the shoulders and the knees, hanging in a dark corner of the store. I'd not noticed it before because it was so faded.

The same day, or maybe the next, it was sunny, I had done my small amount of office work and gone across to the shed.

It was not worth sweeping again till the electrician had been and it was the kind of wood floor you can sweep for ever, but I swept to keep warm. What rose to the nostrils tickled, but not enough to need the clogging mask. I pushed a billow of dust over the sill. What was Martin Somerville up to? Why had he come from wherever – Coventry, Leicester, the names suited him and I knew them very well from maps, green and Olde Englishe, as in jigsaws – why come to Gledhill? He must have suffered tragedy down there in the green and pleasant. He was unreachable and invention was the best I could do, an entry pass, an admission ticket (I was sweeping away and the whole morning lay ahead) to Martin, him in the workshop. A gang of men arrived in the yard in a lorry. 'Where's the gate going?' Wallaces' men, Martians. 'This corner,' I said. The speaker on the other side of the chain-link leant his arms on it and looked at me. 'We've some sheets to put in your roof too.' I made comical gestures and smiled, at the uselessness of my sweeping, from their point of view, at their interrupting a train of thought, from mine. I smiled, completely useless! The man went on, 'We'll not get your roof till the morn,' and I could go on sweeping though maybe disturbed by them at the fence. I grinned and got back to the tick of the clock.

I couldn't fix him in words, sweeping, but the rhythm of the brush, the blood coursing through my arms loosened the brains: I couldn't answer the why, but a reason would be that he wanted a wage and a home where his family could grow up out of the rat race. The sort of thing you read in the papers. The sort of thing that he might say if he knew you; that he might tell himself; he wouldn't be satisfied, but he'd settle for it; the settling-for-it type. Out went a cloud of dust. He should have found the answer at his age. All these men should have found the answers to what they were trying to do, making it clear for us – none of them knew anything – what was the use of them if they hadn't found out anything. This annoyance was good but only part of the sweeping, not in the same league as the possibility of sharing Martin's or anybody's thoughts-in-the-making, looking out from inside him, better than learning what he knew. A grin to the fellows sectioning the fence with their wire-cutters as I pushed yet more dust out of the door and leaned on the brush. So much seething in my brain that I couldn't hold it all at once. A thousand questions about Andy and the furniture business. For instance, why give up what he knew and force himself into this where he always looked anxious, that he didn't know about. Why put himself through diddling the old woman and so on?

One time I went for a drink with him in that place Mailers I was fed up with him at once. He told me plans for supplying furniture in bulk to schools etc. 'Won't that be all tied up?' I asked. 'We'll be cheaper!' He banged his fist on the table. He was quite drunk of course. 'Take my word!' Garbage. He knew nix about furnishing schools, nor me, except I'd picked up from Dad that you'd have to be Prime Minister to get into the business. And talking of the PM: the papers had been saying she held secret talks with Botha the President of South Africa. Nobody could know if it was true if it was secret – the papers 'had heard unsubstantiated reports' or some rubbish and that was the heavies – but Andy knew: 'Take my word!' He didn't admire her or couldn't admit it, but that was by the way; he had this inside knowledge and he knew. He knew. Very square-jawed. Less he knew, surer he was. Ha! Did he try it on me because I was young? But he was an idiot. Sometimes I thought he was an all-purpose idiot, idiocy spreading back through generations, idiocy of adults who hold a wee limp rubber in their lips not knowing the balloon's burst. They know too much and fuck-all. Look at him, will you? He's like this because he's pissed. Isn't that when the true nature shows? Leave that out for now, his nature's what he's like every moment, at all times, it sits across the table clasping its hairy-backed hands and not hiding the greasy folds of chin and down the sides of his nose. The old huddled skin, greasy pimples are magnified through the lenses and the skin round his eyes and those staring jellyfish are enlarged, showing what the rest is like – nothing behind the eyes. They react when they see. They shrank when I challenged the school furniture plan. Only nailing his notice to the shed, they were alright. I didn't remember, but they'd have been alright. A soft big bugger not to know what he's doing! Unfair! Leading honest chaps, me and Annie and Peter and that Drew and the others into a mess because he doesn't know what he's at! Isn't he the leader or something? Whoof! I go to the door for breath, the sun stings my eyes, I don't look at Wallaces' men, turn the other way and hide my wish to be leader.

A glance shows them paying no attention. I go round the side of the shed, a) in the sun, b) hidden. Lean against it holding the brush upright, then slide slowly down its tarry boards, my hand slipping down the brush-shank; sitting partly on my heels, partly on the dandelions growing out of a crack between the brick shed foundation and the concrete surround. On the left is the railway embankment. On the right the bungalows across the road partly hidden by a hump of ground. Ahead waste ground tails to a point where road and railway converge. Here grow weeds and clumps of grass, except they aren't growing, just sitting dead, waiting for the frost to kill them. How can it if they're dead? They must be dead or they'd start growing in the sun. They're in that state, they don't know which, November.

A twinge grips my stomach, spreads into my chest. There's Mum tidying the garden, the garden being tidy, leaves swept or being swept, plants cut down, edges trimmed. What I was getting away from! I'll fall to bits if one of them comes round the corner for a pee, say, unzipping, thinking he's alone. All the same I'm not moving; staying keeps them away, thinking of home also, thinking of an unbreakable circle. Okay being homesick in Leeds – once or twice – but this is home, home country. But think – those days at home can't be got back although they can't be taken away, they don't shift about. You know where you were, I know where I was, where everything was; and it's still there, or here, that time before leaving home, to be looked at but not gone back into, still there.

I drew deep breaths, the end of each, lungs full, easier than the last. The weeds were taking their chance as usual, what else could they do. The past didn't hurt (a trick). Things were in order, home separate and distinct. George separate because he was dead. I put my arms round him. I wasn't sure if I'd done that. The brush was useful to lean on while the pins and needles went from my legs. Going round the shed I was in sight of these men. Manager of this piddling Yard.

Some days later I saw Barbara in the living room, looking out of the window. I went up to her and put my arm round her. I wouldn't have if I'd thought beforehand, but I'd looked in as I passed, not expecting to see her.

I forgot about the last few days as soon as I touched her, but she went on looking out of the window, her face dead in the street light.

'Why are you angry?'

'I'm not.'

'You've been keeping out of my way.'

'Don't you understand? You can't hang around me always.'

'What are we going to do?'

'Do!' She turned from gazing out. 'Nothing.'

'What do you mean?' I asked in the end, longing for her to kiss me. She was like a tree trunk. I didn't dare put my other arm round her. I pressed her hip which I felt quite well resisting my hand. 'Why?'

She relaxed and I began to think it had been a mood of hers and it was over. She kissed me and I moved to kiss her longly, forever, but she held me with her hands on my shoulders.

'No, Michael. You don't understand. The children and Jack.' I didn't believe her, but holding me off was real.

The lights away over there had outlined roads, arching out of town. We stood at the window, my arm comfortable on her waist. Nothing mattered, nothing mattered.

She moved to turn on a light and draw the curtains. I drew the left one to meet her and we touched hands. 'I've some cooking to do.' She flashed her wide smile.

In the kitchen I was sitting at the table with a mug of coffee and she was sieving flour into a bowl. A lump of marg warmed on a saucer on the stove. The curtains were drawn. It was warm, the radio played quietly, Barbara talked about nothing and I was answering; she'd sit when the cake was in the oven, I knew she would, we'd be at the table under the yellow globe light that would shine redly through her hair.

But this was me being turned off. I couldn't do anything to stop it; afterwards I wondered if the two yobbos before had got the same treatment, but at the time I couldn't have thought that.

Jack came in. 'How's it going? You making coffee?' He flopped into a chair. I looked sideways at his strangely shaped head. The oddness of their being together; how could it have happened, how did they choose each other, what had he been like with hair, could they have loved each other? Could she have loved him? Why? What was it about him? Could she have and did she still? Whatever it meant. I knew fine well, though not in words.

Now – which of us? Never mind forever, the moment only, if she chose? She brought his coffee, reaching across the table with it. He raised his head looking for the sugar, and at the same time with an accustomed lazy movement she lifted the bowl from the side and set it on the table. He took half a teaspoonful, stirred it with the spoon from the blue pottery bowl crusted with sugar on its inside, let the spoon drip over his mug and put it beside the bowl. When it had dried he would slip it into the bowl in a sly way.

I was jealous of those slow movements of hers; she crouched to put the baking in the oven; stood up and came to the table, leant her hands on it, forward to me, her head sunk slightly between her shoulders, arms compressing her breasts together. 'How's your coffee, Michael? I'm making myself one.' Her throat moved as she spoke. She was looking at me which had not happened for a long time, her eyes wide and friendly, her smile drawn back to the tooth that pointed differently from the others. I slid my mug across and she rested her hand openly on mine. She reached her other hand across and patted my cheek. 'Good boy.' What a crazy thing to say. But it was okay, sounded okay, in fact good.

'I'll drink it to please you,' I said.

Jack was smiling. 'Aye, an evening at home. Michael, I'm giving up going to pubs – you're not to ask me. That's it. No more beer till Christmas.'

'Oh, drink your coffee and shut up!' She bent to look in the oven. We both looked at her bum, and this was known to the three of us, the knowledge was in the room, mixed with the smell of baking; and that business earlier when her movements had been entirely between her and Jack was wiped out. I yawned and stretched my arms wide.

He started telling her a complicated story about someone who'd come into the shop and their business with someone else; from her listening, she was interested in him, not the story. He said, 'He's a butcher, Michael,' or 'The minister's wife, remember,' to keep me in the picture. I'd forgotten the point of it next day but it had been part of the room with the smell of baking and clean washing on the pulley over the stove.

Jack and I went to watch the TV. Fawlty Towers was on, and she came through later and sat without laughing, enjoying it in her own way.

We were due to open the furniture store on the next Saturday. Andy had explained in Mailers.

'I'm paying cash, by the way. Nothing through Annie's books.' The furniture was coming every week in the back of vans, part-loads in lorries. Odd him saying this about cash, unconnected; it popped out because it had recurred in his head and he wanted to tell me, that's how it sounded. 'In case you were wondering,' he said.

He'd leant back in a casual position, arm hooked over the chair. 'It's just that we'll keep it that way.' His hand flipped indicating the shed. He leant back yet more relaxed, but I didn't appear to catch on. 'What I mean is, we'll not keep records. See . . .' He leant forward and put his fists on the table. 'This is to begin with. I want to see how it goes, so no records, just a waste of time. We won't make a profit anyway! But I don't want to attract the tax-man.' He smiled openly, afraid I wouldn't go for illegality.

The handling of notes! Handfuls of them. A bag maybe like the open bags of the bookies at racecourses, dipping their hands in the notes. 'That'll be great.'

He thought I was kidding because he gave me another look.

'How are you going to work it?' I asked.

'What?'

'We'll have to keep a sort of count. How do you get the cash for buying, to start with I mean?'

'Never mind.'

I nodded.

'Getting a start,' he said. 'It should be self-financing when it gets going.'

I imagined the heaps of notes, sorting them into piles after closing time. Him going away to sales with a thick wad you could feel the weight of – something like what he'd paid our drinks from, but bigger. He'd brought it out of his pocket at the bar, more a roll than a wad – a wad, springiness in the pocket, notes creased, fresh from the customers the day before and warm, almost damp, a pile of greens pressed together, springing slightly in the hand. 'What if they pay by cheque?'

'Get them to make it out to A. Crawford. I'll open a Building Society account in my own name just. A. Crawford.'

'And will I keep the cash somewhere about till you need it?'

'That's right. I'll find you a box for it.'

'Will it be just me there?'

'Yes.' Pause. 'I'll not be there.'

I'd known that. But it was surprising. 'You'll keep me right?'

'Oh aye. Oh aye.'

The drinks were all on him, off the roll, and when he'd paid for this one and pushed the money into his back pocket he got off the subject of when he'd be there, in the shed, before I found out when, at all.

'I'm getting the hang of these sales!' he said. 'Course I'm on the mailing lists now, they send the catalogue. You've got to be quick! Say you mark twenty things in the catalogue – you see them, like them, want to bid on them. There are so many people to talk to and that's important, the contacts. It's bidding and talking you've to do at once. What a tangle I got into! I think some of them were taking a loan of me.'

'Did you buy anything today?'

'Odd things. Regency's dear, just now. And oak – oak's dynamite.'

'I read it was cheap.'

'Where'd you read that?'

'I think it was the Sunday paper.'

'That'd be London. London's a different ball-game.'

'I don't know anything about it. You'll have to tell me.'

'Sure thing.'

The pub was filling up. We were in the Lounge, divided from the Bar by a wood and stained-glass partition, but this partition didn't exist on the bartender's side. When you stood at the end of the bar you saw through. If Andy was in a good mood he'd stand at the end and buy a drink for someone on the other side, asking Bridie or her father to take it along. In bad fettle, he kept out of sight. There wasn't much difference between the sides. The pool table was in the Lounge, the darts in the Bar.

Bridie had red hair like her Dad, freckles and a lovely bum that showed as she whisked round the tables. But something was wrong. What was it? Why didn't she give me a hard-on? She didn't seem to know herself what she was like. She was indifferent or seemed to be. She seemed to think it was of no importance. Someone who loved her – I put myself in the role – cupped this bum in his hands and her eyes didn't change colour. Absolutely nothing. It was strange, I couldn't interest myself, and the fact that first seeing her, when you came in and had been thinking of something else, was always good – she was a beauty greeting you with a perfect smile like the front of a magazine, always; starry eyes, shaped pink lips, white even teeth, crisp clean clothes – maybe those were the troubles. How to get through to her -- was there anyone there anyway? She was popular with the old men. I smiled at her when drinking with Andy, but it was almost a business deal! We dealt in our currency and the others used a different kind: age.

'Get the place built first,' Andy said, hunching forward.

'They've done the roof.'

'Fine! Good tradesmen those lads at Wallaces. I'm feeling the benefit of them.' He paused. 'Rewiring's all that's to do. He'll definitely be there tomorrow. If he's not, phone me right away if he's not there by, say ten o'clock.'

'Will I get you at home?'

'Er. Maybe not. I'll phone you.'

'He's started you know. The electrician. He came and pulled out the old wiring.'

'Ah yes. Quite right.' He dithered with his drink for a while. 'Would have been easier if I'd had my own electrician, eh?' – his son – 'He'd have done alright. I'd have made a good job for him. But no. Away to university and get a job with someone else. Management of course, not getting his hands dirty.' He gave me an inquisitive look; didn't see what he wanted. 'He could have been manager here. That would have been easy.'

I'd got used to being a substitute son even though not good enough, not an electrician – a kind of younger brother, a not-as-good-as-but.

He hunched toward me again and was going to touch my hand, put his on it, here in the pub. People watched without appearing to. He didn't seem to notice. But the ones watching us would be thinking the other thing. I pulled my hand back and his stopped halfway across the table – it would be called square, with gingery hairs at the wrist, across the back where they were divided by thick veins, and on the finger joints; a gold ring on the pinky, a ridged, twisted thumbnail.

Someone touched me on the way to the toilet, a finger up the back of my thigh. It could have been an accident. On the return I studied the people at that table; they watched under their eyelids, ready to look up when I'd passed.

Andy waved for two more pints. Bridie brought them and set them down as if we were special, as if the drinks were on the house for the entertainers, so it seemed.

When I was ten or so I'd been asked by a man who pulled up beside me as I went home from school if I wanted to go for a ride. We'd looked at each other through the open car window for a long time. His car smelt of polish and tobacco. He had grey eyes and his hand was pressing down the leather seat as he leant on it. I'd nearly gone, I think, as far as I remember. But I'd told Mum and there'd been phoning the police, a visit from a policeman who was evil compared to the friendly guy in the car. I'd told her about him just to tell her – well I'm not sure why I told her – but after the rumpus they made, she and Dad made, I was afraid. They didn't tell me the man would stick it up my bum, but I knew there was something I hadn't been told. I swaggered in front of a man sometimes, when I had an escape route, to see what would happen, and wanted to be hugged by one or another – but by then I'd discovered what else, and it didn't attract me.

Being big and strong now, if Andy made a pass I'd kick him in the balls. But he wouldn't. We liked each other and if the father and son aspect was left out we still liked each other. Why do people like each other, I don't know; I would certainly never have chosen him, but he was fine, I really liked him. In spite of picking on his bad points in my mind most of the time, he was my friend. That was it.

A vague sensation – some others in the pub ready to use me to pick on him about the son they'd have known, that Alastair. I couldn't imagine him. Didn't want to.

It was the two of us who were starting the furniture, and we'd play it by ear. The real start: Lines of gleaming furniture. A shedful of customers. The treacly hum of voices. Shed the size of a cathedral, solid deep-glowing floor. We manipulated the mob politely, steering them to satisfy their desires; they'd come to be drugged, the drug, the drug of gleaming furniture, the safe hands of the sellers.

'What about polishing the furniture. Is Drew going to do it?'

He laughed. When he'd done too much laughing he said something about being single-minded; then got round to answering. 'He's too busy. That wasn't such a good idea. He's got too much on his plate, I should have known.'

'The work?'

'Aye. He's senior man there. I don't want to bother him. He's having a bit of hassle with Wallaces. It's natural.'

'What will we do then? Will you show me? Will I buy a tin of polish and start?'

'Don't rush it!' He shifted in his seat. He smiled very openly. 'A lot of it's not worth polishing.' I believed him. 'I've bought cheap. All we do is sell on quick. Get more in. Once they find we're the place for bargains . . . '

'What about the mahogany chests and the clock and things?'

'They need a clean-up, yes. Yes, get some polish.'

'Ordinary polish?'

'Yes for God's sake! We're not in the other business. Not yet.'

'We'll get time to do a bit of restoring later, eh?'

He nodded.

'Have you been fishing?'

He shook his head.

'You said you'd like to do a bit, down in the north of England.'

'Ach no, I haven't got into it yet!' He laughed. 'Fancy you remembering!'

'It's another thing I'd like to learn.'

'When I get organised we'll have a day.'

There was a smell of fresh shavings. The paint-and-dust covered transistor blasted against the saw. Kenny had climbed up the timber rack in the store, the ends of his jeans curled over his trainers level with my eyes. I went through and checked roof sheets, nails, washers etc. The blokes from Wallaces had been using some of ours.

A van had come into the yard and Peter was talking to the little floppy-haired fellow sitting in the driver's seat and hanging out the door. The electrician. He'd been smoking a cigar the last time too, when I hadn't spoken to him, but seen him and smelt the smoke.

I asked Annie to tell Andy the electrician was here, and went to the shed through the new gate. It was a gate for people only and the electrician, seeing me, had got back in his van and driven round by the road. There was a smear of ash on the door post and a stubbed cigar butt on the step.

'The cable's shot,' he said, picking at the end where it came in the shed. 'I've tied it off.' He jerked his head with a flop of hair towards the Nissen hut. 'I can bring it in from your own supply. That staying, eh?'

'That's the office!'

'You're kidding! No, no, okay. I'll take it off there –
Michael, is it? Need a pole in your yard, it's too far for one
span – might pull the old hut over, eh, eh!' He went on when
I didn't say anything. 'Your switchboard goes here, right? And
you'll want sockets, six doubles in a place this size. Smoke?'
He held out the packet and I shook my head. They were dark
cigars not much bigger than a cigarette. 'Right, and it's five
strips you want. I'll hang them off the beams, two each side
and one along the back, okay?'

'Out of sight. Andy wants them out of sight.'

'No bother.' He looked at me with his dark eyes as he lit the
cigar and put the packet into his top pocket. 'What's he doing
here anyway?'

'Furniture.'

'Aye . . . You a relative?'

'No.'

He poked at the wall with a screwdriver, a light in its plastic
handle. 'Just asking pal. Weird idea, eh?'

'What?'

'This place.' He stared at me for a moment, and then said,
'Hold the end of that.' We measured bits of the wall with a
steel tape, and he asked how far it was to the Nissen hut.

'Forty metres?' I guessed.

'About that. There and thereabouts.' He wrote a figure in
his book, eyelids wrinkling against the smoke. 'I smoke too
much.' He looked at me again. 'How're you getting on with
the old fellow, okay? You're alright there. He's alright, the old
boy, so he is.' He finished writing.

I asked Peter, when we were having our ten-o'clock: 'Is that
your son?'

He wagged his head as if I'd been caught in a practical joke.
'Aye! He's no doing bad, the boy.'

'Does he work for himself, his own boss?'

'Bloody right he does. He has a boy started with him too.
Apprentice, ye ken.' Peter shook his head and grinned. 'Got all
his Highers that boy did and he wanted to work for Norman.'

'He's doing well,' I said, envious, of that van especially.

When Andy came at last, I left the shed where I'd been

handing things up to Norman on a ladder and went to meet him.

'Have to make a phone call. Then I'll be with you.'

'Been buying?' I asked when he came out of the office.

'Yes. Not much. But I've been around – Kilmarnock, Ayr, Paisley, Carlisle, Appleby. Done a few miles. Getting my face known. You've got to put in the hours at this job.' His new cap made him look as if he was on his holidays.

'What did you buy?' We were strolling towards the shed.

'A set of ladderback chairs. Couple of carvers . . . ' He continued, and I didn't listen much. The furniture seemed unreal.

Norman shouted from the ladder, 'How's Andy? Life of leisure suiting you?'

'Yup. Have you brought the strip-lights?'

Norman jerked his head, and hammered a clip into the beam. 'Take a look. That's the fittings. Take one out of its box.'

Andy unwrapped a metal fitment. 'But what colour tubes Norman? Where are they?'

Norman ran down the ladder, came over with a smile as he lit a cigar. 'The catalogue's at home.'

Andy scowled. 'If I could have seen them. It's not to be too bright, too harsh.'

'Subdued, eh?' Norman cocked his head. 'There's Warm White, Salmon Glow, Apricot, Blush Pink . . . ' He watched Andy with beady eyes.

'Any of the soft ones. Bring a few and I'll choose.'

'Any of the soft ones,' Norman repeated, writing it. 'Warm White would do you, I can have them here this evening.'

'I won't be . . .You decide with Michael here. If they're alright, put 'em in.' Andy started to leave.

'Michael says you're keeping the old hut there, right?' Norman looked over to the office. 'Well, cheapest way is to bring the power from there, in that case – one pole somewhere in the middle of your yard. If you want to go round the edge you'll need two poles. You'll need to get me them.'

Andy champed something between his front teeth. 'Come across the middle.'

'Unless you want to take it off here,' Norman said, tapping where he'd tied off the original supply from across the road.

'That would make you independent. Make this place independent of the rest. It's not a bad idea. If you wanted to separate the two places, looking to the future, it would be no bother to you.'

'Bring it across the yard – right, Norman? I'll send a pole over.' Andy looked at me to show I was to go with him and strode out of the shed. 'Nosey wee bugger!' he said when we were outside. 'They want to know before you know yourself. You and Peter set up the pole. He'll keep you right.' He jumped into the Triumph and roared off.

At dinnertime Norman sat in his van with the radio playing and the door open. A thermos cup steamed on the dashboard shelf. 'Here you are.' He held out a lunchbox from his knees. It was odd him eating here and his father in the tearoom. I took a sandwich. 'Your old fellow not pleased?' Norman was watching me.

'Andy's not my Dad.'

'No?'

'I'm not his son.'

'I'm not saying you are.' He smiled as if he'd made a good joke and blew smoke at the windscreen from where it bounced back filling the cab; this seemed friendly, otherwise he'd have blown it out of the door where I was standing, leaning my hand on the roof. He flicked the match out past me. 'Changes, eh?'

'I don't know, I haven't been here long.'

'Aye, that's right,' Norman said, 'but you're well settled, eh?' He drank his coffee and offered what was left in the flask. 'Back to work. All this to earn a bloody crust, eh?' He stood in front of me when he got out of the van. By the time I realised that he'd wanted to be friendly – mixed up with speiring, of course, like everyone except maybe Barbara – he'd gone into the shed.

The back of his van was fitted with racks each side for electrical stuff, and reels of cable and bits of TV aerial in the middle space. There'd be room to sleep if they were cleared out. I fancied a job where a van was my home and workshop. The gardening; George's van would have done but it was sold; and his saying I couldn't do the gardens griped me again.

Wallaces' truck brought a pole overhanging both ends. The two blokes undid their ropes and rolled it off; it bounced once, end to end, quivered and lay log-like on the hardcore opposite the Nissen hut. One of them waved as they drove away. They didn't speak.

I dug at the spot Norman showed me. The surface was stone, granite stones that had probably been laid by hand, part of the old station yard. I should have brought the pick. I jarred my wrists getting through the surface but then it was easy till I hit hard yellow stuff. I was chipping at it when Peter came.

'Huh, you'll no do it that way. I'll go for the pinch.' He came back with a heavy iron bar sharpened at one end and immediately began to use it. He was strong although old, and banged it into the yellow stuff and jerked it against the lip of the hole for leverage at the bottom, shaping my ragged hole all the time. I was shovelling out the clay he loosened; it took longer each time as the hole got deeper and narrower; he stood over me waiting to get back in.

But then he stopped, and sweat broke on his face. He leant on the pinch, trembling slightly.

A heart attack? How did you tell? Norman was whistling in the shed. The old bugger would keep on till he died rather than let Andy know he was past it. 'I'll give you a spell.'

He handed over the pinch and hunched and rubbed his arms as if he was cold.

The bottom of the hole was a mixture of hard clay and stone. Sometimes the pinch compacted it, other times I loosened a piece the size of a nut. I stopped for a rest and Peter went down on one knee and cleaned out the hole neatly but slow.

'Here – we must be deep enough!' I said.

He put the spade in the hole; the crosspiece of the handle just showed above ground level. 'Two foot seven.'

'Okay?'

'You'll need three feet anyway.'

'Out the way, then.' I was determined to get the five inches in one go and then take the narrow spade off him to clean it out. But I could only get an inch at a time and we proceeded as before.

I stopped short of three feet. 'That'll do, eh?'

'I'll clean her out.' Before he'd finished – slower and slower – he said, head down the hole, 'Get the fork-lift for yon pole,' i.e. don't stand about doing nothing. He'd shifted from one

103

knee to the other during his digging, the knees wet and muddy and his arms and rolled sleeves smeared with yellow clay. 'Get the chain too, the big one.'

I'd slipped the fork-lift tines under the pole and lifted it; it was too long to go between the stacks. 'Na, na,' he said peevishly and swung the heavy end of the pole sideways, quickly so he didn't have time to feel how heavy it was. The pole lay over one tine only. He started wrapping the heavy chain loosely round the pole and tine and I thought he was too weak to do it tight; but when he'd stood back and waved his hand for up, it tightened as the pole rose, and hung straight and tight. He'd known what to do. 'Gey canny!' he shouted, though I could have heard his ordinary voice.

The creosoted ex-telephone pole swung like a needle pointing skywards, and exaggerated the moves of the fork-lift. Too much swing would slacken the chain and drop the pole, but I got it there. As Peter guided the butt into the hole Norman ran over.

'Hold it boys!' He held a J-shaped bracket. I lowered the pole to horizontal again. 'Fix it here Peter, okay.' He glanced at the old man and marked with his screwdriver through the two holes in the bracket which he held firmly onto the pole. 'Got some wood screws Peter, aye?'

Peter looked at the pole, at the small marks Norman had made. 'Give us that a minute,' he said. Norman handed over the screwdriver and his father scratched a large cross on the wood beside each hole. Then he went to the workshop and came back with a brace and bit and a spanner as well as the thick square-headed screws.

'Are you not putting on your jacket? I'll do it,' I tried, but he was lining up to bore a hole, finding his mark after peering closely; the first curly chips came out dark brown, oozing creosote, then white, then pink wood. He'd done both holes and was turning the screws in; and he'd judged the size of bit and depth of hole right, the screws went home smoothly and the bracket was solid. He signalled me to raise the pole. I'd turned off the fork-lift and the delay seemed to annoy him. A huge effort was needed to do the job right – the digging, the boring, setting in the pole. And I was wondering how it could get like this between father and son, so that Norman didn't see his Dad keeling over with a heart attack and Peter put up with

104

being bossed. I couldn't see it with us, nor calling Dad Arthur.

The pole was in place, and I thought we wouldn't be able to undo the chain; but he told me to jig the tine up and down and that loosened it enough for him to unscrew the shackle holding the big hook. Then he stood astride the hole, arms hugging the pole to his chest, and turned it so that the bracket was aligned between the Nissen hut and the shed. That was it, I thought, throwing earth into the hole, but he stopped me and tumped it firm round the pole with the blunt end of the pinch, pausing between blows. He was knackered but the job had to be done right. I took a shot with the pinch. He insisted on tumping after each few shovelfuls, and stones were rammed in at various points, I thought to give himself a rest, but he was one hundred per cent keen on doing a good job and as it neared finished he looked better; he put on his jacket.

The opening of Crawford Furniture was postponed a week, for two reasons: Norman wasn't finished and we hadn't enough stuff. It had already been advertised.

'Makes you look daft,' Annie said. By you she meant her as well. She'd been in a bad mood for some time and was blowing her top each time she'd had Martin on the phone, as soon as she put it down; she blamed him for the fear of the yard being shut down and this postponement, which was not his fault. It was amazing she didn't blame me too, but she considered me in the same fix as her and Peter. I thought Andy would close down their jobs and keep me on at Crawford Furniture. That was the way the wind was blowing as I saw it. We all had bad thoughts.

Annie didn't take against Andy – the opposite. He'd breeze in: 'Keeping the books straight, Annie?' He'd straddle his legs and grin at her, glasses glinting.

She'd glance at him shyly and say, 'Aye,' like the purr of a cat. They were more friendly than at any time since I'd come and I thought Andy a fine bugger to be friendly when it was him had made the changes that would lose her her job. But she'd decided Martin was the villain.

On Tuesday, putting down his new briefcase, Andy sat on

the counter swinging his legs and telling her about some people they both knew. I dreamt that Barbara was coming with me to Canada.

He jumped off the counter and motioned me outside. 'What are you doing tomorrow?'

'Cleaning up after Norman, and that's it ready.'

'Leave that till next day. Come with me instead. Pick you up here at eight-thirty!'

He was pale and dark under the eyes but wide awake – well shaved, wearing a clean shirt and looking as if he'd had a good breakfast and polished his shoes an hour or so before.

I was having a day off that would start properly when we got to wherever it was, and didn't hardly wake up or say anything till we were out of Gledhill on the road north.

'Where are we going?'

'Paisley.' He pulled round a Volkswagen beetle with 'Nuclear Power – No Thanks!' stickers in its back window, going slow. 'Bastard!'

'Someone not in a hurry.'

He glanced at me. 'Look in there, you'll find some pan drops.'

I opened the glove pocket and passed the bag. He took one and gripped it in his teeth. 'Help yourself,' he said, sucking.

As soon as it was in my mouth I remembered I didn't like peppermint. We drove up a valley covered with dark trees.

'Do you see much of Somerville?' – his voice blurred by the pan drop.

'Not really.'

'A smart fellow. Up to date with computers. You any good at that?'

'I did a bit at school,' I said, not mentioning the easy and boring business course I'd dropped out of.

'Don't understand them myself.' He looked for the pan drops and I got them out again. 'So I'm a wee bit in the hands of those who do. But . . . think he's alright. Leave them here.' He patted the ridge between the seats.

'He seems a nice guy.'

'Very able fellow. You've met, eh?'

'Of course! But that was a while ago he came over.' In his green English suit in the workshop.

'He's important to me.' I wondered what he was getting at. I could do computers no bother but didn't want to work with them and this might be the beginning of being sucked in; this might be deadly business while we were side by side looking ahead at the road, supposed to be only going to Paisley. I might be a WP operator when we arrived. It was best to say nothing.

'I don't understand half of what he says!' He was still on about Martin. 'I don't like what he's doing, but I can see he's right. He's got his head screwed on. You know this' – he touched my knee – 'he's stopped making window frames. He turns them down – the people! All he'll give them's a factory-made one. I've a red face I can tell you, meeting folk who can't get things done the way they want.' He shrugged. 'He must do it to keep up, I can see, I can see. I would have had to do it, but I couldn't, that's why.'

'There's not much doing in our yard. Could you start making real windows there?'

'It's complicated . . . ' Flat countryside whizzed by and he chewed sweets. 'Matter of fact I'm in debt to him for this.' I half-listened; a gap between the car door and frame caused continuous drumming and hissing. 'I get the cash through Wallaces. You know,' – he went to pat where the roll was but his pocket was covered by the seatbelt – 'this. He puts it through the books as casual labour. Very decent of him. Understanding. We'll sort it out of course. A business like this needs bankrolled to get a start.'

'Yes. Oh yes.' I was falling asleep. The motions of the car, the rushing, and now the twists; he was taking them like a racing driver and it was that kind of sick sleep I was falling into.

'We'll take in enough to pay him back once we start – and have some over to buy more!'

'Yup.'

When I woke up there was a town, small compared to Gledhill, but immediately becoming another one – the old main streets, and new buildings shouldering through; old black-covered grass; the low grimy buildings – like the edge of Leeds.

We'd arrived in busy streets, I must have dosed off again, it was later. At the lights, two old women in heavy coats, with bags, one wearing a round purple hat, a moth-eaten affair, waited for the green man. Three girls came up behind them, all with blonde hair sticking out, blusher on their cheeks, black clothes, luminous socks. Not like Gledhill. The buildings here were tall and grey and falling-to-bits, and the girls like tropical birds. We seemed invisible to them. We both stared. At home someone would have been watching Andy watching, it couldn't have been done.

His big hands guided the car as he concentrated on the streets and crossings. 'First time through here I followed a wagon,' he shouted. 'He showed me. This is it.' My head was dull from the noise of the car. We were in a car park.

The narrow street was crowded with people loading and unloading furniture from vans and pick-ups. Andy nodded to a man tying a pile of armchairs and settees onto a small truck and the man raised his arm from the rope. I asked if the sale had already started, seeing that this man was loading up.

'Some of them deal in the street.'

'Is it okay?'

'I don't think so.' The street came to a square where some wagons stood. 'There's Tom. He's usually here. I could have got someone else though. Dammit!'

'What?'

'The pan drops – left them in the car.'

'I'll go back.'

'Thanks.' He gave me the key. 'See that door. I'll be in there.'

All the people in the street were different from us, and we were only an hour or so from Gledhill. They were town people like in Leeds, small, Army and Navy Store clothes or real town grey, occasional sheepskin. Hands and faces pale grey and mostly frightening, as if they were alone. What was it? They didn't look at the rest of the crowd. Mum would have said riff-raff, lightly – she had a weakness for what she called rascals. Sterner Aunt Jean would have said the scourings of the gutter. They were people who'd always lived somewhere else. I didn't think one thing or the other about them except that I was rather afraid; and didn't make eye contact. They could survive better than us here. I probably looked funny and Andy striding in his cap a man from another country – the country.

There were thousands of them in towns that joined each

108

other across the country. In Gledhill they were foreigners; they came twice a year with the fair, that's when I'd seen them before. Fat and motionless or quick as rats. Through the door a passage was narrowed by furniture stacked along either side; not only furniture but lawnmowers, garden seats, ladders, bikes, freezers, with cattle-sized numbers stuck on them. It had a feel of the cattle market where I'd gone for a job. The passage led into a room with a high glass ceiling. All the space was filled with voices twittering like birds under the warm glass, in the space after the passage. Andy was at the end of an aisle through double rows of furniture two-high. One hundred and twenty-two, pair of small lamps, stood on top of 123, chest of drawers. Across the aisle 313 was above 314, but 315, standard lamp, stood tall by itself, boxed in at its other side by two basketwork chairs on top of each other.

The wall was hung to the roof with chairs. All that could be seen of the higher ones were the legs and the underneath of the seats. I bumped into people as I looked up, and touched my pocket to check for the plastic wallet, easily felt through the anorak. The number of people was the thing.

Andy had unbuttoned his overcoat and pushed his hands into the pockets, speaking to a middle-aged woman.

'This is Michael, who's going to run my place,' he said. 'Mrs Shanks.' I gave him the sweets. He opened the crumpled bag and held it on his palm. 'Pan drop?'

Her hand which reached out was rough and slightly dirty, her coat-sleeve threadbare at the cuff and her face worn too as if she didn't expect an improvement, but she looked kindly. She was a dealer. She moved off, giving a light tap to Andy's lapel with the spine of her red business book.

'What do you think of it? Some place?' Andy smiled broadly. 'She comes from down Ayrshire. A real decent woman . . . Mr Slater!'

When we'd been introduced Mr Slater said, 'Fine big lad.'

'No relation,' Andy said. Mr Slater wore a maroon cardigan under his jacket. Like Mrs Shanks he was completely at home. Most people pushing up the aisles were just buying something for the house or looking around.

Andy looked at Mr Slater.

At the end of the room, beside a glass-walled office, the

auctioneer was climbing onto a rostrum and a woman clerk had settled at a table below.

'The mahogany writing desks,' Mr Slater said.

Silver, brass, jewellery, china and glass were laid out on a huge table. Each item was held up in turn by an old man in a brown coat. The auctioneer, suit falling off his shoulders, drawled a description into a microphone, said a figure, increased it once or twice, tapped his hammer and spoke to the clerk, quick and monotonous; I couldn't catch it. The bidders would be among the scruffy old men round the table talking and laughing. It was bad to think of these things on a mantelpiece in someone's house and the same week sold like this, for slaughter, melted down, thrown away. Though that couldn't be true it felt that way, a melting down and slaughtering place. Some might be lucky, on a new mantelpiece, perhaps in America or Canada.

I could buy Barbara an antique for peanuts if I knew what to look for – it was all jumbled though, and I couldn't tell. I always thought of her when I thought of Canada.

It would take hours for the whole table. As time went on I saw bidders and heard the words, and the prices – some scruffy looking things went for hundreds.

'We'll look at the furniture.' Andy lifted his shoulder, moving away to the passage.

'Look in that box.'

I moved a china dog onto the floor and lifted the lid of a blanket chest with brass handles. A spiced wood smell came out.

'Any worm?'

'No.'

'You've got to look for worm.'

'There isn't any.' I had brought a notebook. 'How much?'

'I'll go to forty.'

I wrote it in the notebook. I wondered if he'd have noted it down if I wasn't there. We came to a mahogany chest of drawers, the kind he'd bought before. He passed on – he'd agreed not to bid against Mr Slater, but wasn't that writing desks? He passed more that might have been off-limits because of an arrangement with Mrs Shanks perhaps, or he missed them. I couldn't talk to him, he'd withdrawn. He walked beside me but wasn't there – coat, trousers, shoes, glasses, cap, face and hands the same, but inside, someone you didn't know. His eyes didn't see me. He'd gone so far inside himself he'd vanished.

'These lamps, Andy?'

'Put 'em down, fifteen.'

'Each?'

'The pair.'

'What about these?' – a couple of school desks.

'No.' – voice from space.

'Hey, people like these for baking!' – a marble topped washstand with a basin and jug on it. Mum had wanted one, she said it was good for rolling out pastry. 'They use the basin and the jug for flowers.'

'It'll be too much.'

'If you got it for . . .'

'No.'

By now people were moving away from the big table towards the furniture.

'What about that, then?' It was a carved wooden figure, I guessed African, so twisted it might have been male or female. He laughed. 'Old Lindsay'd go for it for his collection. Put it down at a fiver.' He'd been switched on for a moment, then he hid again.

The auctioneer could not see the items at the end of the passage. "Two hundred and fifty-three!' shouted someone officially. It would be the man in the brown coat. The auctioneer gripped the rostrum, the knobbly stick he banged down at each sale sticking forward from his right hand, and turned to the crowd. 'A washing machine!' he shouted. It sold quickly. Two hundred and fifty-four was called and soon the old man, and the people moving with him, came from the passage into the room.

'You've all that written down, have you?' Andy took my arm. He put his head close. 'You bid for it, eh. If you go a bit over, don't worry. I've seen someone I've to speak to. Shouldn't be long.'

And the old man with his pointing stick was nearly at the blanket chest. 'Two hundred and sixty-seven. Standard lamp. Fiver for it – three – two then.' The auctioneer had it away for £6 in a flash.

Andy was leaving the room by a door opposite where we'd come in; probably a bar. But he might be going to meet someone. I had an idea of questioning him later. Meanwhile I checked in my book, yes, forty for the chest, and followed every stage of the next lots. I remembered running downstairs because Dad had brought new bread warm enough to melt the butter, and to get the crust I'd have to be there before Helen. My bare feet, pink from the bath, felt the stair carpet, and the silky cord of the dressing gown slipped on itself as I tried to tie it, running. But nothing had escaped me of the sale. The stick tapped our chest.

'Two hundred and seventy-two, blanket box. Who'll give me sixty pound? Thirty? Twenty? Fifteen bid.' He went up in twos and threes.

I looked at him and waved my hand. The clerk pointed at me. 'At twenty-five, twenty-five, twenty-five, twenty-seven, twenty-seven – THIRTY! . . . two . . . four.' Oh Jesus. I was there somewhere – he looked at me, but which number? Below forty, anyway. Then he was at forty, one, two; he slowed down. 'Three – four – five,' a pendulum ticking between me and another bidder. He looked the other way, at the person I could probably see. Turned back – 'Forty-six' – banged down his stick and pointed it at me.

I went to write the price in my book. I was nudged. The auctioneer was staring. 'Crawford' I croaked, and someone repeated it to him.

I replayed the blanket chest. Was £46 too much? Would I have gone on? Meanwhile I bid for some items in my book that went above our price. Then I got a bookcase for less; it balanced the chest. I bought something more and the auctioneer knew me, he said Crawford to his clerk.

Smells of peppermint and whisky impinged and Andy was back. I wasn't bothered why he'd gone away now. I'd written the prices of my buys in the notebook, and told him the rest had been too dear. 'You do it now,' I said.

He nodded. No mention of anyone he'd met; he was still absent, but I didn't mind now I'd done the buying. He looked at the book I held open, licked his lips and got into a slight boxer's crouch.

He bought a pair of bedside tables; the auctioneer's glance

was puzzled for a moment. He bought something else, and something else. Once he'd started to bid for something he went on till he got it and from my experience (ha!) that was stupid.

No-one could stand up to him, but he exhausted himself, in his boxer's pose. I remembered how solid and easy he'd been in the yard the first day – the efficient, dull guy with the pencil behind his ear. That man had known what he was at, measured, written with the flat pencil in the black dog-eared notebook. The man beside me without notebook and pencil, a briefcase in the car, brown boots changed to black brogues, and the great overcoat, was a Russian leader or a hero of the proletariat in Red Square. He was someone in a photograph, not real; tone-deaf to furniture, playing another game. Meanwhile he bought a round coffee table with scooped edges from beyond the aisles we'd inspected, beyond the range of my book – a table that shows you are respectable, which would sell in Gledhill but for less than he'd paid (I thought). The same with a mirror and then he said, 'Come on. I met a fellow can do us some good. He should be back now.'

We went to the bar. 'Have a pan drop,' he said in the doorway and took one himself. He went ahead through the drinkers and I didn't realise that the small man on the stool was the one. I was looking for somewhere to dump the pan drop I'd wrapped in a tissue in my pocket. 'My assistant, Michael.'

He sat with his feet on the rail of the stool, elbow on the counter and nodded without smiling. It seemed right Andy had picked up someone unimpressive, in his frame of mind since we got here. Had he felt sorry for the guy I wondered? That couldn't be if he was to do us some good, whatever that meant. The man was pale, in a light-grey shiny suit. A cream shirt joined it to his face. Steel glasses rimmed pale grey eyes. He paid for our drinks and his fist stayed clenched round the change in his pocket.

The bar had been brought in for the sale. Someone had set up the gantries and put the counter in front. The room was bare and square, painted brick, like an empty government office.

'Find your transport. We'll go,' the man said.

Andy went out and I remained leaning on the counter. The

grey man had spoken and Andy had gone, beer still in his glass. Maybe he spoke for someone else, was that the reason for Andy's obedience? Andy shouldn't have gone off so quick to do what he was told; he could have sent me, or looked at the guy and smiled like he would in Mailers and we'd have gone together in a normal way. That would have been okay.

'Have another.'

'Yes. Thanks.' I'd answered before I thought if I wanted one and it came on me that I'd been told what to do, too.

The barman stopped getting the drinks to answer an old black phone that must have been sitting on the floor when the room was empty. Now it was on the trestle table below the gantries. He moved it to the counter and handed over the receiver. 'For you, Abe.'

Abe listened, said yes, no, aye, uh-hu and put the phone down. The barman removed it.

'That's the way it goes, eh?' Abe said to me.

Under his grey eyes I tried unwillingly to live up to his stupid sentence, and tried to drink in the right way; but I'd vanished. He was staring at the bar.

His heavy brown shoes splashed with mud didn't go with the rest of his clothes. If there was a bit of him I liked, it was the shoes.

Andy came back. Abe's whisky glass was empty and I quickly drank the beer.

'Let's go,' Abe said.

Our car was in the parking space outside the saleroom.

'He'll meet us out there,' Andy said.

Where it had been all day in the space reserved for it was a big, polished, metallic-grey Volvo. Abe started up. It glided out of its bay like a shark.

'I've been there before but I'm not sure of the way. We don't want to lose him.' Andy was turning in the tight space.

'Where are we going?'

'His place.'

'His house?'

'Warehouse!' Andy pulled the seatbelt across and felt to click it as he watched the Volvo two cars ahead. 'He's a big dealer, boy.'

We passed red tenements, grey ones, waste ground, weedy

114

mounds of earth tracked by red and black slides, broken bricks, mattresses and tins and rusty iron. At the edge, between the advert boards, a blackened hedge was stuck with ragged polythene. One of the worst places I've seen. Not many people about, in the afternoon.

Tenements became bungalows. The Volvo turned between them on a narrow track to an old railway yard with remains of platforms and some brick sheds. A hangar of rusty corrugated iron stood at one side. The Volvo rolled through black puddles in a surface of coal and broken brick, and Abe had opened a heavy door and gone inside the hangar by the time we arrived.

'He's got some really cheap chairs,' Andy muttered. He'd disappeared into himself again, and his outside was imitating Abe's movements and muttering speech. I could have talked to him on the way, but it was too late.

A plywood wall divided the hangar and perhaps the other end belonged to someone else. There was one pile of furniture – some had been thrown up on the rest, like corpses. I tried not to be there, and thought Andy was doing the same.

Abe's part alone was bigger than our shed, and most of the pile was ordinary wooden chairs. We looked at them while Tom's wagon crossed the broken ground.

'Pull that door open. Get him backed up.' Andy jerked his head.

The engine had stopped as he spoke and when I got out there, Tom was having a cup of tea in the cab. I tried the hangar door. A semicircle was scraped in the solid coal dust where it had been dragged on its wonky hinges before. I needed help but Andy and Abe the terrible twins were waiting and I heaved it a bit at a time; got it three parts open, hanging in at the top.

Tom gestured with his flask. I had a cup and went behind the wagon for a pee. The Volvo shone like an advert against the brick sheds. The rust along the bottom of our Triumph matched the old hangar.

The engine coughed and the wagon backed up very slowly, sides creaking. There was furniture packed in the front. 'Not for you,' Tom said.

The space that was left wouldn't hold the sale stuff and many of the cheap chairs. I couldn't see what to do, couldn't see why we were doing different to what we'd started on. Andy'd thrown his overcoat and jacket onto a chair they'd pulled out. They were discussing their deal in some way, Andy waving his arms; he hoisted and disentangled another chair with his thick forearms. This chair was a different shape, there were several different shapes. There was no-one to buy as many old chairs in Gledhill and we hadn't room for them, tatty, old, secondhand chairs. Why did he want them? It must be somewhere else they were for or he'd have told me. He should have told me where they were for. He dragged out another and they discussed that. If you ask me he didn't want any of them.

Abe's hands were in his pockets. He was still and impatient. When I went up he said, 'Here's your assistant,' and smiled – big, spaced white teeth, pink tongue and gums, a sudden blink, a lion's mouth or a big dog's – pow! – open-mouthed, pink, slavery and panting! Breath! I wouldn't like to stand next to him in the changing room at the baths either. He'd clapped his mouth shut into a kind of smile, calculating the effects of saying 'assistant' and smiling that horrible way.

Andy had told Mrs Shanks or Mr Slater, 'no relation' about me; it made you think of a hushed-up family scandal, bastard son, son of a gipsy woman found on the doorstep, son of a crazy brother in a mental institution – who was I? There was Andy flushing and blinking under Abe's eyes, and the other suggestion in Abe's voice that we were gay . . . like the people in Mailers. But it wasn't that! The big goat was embarrassed at me not being Alastair!! I laughed, standing by myself between them and Tom.

He must have agreed to Abe's terms for he nodded and said, 'Start getting these in, Michael.' He didn't like me laughing. At the same time he raised his arms, drew his elbows back to stretch his shoulders and dived into the chairs, to sort out the ones he wanted. 'Take these I'm putting here. Not these. Tell Tom to stack 'em tight, there's a lot.'

Abe stood watching. After a while I saw he was counting. The smile was unimaginable when he was straight-faced, that was one good thing. He brought out a bulky order book that had been a sag in the pocket of his suit, folded it open and wrote with an expensive-looking pen.

116

Andy and I worked away. Tom eventually remarked, on one of my trips to the wagon, 'You'll not get many more.' Lifting one under each arm and one in each hand, I told Andy that was enough.

'Right!'

'You said you'd take the lot,' Abe said.

Andy stood there. It looked as if he didn't know what to say.

'You're waling them out too, that wasn't our bargain, you were to take the lot.' Andy still didn't say anything.

'You'll send him back for the rest.' Andy shrugged. 'Or you'll take something else to fill up.'

'I've stuff to pick up at the sale, for God's sake.'

'Up to you.'

Tom and I sat on the back of the wagon. I was hungry, thirsty and wanted to go home. I thought of the road outside Barbara's house and the graveyard – bits of friendly Gledhill.

They had lifted some things out of the pile. They were discussing a desk that was still up there. Now Abe stepped forward with Andy to lift it. He moved like a working man. The suit emphasised his vigorous movement, he was still strong though he probably didn't do much of this; and his muscles, the shape of his body were clearly seen.

Most likely I noticed this after, remembered, and at the same time remembered Dad changing the wheel of the car in the feeble, stick-limbed way of an academic person, quite old though maybe not older ... Dad was so different to Abe. I was surprised at having to choose and a bit surprised I liked Dad best; I'd never thought much of him, compared to other men. Abe's back under the shiny jacket stretched across the shoulders – the memory of it later, the bomb exploding inside the suit that had been motionless, sickened me and made me afraid.

Abe's book was out. He wrote quickly and I saw the neat sloped writing before he walked away, writing as he went, with the expensive pen.

'Come on,' Andy said.

We took an end each of the writing desk. It was soft under my thumb where the back dovetailed with the side, full of little holes. I ran my finger over the beautiful dovetailing, then moved my hand to press the middle of the holey bit; a section bent inward. 'Come on,' Andy said.

I hit it with my fist and it caved in like breakfast cereal. A shower of powder fell on my sleeve.

'Come on!' He lifted his end and jiggled it, he hadn't seen.

I kicked it gently. More of the back broke with a cracking noise and the bottom drawer jumped out, skewed.

'No need for that.' Abe arrived suddenly beside me. Andy came round and had to look at the broken bit. Then he straightened and pulled out the drawer. It landed with a clunk onto the floor and dust rose from the back, completely rotten too.

'The worm,' I said, maybe aloud.

Andy looked into the drawers, inside the lid, everywhere, for ages; the seconds dragged. He fingered the edge of the hole. 'We'll have to reconsider on this one!'

'Your assistant put his foot through it.'

'Look at it, Mr Mackie!'

'Put a new panel in. You're getting it cheap.'

'I'm not selling that,' I said.

Abe ignored me for ten seconds. He said to Andy, 'It's antique, you're getting it for a song.'

'Put it in, Michael!' Andy walked a few steps away and back again. He waved his arm at Abe. 'Add it up. That's it.'

Abe looked, without expression, and turned away to tot up.

'You and Tom put it on,' Andy said.

They got into the Volvo. When the car door had shut it was quiet. The only sounds came from out beyond the yard in the dusk – people going home in cars and buses, the day's work over. Tom lit a cigarette and we rested on the floor of the wagon, the small area at the back that wasn't filled.

The car door opened and closed. Andy walked over.

'Come on, boys.'

Tom stubbed out his cigarette. There was a pause of a mini-second, then he slowly got up to pull grey blankets out of the slats at the side of the wagon and stuff them between the chairs. Andy and I gripped the oak writing desk once more. 'Two, three, hup!' He puffed, from disgust not weight.

'Looks good from the front!' I said as Tom jammed it against the chairs. I was laughing.

Andy went into the hangar for his coat without answering. 'We'll get back to the sale-room.' He motioned me to go with him.

Tom said 'Go ahead and Michael'll give me a hand here. I'll be there behind you.'

Abe was in his car. His jaws moved as he ate, then he lifted a phone and spoke into it. From his point of view we'd gone.

Tom roped the furniture without me doing anything. He was whistling to himself all the time. He ran the engine a while, then drew forward and I shut the doors. I dragged Abe's doors and he never looked over. I left the padlock hanging and climbed into the cab.

The ashtray was full and a folded Daily Record quivered on the engine between us. I'd moved his piecebag from the seat and held it between my feet. It was too noisy to talk. The view was great – sunset behind the black shapes of hills and church spires and tall buildings, and in the remains of that rosy glow the streetlamps made bulbs of light around themselves. People moved along dimly lit by both these lights.

The Triumph was parked near the sale-room and several wagons were queued at the door, but Tom stopped a distance away and seemed to be in no hurry. 'We'll go for a cuppa,' he said. I didn't answer while the situation adjusted in my mind. We should have gone in to help Andy.

We had tea and rolls in a café. I went for another cup and two rolls, pork and chutney they were, while he smoked, leaning back, and asked: 'What'll he do with the chairs?'

'I don't know.'

'Abey got them for nothing, boy.' Tom opened his packet again, one-handed. 'I used to do his work. I did all the bugger's work till we fell out. Wanting you all hours of the day and night so he was. Couldna put up with it.'

'How d'you mean, for nothing?'

'He got them for nothing! Nix. Cleaning out a church hall – mebbe charged them for doing it!' Tom stretched. 'That was a while back. He'll have been looking to get them away. Likes a quick turnover, Abey. He'd want to cash them and he'd want space, but that wasna the point' – he pointed the cigarette held between his fingers at me – 'that wasna the point! You were to be got out of the sale. Aye. He was doing a favour for someone else, maybe that cunt Slater.'

'Eh!'

119

'Thon Andy should have left you there. To buy, see.' Tom sniffed.

'Oh I see.'

He stacked the crockery and pushed it to the middle of the table. 'He's not smart enough for the likes of Abey. Nice enough fellow mind.'

I was really exhausted.

'There you are!' Andy cried.

'Tom's getting into the queue,' I said, and couldn't look at him, with what I knew. Everyone in the place must know. I didn't want to look at anyone.

'Give me a hand here,' Andy muttered, striding to the back of the room. I caught up with him and he was already raising one end of a heavy table.

'We got held up,' I said.

There were not many people, but they were thick at the door, coming in for their stuff and carrying it out like us. There was a certain pace everyone went, except us – Andy first, walking backwards, assuming that because he couldn't see where he was going everyone should get out of his way. If he was going to bang into someone I held back – he pulled harder because we weren't getting on. No use speaking to him. He turned and grinned and nodded if he hit someone, as if all were in the same job, helping Andy get his table out. When he looked and grinned at them he didn't see them.

We weren't far from the door; he'd stacked our other stuff there. And now it was mostly people carrying single items to their cars and away along the street under umbrellas of thin misty orange; and there must have been a lull in the queue of wagons because Tom was there and had opened the doors.

'Hold on a minute!' The way was completely blocked and I put my end down, forcing him to as well. We started again and he tripped back onto a man's foot. I saw the guy's face, and felt the steel heel drive down into his foot as Andy swayed back – forwards – got the weight onto the other foot, and set down the table. 'Sorry, sorry,' he said, ready to start again now he was balanced.

The man doubled up swearing. A fight was coming. Andy putting down his end. I shoved mine to keep him moving and it was me causing the banging into people now but we had to

120

get out. I didn't look at anyone or listen. I would never see the place again in my life. We put the table up to Tom and the rest of the things quickly after.

We were outside and Tom was roping. The dirty blue-black doors were closed.

'See you there,' Andy said.

I made for the car and slumped into the soft seat. The bastard meant to unload when we got back, I couldn't believe it.

I woke in a place with no lights. Only a few headlights coming towards us. Great black spaces of the hills and the line of their tops below the sky. Mist below in a deep valley and one light, a farm or house. On my other side, Andy's dog-like profile. I turned from him so that the headlights didn't reflect from my eyes and show I was awake.

He'd pulled in at a Little Chef.

Everybody was pale under those lights or maybe it was the blackness outside. He squashed into one of the fixed seats at a centre table in his overcoat, laid down his cap and glasses on the seat beside him, put his elbows on the table among the cutlery for a full meal and rubbed his eyes. I took the shiny menu from its plastic holder.

'Strong coffee.' He rubbed his forehead, put his glasses on and blinked. I asked for coffee and we didn't speak. I suppose he wasn't unusual to the waitress. They'd get all sorts dazed by travel, their minds either before or behind them. The Little Chef was a spaceship and I could stay forever without going forward or back.

She brought the bill and at the desk he was patting all his pockets, so I paid. We took to the dark road again. We turned for Gledhill with half an hour of the journey to go, and nothing came towards us. I shut my eyes because they were sore, but I was wide awake. He nudged me and coughed. 'Hard day, eh?' We passed through a tunnel of trees with bare black branches, the yellow star of a leaf clinging. 'You get them like that. Always learn something.'

What did you learn today, pal, I wondered. My head

121

couldn't hold all I had learnt, it ached.

'The chairs are a bargain!'

'Where are you going to put them? There's no room in the shed.'

He was watching the road unreel; a rabbit jumped from the verge and it was a while before he answered. 'There should be room at the back.'

I shook my head. 'When today's lot's in, and the load coming up from England, it'll be full.'

'Is that right? It's coming tomorrow by the way.' He was so dreamy.

I could have done with thinking about anything except these chairs. But the great pile of them was there in front of me. I could readily have gone to sleep but couldn't shut my eyes for the chairs which crept in under the lids. Why was I thinking about them? It was his problem. 'Stack them in the workshop.'

He shrugged.

'There's nowhere else.'

'I bought them to get in with Abe. He's a huge business. Any deal you can do with him, it's a way in.'

'Are you meaning to take them off tonight?' I asked in a very draggy voice.

'Aye.' He butted his head at the windscreen. We were at the edge of Gledhill. 'I'll tell you this, Michael, it's a gamble. The whole furniture carry-on. I don't want Peter and Annie out of a job any more than you – all credit to you. I had to do something for myself. Had to get my head up from the carpenter's bench. That sounds showy-off, but you know what I mean.'

'Yes.'

'So I borrowed a lot of money. They wouldn't have lent it if they thought I was daft, I suppose.'

'No.'

The part of Gledhill we were passing through was deserted; folk had not come out after their tea. His driving was loose after the long spell, as we drove up the familiar road. 'Wife wants me to retire. Go and live at the sea.'

'Ah. Do you not –'

'There he is.' Tom must have passed while we were in the Little Chef though we hadn't seemed to be there long. Had we

122

missed time sliding by? Something blurred the edge of now, Tom smoking at his blue wagon, waiting for the shed to be opened.

What a homely place! I knew everything in it. The lighting was finished enough to see, and we didn't take long after all – the writing desk scribbled a trail of powder on the steps. We put the chairs in the workshop. Tom went to deliver his other stuff – what a life – and we were standing in the dark outside the locked shed.

'Coming for a drink?'

'I better get back.'

'Landlady expecting you?' His voice a physical pressure in the dark, almost a hand, and I blushed; I glowed in the dark.

It came out in my voice: 'Nothing like that.'

'Eh! Boys will be boys. I'll away down to Mailers and see what the lads are saying.'

I was heading for home, but remembered to ask if he'd be in the next day.

'Afternoon maybe.'

'Right, goodnight.' I walked away. The slippery bastard, two days before opening and a pile of work to do.

I burnt along in the dark and then the quiet town took effect on me. In the uninhabited dark I could keep it there or not; Gledhill would move away or stay while I was solid. What if I'd hitched a lift from spaceship Little Chef? – the black, bitter coffee, the darkness outside – to another part of earth, down the road with somebody, anybody in a car or van or lorry but a stranger, heading into England, warmer as it was south, to the beaches. Light, sand, sun. Away from the greasy chair-arms and the dark-red, dirty carpet in Mailers, the smell of cooking coming out of the walls, the men crawling round over each other like crabs in a box. Andy yarning away in there ... the town was crossed and threaded by fine webs and ropes of information that touched everyone but me. They passed messages between themselves unconsciously; they'd known each other before they were born, in a way, and how was an outsider to get into that? Did this web even reach underground to the dead? (There was traffic now at the riverside.) And yet they made a balls of it! By Andy's age I'd have sorted it out! They were all in the same trap; Jack the master web-man at the

123

junction of all the webs in his basement! What for? Nothing! Turned-in on themselves with their questions, smart answers, turning it back into the middle, the ball they couldn't get out of their court, prophecy, smugness . . . I was beyond myself, the voice was Dad's sermonising within me, unheard by people now passing – not many, one now and then, a couple. But because it was only me and them in that bit of street there was a connection, it was quite likely they *could* hear the inside of my head.

I passed along, nearer home. A man approached. He probably lived hereabouts and knew who I was and where I stayed. Did he know about Barbara? After a glance he turned away.

I repeated the business with the next person I met, that is, stared at her. She returned my look as the man had, and then her gaze seemed to break down into a curious look; frightened, but willing to submit to something I hadn't asked. There were only us two in the street.

The passage was lit, full of the house's particular smell – which I could never remember when it wasn't in my nostrils – and the cooking, the tea which had been cooked for a while.

'Yours is keeping warm,' Barbara said. I opened the heavy iron door of the oven and out wafted the smell of hot china and macaroni cheese.

Norman cut holes in the wall for sockets. A Wallaces' man was banging on the roof where one of their clear sheets was leaking. An ancient wagon nosed up the road with the stuff from England.

It was better than Paisley's, and there was a lot. A lot of oak in my opinion. I asked the old driver where it had come from.

'Harris's, mostly,' he said. We were carrying it into the shed at his pace though it had begun to spit with rain.

'Wouldn't let it away till he got the cash, old Bert Harris,' he said on the move past Norman, who was standing in the doorway stripping the outer core off a cable, letting the grey and black and red and green-and-yellow bits fall on the steps.

'Some of that's in a bad state. It's chipped. Look at it,' Norman said.

'No, wouldn't let it go till he was paid.' The old chap turned back and got into the wagon, putting his knee on the floor and pulling himself up straight-backed by a chain hanging at the side. The last bit was a round table whose top folded down in two flaps. I carried it in as the rain increased, and gave him a hand to close up.

I was in his way putting the warped doors together – they could only be shut by someone who knew them and I stood back and let him do it.

'Your boss new at the game?'

'We're starting, yes.'

He pulled a filled pipe from his pocket and lit it. 'You want to watch. Some of them's taking a loan of him. Not Bert, he's straight.' He tilted his head. 'Them at the auction.'

'I'll watch out. I'll watch out for that.'

'You're welcome.' He looked at me with blue-ringed eyes, the pipe bowl hidden in his oaken hand, and climbed painfully into his cab. The rain came down harder and his wagon blurred to a brown ghost with two red tail-lights.

Norman switched on and the tubes buzzed and flashed into their pinkish glow – 'Hope he likes the colour!' He rubbed his hands because of the cold. It was cold because the door had been open for the furniture. I'd lit the paraffin stove earlier and he held his hands over it. 'Christ, this smells! You'll chuck it, eh? Get in convectors. Should have thought of putting in storage heaters so we should.'

'I like the smell.'

'Like it! . . . your customers won't, boy!'

'It goes with secondhand furniture.'

'Oh aye.' Norman thought this was deliberately being stupid. He went back to his work. Maybe it was. But the smell went with small shops too, the cobblers and the watch-menders, Jack's workshop. An old Gledhill smell that would draw the old ones to our furniture. Trendy people like Norman would go to superstores anyway. I didn't say anything to him, he'd have made a joke about cobblers.

The paraffin stank mainly because it needed a new wick, and the ironmonger had said that kind was out of production. I didn't believe him. I'd been down the town, buying sticky labels to mark the prices of the furniture. 'Don't pay out of your own pocket!' Annie said. 'Give me the receipt.' Her finger

125

stabbed the bag from the stationer. There was a receipt in it and she gave me cash in exchange. 'These things should be kept bloody track of!' she said. She knew the size of my wage.

At the beginning of the week I'd put up posters – red letters on yellow paper, done by a friend of Jack's with a printing machine. I stuck them in the windows of shops that would have them. CRAWFORD FURNITURE. OPENING! SATURDAY, 6 DEC, 10 AM. An eyecatcher. We'd have included the regular opening hours if I'd been able to make Andy decide what they were. 'See how it goes,' he kept saying.

He had not come to the yard by late afternoon and I phoned Wallaces. He wasn't there so I phoned his house, a few miles out towards the coast. I'd seen it from a distance; his wife would be sitting up there on the hill looking at the lights coming on below.

It was the first time I'd spoken to her. He wasn't there she said in a calm, slow voice. We discussed the shed and furniture in general, and I got the idea she knew more about it than him. She didn't expect to be at the opening day which I was sorry about from the sound of her. She'd come another day, she said.

I spread the English load among the rows already laid out. We'd dumped it anywhere because of the rain coming on. Now the rain had stopped and the man on the roof and Norman had gone. The work was not much as I'd left spaces, and the new lights made the shed cheery on the gloomy afternoon it was, and warm with the door shut. I dusted the new stuff except for labels and chalk marks that might mean something to Andy. I was going to need a desk where I'd sit and keep the money. The obvious thing was near the door, I'd not dragged it far because it was heavy, a roll-top 'bureau' I suppose it was; drawers each side, a space for your legs in the middle, the rolling bit and a flat top. I put my fingers under the slats and rolled them back – a smell of old leather and tobacco – and the scuffed green leather with worn gold pattern round it, and drawers and pigeon holes. I smiled, not for anyone and continued to smile as I looked over all aspects of the desk, an internal smile on the outside. I recognised this desk though I'd never seen it before. There was nothing in the drawers except a rubber band, a paper clip and dust that must have been there a long time, clinging to the sides and bottoms of the drawers.

126

In the dark it could have been rearranging itself. The smell of dust and wood put a bottom in me as George would say, and I felt better in myself, to use one of Mum's phrases. It was all coming together and I ran to the workshop and picked a good chair.

The shed looked good enough for opening from this viewpoint. There were scruffy items, really too bad to sell, but I'd put them in a bargain heap at the back, 50p or less if Andy would agree. All it needed was prices.

He came on Friday. I was standing over the stove warming my hands in the fumes it gave off before it heated up.

He liked the look of the shed, but didn't like the idea of a 50p heap and didn't remark about the bureau. I showed him the labels.

'Good idea,' he said. I don't know how he'd have gone about marking the prices otherwise.

He said the prices and I wrote and stuck them, clumsily at first, but keeping my mouth shut. That was my policy as far as he was concerned. He did it by guesswork, not by what he'd paid unless his memory was amazing, but I didn't say anything although I thought he was on the cheap side.

The clock had stopped and I'd never got Peter back to it.

'Wasn't this going?'

'It needs winding. Peter started it for me.'

'Peter? Christ.'

'He knows how to work them. He put the weights on and wound it. It's been going fine, it's just that I haven't wound it.'

'Heh!' Andy hunched further into the collar of his overcoat till his specs were almost resting on it.

I opened the case and wasn't sure, from the position of the weights, if all it needed was winding. The key was on top behind the broken bit of wood carving. 'Shall I wind it?'

'No! It can't be right. Um – '

'Is it out the sale then?'

'Yes. Put a . . . a cross on it. On your label.'

'I know a guy who'd mend it. My landlord, Jack Fulton.'

'Fulton?'

'D'you know him?'

Andy made a face.

'He'd look at it. He's a nice guy.'

'Know anything about clocks though? You could ask him to look at it, I suppose. He'd have to give me an estimate,' Andy said but he didn't want Jack in the place at all. It wouldn't stand up to what Jack would say about it later in his basement but it never would have, even if it had been perfect which it wasn't – it was a joke looking round properly, not from my crazy viewpoint at the desk. No wonder having Jack in didn't appeal.

The clock had been our last item and he was heading for the door.

'I'll fix it up,' I said, putting a cross on the clock. 'When do you want me here in the morning?'

'Your usual time. There's nothing else is there?' He looked round. I was staring at him. 'I'll be in when I can,' he said, looking back. He held my eyes for a second, then he turned and walked to his car, raising his hand as his back was turned.

He wasn't going to be here when the doors opened at 10 am next day. I'd known, more or less, and didn't mind too much. He'd said in his look: this is how I am – and asked for help. But the next time we met he'd seem not to have admitted such things, and I'd go on pretending he was teaching me the job. I had known, I had known all along this was how it was.

I twitched all night with the dream or waking imagination of people passing and passing the same pieces of furniture while I couldn't get out of my chair at the desk or speak to them – if only I could have, they'd have bought something and the process would have unjammed – but I was distracted, a distraction repeated, after me thinking for a second I'd got rid of it. I wasn't sure what this distraction was altogether, but one part was the stove – switch it off because of the smell, or keep it on because of the cold? This I couldn't make up my mind about.

I got up before daylight, made tea in the kitchen – I didn't use the cooker in my room now – ate a slice of bread and set off for the shed. The town was peaceful early on Saturday morning and my head was clear.

First impression, opening the doors, was that it was not so bad at all. Not bad at all. Only an ex-church hall, not even an ex-church, but it had a church-likeness; the light came dimly through the roof sheets and might have come from tall peaked side windows, the same kind of light; and the furniture in rows was pew-like. And you got balconies in real churches.

I had thought of putting some of the goods up there, but it had creaked each time I'd been up, and in the end I put a rope across the bottom of the stair.

I strode about looking at the array from different angles and trying to keep warm till it got light. Plenty time and nothing to do.

No-one in the yard. No-one came on Saturday, except sometimes Peter who'd bring his car and wash it with the pressure hose. He'd wash the joiners' vans too – they never bothered. I used to hear them shouting as they knocked off on Friday, 'Mind and give that van a wash, Peter!' meaning a joke at first probably, but now only partly a joke, because he'd been doing it and it seemed part of his job. There was a van, drawn tight against the staging at the workshop, but it didn't look as if it was going to get washed. Anyway, if he came it would be before ten o'clock because I thought he was embarrassed, like Andy.

I was still tangled in dreams. There was a violent one – I couldn't remember the shape of the violence, a dark cloud I couldn't enter, but suddenly I did – it slipped round me and I contained it. Inside me were the killer, the victim and the investigator, but it would not move, stuck in the same groove – the investigator was always outside the hut where the child's body lay and he wouldn't go in.

There were things to do if I could think of them. The clock. I felt for the key where Peter had put it, opened the glass door of the face and didn't remember which hole wound the movement – the other was the chime. Both weights hung at the bottom and looked the same. Chimes wouldn't be good during the sale, specially if they were haywire – there'd be no way of stopping them and some know-all punter would have to show me. My hand went to the hole that Peter could have used – that solid ratcheting noise again and one of the weights came up smoothly – the key back in its place and without thinking I'd moved the pendulum across – it swung back with a clicking tick – the second hand of course had started too,

129

and the cogwheels behind the face would all be in their steady motion . . .

It showed half past five and my watch was dead right on ten past nine. I pushed the minute hand but it wouldn't go, bent and sprung back. I left it.

It could be a good day. It was quite fine. The sun was peeping through low bandages of cloud though not exactly shining, and there was no wind that would maybe have kept them away, so they would probably come. But no-one was to be seen yet.

Money! I'd no change – they'd want it, some things being in pence and them handing out a fiver for a £3 thing, £10 for £7 etc. In my backpocket my wallet had two singles in it. Among my house keys and jammed into the slit of my penknife was about 40p. That useless bastard! Then I remembered the look we'd exchanged, shifting everything onto me, absolutely everything, including this, and why hadn't I . . . but the bank would have been closed. Why hadn't I thought about it! I was heading for the office and feeling for the key on the dog-lead clip of my belt.

Then, it began to level out. I knew where the key for Annie's cashbox was. I switched on the kettle, and began counting the money. I would take the whole box over, and a clean notebook too. I noted the sum in the box and wondered what she'd think about me taking it and knowing where she kept the key; her view of the sale which I only guessed from her saying nothing about it was wait and see and expect the worst.

I went back over with the box of money and the notebook and the coffee spilling on my hand. I sat on the stone step of the shed burning my mouth and spilling it again on my clean jeans. The hot drops seeped and turned freezing. Nine thirty.

My eye singled out the things he'd bought from the couple, the day he diddled the old woman out of the clock. I was vaguely surprised that I'd been sorry for them, and her, since to begin with I'd put another injustice on her by admiring his cunning in cheating her.

That was the past; now I was one against hordes. I got off the cold step, put the cashbox in the bureau and waited.

I was watching figures coming up the road. They didn't walk like people going home and they carried no milk or

130

papers, but it was still probable that they lived in the houses over the way. I was hypnotised by their strides as they advanced on the other side of the road, and glanced back for the traffic that might have run them down, and crossed. Everyone round here knew it wasn't a traffic road. They were twenty yards off. My eye's photograph developed instantly, and I saw myself in the mouth of my lair, and a woman and two men standing at the steps.

'Are you open?'

'Yes. You're my first customers.'

They came in, looked round quickly like the dealers at Paisley and I felt sickness in my stomach thinking of that. They saw at once what a mess . . . I stayed at my bureau, facing out the door, and also seeing them, down at the back, going towards the back under the balcony almost out of sight, and I was afraid they'd get out of my sight altogether and lift something. They seemed to whisper.

I strolled back and pretended to look for something – still couldn't hear and I went closer.

The woman said something in a heavy accent. I didn't understand and asked her to repeat it, then didn't understand again. 'Sorry?'

'Ur ye the boss?' she said loudly, echoing round the shed.

'No.' I laughed.

'Giving a bit off?' one of the others asked – 'Are you knocking the prices down, son?'

'No.'

He shook his head.

Talk of knocking, my heart was knocking. I didn't know how to continue this conversation and roamed the area between them and the door . . .

They were beside me and one had the stem of a small round table in his enormous hand. He held it toward me.

I found the sticker. '£7.'

He handed me a tenner and I gave him change.

'All right son?' he said.

I let the thing settle in my mind when they'd gone. They weren't Gledhill people – maybe from a tribe of sale-goers who were only seen at sales. It felt as if it had happened in a place that wasn't Gledhill or anywhere recognisable, known only in

131

a dream far back in the head.

Just short of ten o'clock, I'd taken £7 and felt terrible. Nobody about! No-one I knew. Peter hadn't come to wash the van, all those people living across the road seemed to be deliberately not looking, and I was hungry and there wasn't time to go to the dairy for rolls.

Those people on the other side of the road were doing Saturday morning things, washing their cars and slowly exercising their dogs, different from the weekdays, chatting over their hedges and railings, and so forth; ignoring the sale. I opened both doors which made it cold. I should have had a sign at the door in letters thick as a python, SALE!

I kept moving to occupy the shed. Then was aware of them.

'Come in!'

They hesitated – five or six of them – maybe because of my excessive welcome. 'You're the first!' I told them as if it was a prize-winning feat, as well as untrue. They were too far in to back out; they gave themselves up and wandered through the shed.

It had changed suddenly from too few to too many. I stayed at the bureau, cracking up because nothing happened – in the way of buying things I mean. They moved silently out. More came in and I couldn't smile.

This grey period had gone on for years when someone bought something. All at once I was busy. A continual smile now.

Someone called, 'Excuse me!' He was at the clock, hand raised to attract attention.

'How much?' He pointed to the label.

'Not for sale –'

'What do you mean? Who do I speak to? Where's Mr Crawford?'

'It's not for sale at the moment.'

On the side of his face, as he stared at the clock, the flesh seemed to flow so strongly past his ear that it was creased. The clock tick was loud. 'Alright, is it? It's at the wrong time.'

'It needs an overhaul. A kind of service.'

'Why's it here? Should be for sale – give you a hundred for it.'

I began to get tense. 'It's not for sale.'

132

'Where's Crawford? You in charge?'

'I expect him soon.'

He opened the clock case and shut it. Then he held out a little card. 'I can't hang about. Ask him to contact me, would you.'

He turned to look at the rest of the furniture as if I'd vanished. Anyway I was being smiled at in the way that means come here, I want you, but is a smile all the same, by a woman who asked, 'Would it be possible' – she was being gracious to show that she needn't be – 'to keep this chest for me? My husband will collect it later.' She varied the smile – a woman about fifty, give or take a smile, with lined but soft cheeks, firm lips with the lipstick flaked by the moistness of the naturally pink lips, as if it could not get a grip on those damp surfaces, and intense blue eyes.

I went to the bureau for the roll of stickers and wrote 'Sold' on one, and stuck it below the price on the chest. I got another gracious smile. She was so good at this smiling, and perhaps didn't know that her blue eyes, with a thoughtful look such as you see on people choosing their sweet in a restaurant, wandered down to my crotch without exactly leaving my eyes.

'I'll pay you now,' she says, taking a cheque book automatically from her bag.

We're at the bureau and I hold out a pen to her, watch her hands as she writes leaning on the flat top part. They're slightly tanned, their backs smooth skinned, youthfully blue veined, wrinkled between finger and thumb. She'll have slim ankles I haven't seen. She gives back the pen holding it for a moment. Is this habit? 'Oh yes, you want to see my card.' We are joined by this other bit of plastic – I feel the shaking of her blood. This old bat! I'm ready to be fascinated.

On the confusing cheque card her signature doesn't look like her name, but of course it's the comparison with the signature on the cheque that keeps the world turning, and I'm saved by seeing the words 'card number' in very small writing. Anyone should know this. I've often seen it done. I write that number, off-handedly, on the back of her cheque, and begin to hand her back her card, unable to look above the button that pulls her jacket in, then skipping my gaze to her face for the full blast of the eyes. I catch my breath and she too I'm sure.

133

There's no reason for her to stay, and she goes.

I put her cheque in the cashbox. Mrs Fletcher. The man from the clock walked out too, frowning to himself without looking at me, and I put his card from my pocket into the box. Major Black. An address near Gledhill. The little card was threatening. A Government man from some sales regulation office? A detective working for the old clock woman, with his questions and his offer? I'd imagined an exhausted old working woman, but now she was a crazy gentlewoman, a country lady in that cottage – I discarded her – she wouldn't have been crazy enough not to know the value of the clock even if she was crazy. She could have been temporarily crazy and employed this expensive Major – she could have been anybody . . .

Sitting at the bureau, taking money and giving change, writing numbers on the back of cheques; on it went. Mixed voices, plenty people, I saw them more or less all at once and could spot everything . . . a man had passed the bureau carrying a hold-all . . . he went out down the steps and for a couple of rapid strides . . . I ran after him. The zip of his bag had closed before he passed me, while he was in the shed – this sound was with me as I ran.

'Excuse me!'

He stopped, I caught up and was face to face with a man I'd seen around town, middle aged, in a neat tracksuit top though I'd seen him in overalls; but a boss, and not to be messed with, a rather tense man.

I was saying, 'Is that your bag?' and adding, 'I wonder if I could see in it?' The sound of it being zipped was still in my ears. He paused, bent, put the bag on the ground as if demonstrating an exercise, and pulled the zip in one move-ment. There were neatly folded clothes. I stopped before I rummaged through them, but nearly did, because of following it through, the situation was pushing me. 'Sorry, I thought you might have taken something by mistake.'

He closed the zip slowly and stood up, staring at me, and intensifying his expression for a moment, bringing it close to words, but he turned and strode off.

No-one looked at me. I still saw the bag lying open and the trousers and skirts, grey brown and beige, collected from the cleaners. Why had he opened it in the shed the crazy goat?

Peter approached from the back of the shed where he must have been and maybe hadn't seen this business.

'Hey, Peter!' I was really glad to see him.

'You're doing alright!' He wore a dark, thick suit, blue shirt and tie close up under his adam's apple, and might have been for a haircut – his hair seemed shorter than usual, hardly there at all, like the men at the funeral.

'Are you buying?'

'Me! I don't need anything!'

I was going to ask if he'd nip down and get me some rolls, though I didn't want to as he was dressed, and more himself than going about the yard with that damned brush – but he was wanting to say something: 'Your clock's no at the right time.'

'It was stopped. I wound it this morning just. I was frightened to push the hand.'

'Have you not been winding it?' He scratched at the grey stubble above his ear. 'I'll set it for you. Andy here is he?'

'He'll be along later.'

Peter nodded. He brought out his watch. 'Half past twelve. I'll fix your clock for ye.'

He'd started away when five or six well-off, belly and grey hair types came in – oh yes, one of them was Maxwell – they'd be Andy's pals.

'How're ye, boy?' said Maxwell.

'Where's the free booze?' one of them shouted, quickly as if he wasn't sure. They stood close together, grinning at each other like big fifth-years. They weren't keen to go further in and I guessed they didn't know what to do next for the moment. They were right by me and one said, 'Is Mr Crawford about?' in a posh voice, trying to take the piss because he didn't know what to do.

'He'll be along later. Are you going to look round?'

They didn't move.

'He's let a lot of light in, you've got to say that.'

'There's old Duncan, see.' They leered at a man who was with his wife.

'There'll be some nice stuff here.'

'I ken nothing about it.'

'You'd think he'd have launched her with a bit of a splash.'

135

'You'd think he'd have been here.'

'There's old Peter!'

They surrounded Peter at the clock, Maxwell on the outside of the group filling his pipe, watching everybody while standing still and seeming to be busy entirely with the pipe. Peter moved his arms and he'd be telling them the points about the clock and maybe his own at home.

They were too curious not to have come; they were for a bit of fun and the free booze. Why not? They'd have a laugh at Andy's daft idea – but they didn't know this trade; and apart from no free booze there was no fun – families searching among the stuff, looking quite at home, and no Andy. I doubted if I could handle these guys. They'd looked at the new rooflights, the striplights and the rope I'd put across the stair. They would remember the damn whists and bowling and the hall in its old way. If he'd been here he could have handled them.

One of them untied the rope across the stair. He'd had a drink or two, him, or it was more noticeable with him, perhaps they'd all met in the pub first. He was by himself anyway. He'd left the rope dangling and was going up.

'Come down off there!'

He looked at me over his shoulder, taking in the rest of the people too, though his eyes remained on me. Most people were looking at him and he went to the top of the stair.

'Didn't you see the rope?' I was holding it, standing on the bottom step, and my neck was sore from looking up, my eyes screwed tight.

'Aye, I saw your rope.' He went along to the middle of the balcony. He leant on the rail and looked down on his friends.

'It wasn't there for nothing. That's dangerous!'

'Don't tell me it's dangerous,' he answered. It didn't seem to be. He was standing at the edge, leaning on the rail, a heavy man, and it was perfectly alright; but it had been creaking and cracking when I was up there.

He got angry. 'I was up here before you were born!'

'Would you mind coming down, please?'

He moved further along. I started up the stair and then stepped down because that would be daft. I was stuck. They were looking up at him, though Maxwell looked at me, the thin pipe with the small bowl sticking straight out from his face.

'You mind Sunday School, Bob?' the one on the balcony said, leaning over as if he didn't want to be heard by anyone else after all. He got an answer I didn't hear and stood straight and spoke to everyone. 'Old Miss Thomson, eh? "Now pay attention boys and girls!"' There were laughs at this imitation. 'She didn't know half of us were up here out of sight, poor old blind soul!' A general chuckle. He kicked the front of the balcony. 'Solid as houses!'

The new roof sheets seemed to make him angry again and he grasped the rail. 'Pokes of sweeties we had up here. Ration sweeties! Aye we were rationed in those days, and better for it. This old hall was used every night, with blackout curtains in the windows . . . some of us remember!' – he waved his hand. 'Often enough I've been up here. Never thought I'd be up here making a speech, but ladies and gentlemen, in the absence of our good friend Andrew Crawford . . . well someone's got to declare the place open! In his absence, we must congratulate him on his initiative, on bringing the Hall back into use, with modifications. He deserves credit – and it would have been better expressed, no doubt, if my friend –' he peered over, down, looking for Maxwell – and there was a loud crack. The balcony had moved out from the wall.

But no further, and the big man hung over the rail and dared not move.

People drew back from underneath.

The beams were rotten where they joined the wall – some right through, others holding by a core of wood that might be rotten anyway. The whole thing was held up by the stair at one end and a small bracket at the other.

'Go back against the wall,' I called. People were giving advice, but he heard me, and keeping a dignified look as if he'd finished reading the lesson, he moved backward, only the legs moving.

'Come down off there, Ramsay!' someone shouted.

He'd stopped. He shifted his weight to one foot and gave a little downward pressure on it with bent knee, testing if it was safe to move. He started again along the rail, and there was another crack.

'In to the wall!' I shouted, but he clung to the rail and eyed the distance to the stair as if he'd rush it – I imagined his fall, and what I'd do was: run to the office, 999, ambulance, Station Road – but he may have felt the boards give as he crouched to jump, and he began to shuffle.

'Keep to the wall, you old fool!'

'Wheesht,' Maxwell said.

I stood away as he reached the foot of the stair and Maxwell took his arm and led him away. I tied the rope and someone said, 'Quite right, son, he shouldn't have gone up.' I smiled but I was mad. Was there a special rule for silly old men? Trying it on! The blackout, the rationing! The fucking war! They'd soon all be dead. The sooner they were all dead . . . and so on.

People got back to the furniture. I was on my way to the bureau where people were waiting, and there was Peter looking at me as I passed – no word – another of them – I knew that stone war-time face. He sided with the war-time people when it came down to it.

I'd left money when I dashed away, but not folded and put under the book; that was something I wouldn't have done. An old man holding a vase said, 'I put that under there in case it blew away.' The old swine.

All afternoon I was dazed as if shut in a plastic bag – couldn't see well, deaf, slow at adding. My eyes began to shut as I watched the clock. At four I knew he wasn't coming. It was bad him not being here on the opening day of his new business (the fellow on the balcony had been right). . . Was it that he didn't care, or couldn't he face the people? I wanted him to come and end it. How was I to manage? When? I couldn't think as I mechanically did the job and said again and again to myself that it was unfair.

'You're having a good day,' a woman said to me. I knew it was Mrs Crawford at once. 'I'm Phyllis Crawford. Andy's wife.'

My sight and hearing perked up immediately. I'd expected a big woman, her deep voice on the phone had made me think of a big slow woman, but she wasn't; active-looking and quite small with grey eyes, so kindly that the rest of her which might have been ordinary, dull, nondescript – if she'd been looking at the furniture, head down, she'd have been invisible, she might have been here for hours – was wonderful; absolutely wonderful; never seen before. Small, and stocky with it, not fat or thin. A weather-beaten face, a big nose and grey hair.

'Have you been here long?' I was asking her.

'I popped in earlier for a minute. You've sold a lot. Have you had anything to eat?'

'No.'

'Give me your key and I'll make you a cup of coffee.' She had seen the mug on the bureau and I suppose the key on my belt. She went away across the yard and the way she unlocked the office, I knew she'd been there before, and knew about the coffee and the rest of it, but I was too thirsty to think much about it. A bucket missus, a bucketful!

Someone asked if the chair I was sitting on was for sale.

'I can find you another if you come back next week. Seven pounds.' I was alive! Mrs C and the thought of coffee had stimulated my brain.

An Estate car backed to the doors. The active businessman opened his boot and trotted up the steps. 'Blanket box for Fletcher,' a smile stretching his moustache. Mrs Fletcher from long ago. We carried the box out, put it in the car, and I smelt her. I thought of him taking the loot home to her in their cave.

Mrs Crawford came back carrying a mug and a paper bag. 'I nipped to the dairy while the kettle boiled and got you something.'

'Thanks,' I heard myself say. My arms had already reached out, and my hand had closed round the mug, taken it to my mouth and delivered a burning gulp. The other had fumbled open the bag on the bureau, wriggled in like an animal and was carrying the egg roll on which I could see all the little bits of crust sticking up, and the butter glistening between the porous ledges of bread, to the back of my throat.

I ate and drank, and she stood turned slightly away.

'How much do I owe you?'

'Don't be silly.'

We went out onto the steps. The sun had sunk and cars had their lights on, there was no wind and it was pleasant standing in the fresh air looking at the stars in the clear dark above the dim lower part of the sky.

'You didn't think you would come.'

139

'I was going to be busy,' she said as if she hadn't forgotten our phone conversation.

'Oh yes.'

'Here, help yourself.' She fished a packet of biscuits out of her bag. 'More coffee?'

'No thanks.' I didn't want her to go over there again, to have the bother, though mention of it had made my throat dry. 'Did you see the fellow on the balcony?' I asked her.

'No–o.'

'Some guy went up there. I think he was a bit – it began to creak and he came down again.'

She looked at me and I wondered if she had been there.

'You see I don't know any of them. There was that friend of Andy's, Maxwell.'

'Oh, they're a wild crowd.' She spoke of them as if they always went around together. They maybe did and they'd have been at school together; maybe her too. But if that idiot was a friend of hers so what.

'A fat guy with a boozy face.' That wouldn't distinguish him. 'He had a scarf tucked into his jacket. No coat. A dirty, coloured scarf. I'd got a rope there you see, but he untied it and went up. Made a kind of speech.' Did she mind me telling her? She was looking at me. 'More or less saying he thought Andy should have been doing the opening. They were shouting about free booze when they came in.' I felt sick from eating quickly. 'He hasn't been here all day.'

'He's got a lot on.'

'I thought he'd come. He said he would.' I began to shiver. I was looking at her shoes – clumpy affairs, real leather without question as in the adverts in the Saturday papers among the wicker commodes etc. Here I was talking to her.

'Come on, I'll help you get finished,' she said, her face freckled on the cheekbones and then she looked into the shed and at the new angle the freckles disappeared and fine down showed on the ridges of her jaw and cheeks – her eyes were shadowed. It was a mask or skull at that moment. I always had some awe of her after that, in spite of her grey eyes and quiet seeming ways – Mrs Blackbird in her dowdy feathers hopping under the bushes.

'I suppose we could stop at five thirty. There wasn't any

140

time fixed,' I said.

'I think you should close now' – it was five o'clock. 'They've had a good run for their money. They can come back another day. You gather up your money. You'll be going to put it in the safe? I'll chase these people out.'

She went quietly away round the shed and I started counting the money. I heard her talking as if she knew the people. Maybe she did. There was more money than I'd thought, more than £600, and it almost tallied with the book.

She herded them to the door, like a dog behind sheep. 'No more pound notes for you here, Michael!' They were grinning, everybody knew each other.

She'd turned off the paraffin when I came back from the safe.

I told her there was a man coming back with his car, and I hadn't said what time we were closing.

'He'll come another day. A Gledhill man?'

'I don't know.'

'Did he pay you?'

'Yes.'

'He'll be back then.'

'Maybe I should wait a wee while.'

'Well, if you like . . . these chaps . . . he's probably in the pub!' The boys-will-be-boys look again, not to be taken at face value. Layers of it.

'Did you know it in the blackout?'

'It was long after the blackout I came here!'

'Sorry, I didn't . . . '

'I came here when I married Andy. Long after the war, you know – no, you wouldn't know. I remember it.' Her mouth twisted at one side when she smiled. 'They started with that.' She pointed to the Nissen hut.

'I saw you knew your way to it.'

'I kept their books for them so I was in there for a year or two. It was simple in those days.' She was looking at the workshop and store, the bays of gravel and the stacks of materials, easily seen in the light from the street lamps, and seemed to have forgotten me.

'You'd see them being built,' I said of the buildings.

'Oh yes. Your man doesn't seem to be coming. I must get

141

away home.' I went out with her. From inside her car she said, 'You must come for a meal some time. I'll fix it up. Andy thinks a lot of you, you know. He depends on you.'

'Oh!' What could I do but make a face.

'Don't stay long,' she called out of the car window.

When she'd gone I took her advice. There was no point hanging about.

The man turned up on Monday morning, but nobody else came. Still, Monday. I straightened the place up. We needed more furniture and I wondered if Andy had been buying on Saturday.

A couple appeared in the doorway as if they thought there was no-one there. I startled them and the man barked 'Are you open?'

'Come in, come in, open all hours,' I was saying, falling into it as if this was about my twentieth year, blah blah blah, and immediately hating this man who wore a sheepskin coat and a narrow-brim hat that looked like suede, with a ribbon round, and a blue feather in it. He had a stern face and small moustache, a small head and big ears, he was old enough to be retired and this was Monday.

'Just a look round,' his wife said, forward from the door with a quick glance. They'd come to see what kind of a mess it was.

'You've not many customers.' He smiled dourly.

'You should have seen it on Saturday. Place was full.'

His wife paused, and he and I went on and stopped at the clock. 'Not bad,' he said.

'There's been a lot of interest.' What did I mean? Was I going to be talking nonsense to idiots for ever? It had come out of its own accord – I pinched my leg but that didn't reach my head. We drifted along the wall at the back and I stopped at a barometer. 'This is a nice piece.' I was overdoing it – he looked sharply to see if I was taking the piss. However he tapped the glass, the needle jerked up, and I glid away to his wife who hovered at a wash-stand. Could I help I asked, low and creepy. She stood away from it and said she was just looking.

142

It would have been good if the shed had been full of people again and no time to think. Why not a big day every Saturday, special prices? . . . nothing could be done without Andy. The idea should be put to him at once to allow time for gearing up for next Saturday. If it got to be a regular affair there could be a tea-stall. That would certainly be a good idea. And possibly room for people to sell crafts or something. But nothing could be done without Andy. I was seeing a deadline – one o'clock. If he wasn't here by one o'clock . . .

They were both at the barometer. I continued my walk to be nearer them, threw open a wardrobe within a short distance and fiddled inside it. She said, 'Excuse me . . . could we?' leaning toward me, her hand raised.

I seemed to remember as I wandered deep in thought, and brought my attention to them. 'It's a nice one.'

'Is it good?' she asked, coaxing.

'Yes! Mahogany and solid brass!' I smiled. 'Early this century. If we'd had time to clean it up, would have been twice the price. It doesn't look its value. As you see, it just needs . . . came in a couple of days ago.' I rubbed its dirty surface.

'Well,' she said. We looked at her husband, at the side of his face. 'I think it's very nice. And when I've polished it . . . hanging in the front hall? I think we should . . .' He nodded. 'We'll have it then.' She smiled on me, a parting-with-money smile.

I lifted the barometer off the wall. It was £12. He paid cash from a leather wallet like Dad's, and said I'd no need to wrap it, they had the car.

When they were out of the door he said to her, as if I was sealed off and couldn't hear, 'Wouldn't give wee Crawford long in that place.' She only shook her head, perhaps because she knew I overheard.

On the face of it it was ridiculous, a wee smout like that calling Andy wee. That little man maybe thought he looked impressive, his hat etc, but you'd have to be in a low state to be impressed – like I'd been in Leeds, for a day, hour, minute, second, and when you knew there was nothing in behind the mask it was okay. That man had been born retired, wearing his blue-feathered hat! And then in his same job clogging his bit of a Government office or some other building to the best of his

143

powers. The barometer had been unlucky, there'd be no escape, the wee shite frowning and tapping it every morning. Imagine that to look forward to every morning! Worst thing about him, though, was what you couldn't argue with: wee Crawford.

The wee monster was right in his wee way. I went to the office to see if wee Crawford had called. He hadn't. My status with Annie had gone up because of the money. We had divided it that morning and the shed money was in her box with a rubber band round it. I took it back to the shed and put cheques and notes separately in two of the bureau's small drawers.

There was wee Andy and big Andy – shorter than me but his breadth more than made up for it and a stranger would have said at once that he was the bigger of us. I was glad to see him, I didn't have to put a smile on and he was smiling too. 'How're you doing, Michael?'

I concentrated on him, while my systems automatically recorded: the floorboards' raised and rubbed edges, the footworn stone at the door, grey cable sliding along a beam – a shed full of air, paraffin and silence, balanced round us. The smell of him, the soap he used and his skin.

'How'd you get on?' He was looking and seeing how much was gone, shoulders thrown back and hands in his pockets.

I gave him the notebook, with the total pencilled in, and the barometer entered below at the day's date.

'My God!' he said, and while I opened the drawers for the money he poked the bureau with his finger. 'Hoho!' He'd forgotten it being here on Friday, or not noticed it. I handed him the cheques and the banknotes. 'You've done well,' he said.

'I could have done with you being here.'

'Sorry, I was held up.' He slotted the large wallet back into his pocket.

'I don't think you meant to come.'

Andy frowned. 'It's been difficult.' He walked up and down while I sat at the bureau. 'The way I see it going, I mean, this is a most encouraging start. If we stay open six days a week at low prices we'll keep the punters coming in. There's a lot of people in this town and they've not had a place like this.

They'll be telling their friends about us. And once it's going' – he stirred with his hands, mixing flour – 'we'll get into better stuff. It's cheap up here. Some of those boys from the Midlands of England . . . their appetite down there . . . you can't keep up with it. Lorryload at a time of the best – and they mark it up 100%.'

'If I'm on my tod here I want more money.' I hadn't meant that but him changing the subject . . .

'Oh, of course.' He came towards me holding out his hands like a –

'You should be here too. It would be better if you were here. Wasn't that the idea?'

'Now, look, you must have –'

'You said you'd get me an assistant and you haven't, and I needed one Saturday. I bloody needed one! They were laughing too.' I'd got his attention. 'Just laughing, you know . . . about the stuff . . . and the price. Saying it must have fallen off the back of a lorry, you know.' Why was I saying this? I hadn't meant to. Did he know about the man on the balcony? If he did or he didn't there was no good me telling him; but I'd have said it if it hadn't stuck in my throat.

'I appreciate what you say about Saturdays. Working Saturdays. On your own.'

'It's not the money.'

'But you're right.'

'Well are you going to be here then?'

He spread out his hands and opened his mouth, but didn't say anything. Why had I said money? He sighed. He was moving his feet although they were out of my sight. I leant my elbow on the bureau's leather, my chin in my hand, pulling the sulks, and it was working. The silence existed between us. What might have been said passed through it. I knew he'd never be here in the shed.

I started a new conversation: 'I've got some ideas, about mebbe each Saturday. Why don't we talk about it?'

'We are.'

That was the end of that one.

At that moment I was thinking that I'd finish the things that needed to be finished, like the clock, and then leave, get out of the town. I was pacing round and had reached the clock. 'Do

145

you want me to get this fixed for you?' I asked. He gripped a fold of his cheek and rasped the bristles. The porous skin and black shadow of his chin gave a shallow transparence, his lip another platform repeating the chin like in a silhouette. His mouth opened a bit when he'd swallowed and a string of saliva led from a yellow tooth up and out of sight. 'Will I tell him to go ahead with it?'

'If it's more than £50 tell him to send an estimate. Jeez, it's cold in here!'

'I'll shut the door.'

'No, I'm going over for a cup of tea.'

'I need a kettle in here.'

'Good idea. Go ahead and buy one. Get them to send a bill.' He paused. 'Eh . . . I'll give you something for Saturday.' He was holding open his jacket, peering in, feeling with the other hand for his wallet.

'No, no.'

'Aye, here you are.' He pulled out notes and handed them to me crumpled up. I put them in my pocket without looking. 'You did well,' he muttered and swung his arms, almost choking the words: 'And keep selling the stuff!' He faced me. The big ball of his thumb rubbed his temple, wrinkling and stretching the skin. 'You could be better at this than me! You do the prices next time. Put 'em up a wee bit if you think, but not much mind.'

'Okay. But tell me how much you want for the clock, when it's mended.'

He screwed up his face. 'Four hundred.'

'Four hundred pounds?'

'Four hundred pounds.' He rubbed his hands.

I remembered the card left by Major Black and gave it to him. 'Huh! Him,' said Andy.

'D'you know him?'

'Know him alright. What did he want?'

I told him what had happened between me and Major Black, not mentioning Major Black being a detective – it would be okay if Andy knew him. 'You're to get in touch with him.'

'Oh, aye.' He rubbed his hands again for the cold but wasn't really minding it now.

'You better go and get your tea,' I said.

I watched his short, sharp, stumping stride cross the yard, like anyone's of that shape and age in a big coat, but I could have picked it out of a thousand, as unique as a fingerprint, and I was proud of that.

I had a customer. A customer! He bought a pair, almost matching, of Abe's chairs (£12 the pair) and a folding card table.

Barbara was coming in the afternoon, although showing her the shed, being with her and admired by her, had changed now. She'd be impressed by its rubbishy nature, with 'good stuff', but between us it was shot, it was over.

I knew but couldn't admit it, so I imagined how she would look at me when she came, from under her brows, whether or not anyone else was here.

She'd said two o'clock. Warmth was better than cold with the door open but the stove made the air stuffy. Those windows should have been scraped of paint so that they'd open. The pole with the brass hook on the end had been there all the time, perhaps not used since the summer evening whist drives. A scraping away of the outside paint and I could have opened up on the side away from the wind – rising, cold. But it was twenty minutes to two and I gave up that idea of opening a window. No possibility of turning off the stove because just after turning off was the worst smell, worse than immediately after lighting.

I repositioned some furniture to make it better when she entered. I got it looking its best, did my best – result? It was scruffy, should have been junked – well-arranged, you could say, as if it was a Japanese art, the art of arranging rubbish furniture in an old shed, the angle of cobweb etc, but there was more than a chance she'd miss this delicate aspect – which would be destroyed if I mentioned it. It had to be felt; felt in the bones, in the bones; she'd feel it immediately, otherwise it would die.

I saw her; as if a curtain had been pulled to let in the daylight, I couldn't see any more what I'd seen in the dark. She

147

passed the Nissen hut, walking anxiously I thought towards the shed, me at the window. Then I was holding the door open.

'Wheee!' she went, suddenly on the step and through the door. 'What a wind, I'm frozen!' She said it in such a way that I was to make it better at once. I'd caused her this unnecessary pain . . . eh? Oh dear, oh dear, it was an average wind, what everyone would expect in winter, and anyway she was wrapped in a big coat. Oh God! She came in. I shut the door and noticed the magnetic repulsion; she couldn't look at me, couldn't look at the furniture or the place although her eyes were open. She turned from side to side as if chained and wrinkled her nose at the paraffin smell . . . a bit much, Jack had it in his shop. Then I thought: she never goes there.

'It's the only way of keeping warm.' I laughed.

She had her back to me, walking along a row of furniture, and she stopped and looked at something. I saw her sharp profile. And then when she turned back to me, the width of her face round the eyes, the delicate heavy chin and red mouth. This charming face, surrounded by reddish-brown hair, peeped out of the tweed overcoat she wore over her black trousers.

She glanced slightly at me again and said, down into her coat: 'Junk,' seeming violently depressed, in behind the red mouth and pale face.

I said to her, 'It's not meant to be antique.' She didn't answer. 'It's cheap, for people to furnish their houses. Nothing wrong with it.' She looked at me as if I'd said something unbearably stupid. I thought she was going at that moment, without seeing the clock, but she'd opened the door to get some air apparently. 'You didn't see the best stuff,' I said. 'It's right at the back. The clock's there too.' She must have seen it in the middle of the back wall opposite the door.

Her body swayed without the feet seeming to move. But she followed. I led her past the rest of the good stuff before the clock. Occasionally she touched a surface and made an indifferent noise, maybe to occupy herself because I was in front and she couldn't pass me in the narrow space.

At the clock she stood upright for the first time, her arms hung down instead of folding the coat round her. I knew, though it was hard to believe, she'd been nervous; she hadn't

148

been able to look at the clock till assured about something. And now she was looking at it intently. Perhaps she'd thought I'd attack her . . . no, ha ha, but some fear connected with me, that I'd behave badly, try to kiss and cuddle her and be seen by people who knew her and Jack. I admit I'd thought about cuddling her, but that fantasy had gone away in the face of what she looked like when she came . . . it was knocked out by her real face, not the fantasy one that was motionless, and could be studied, and didn't look at me.

She looked at me again and said, 'Hum,' her hands in her pockets, head poised on one side. The blood flowed into all my vessels which had been screwed tight shut. 'Well, I thought you said it had stopped! It's certainly a good one or has been and they can repair anything these days – except the crazing on the face. I don't think they can do anything for that. These are jobs for furniture people of course, not clockmenders. Tuxford of Boston – very goo-ood! Of course it may have been cannibalised . . . unscrupulous guys often get the case of one and the works of another and the face of another and put them together. Did you know that?' I wasn't listening to a word. She opened the case and shut it again. 'I expect the works need an overhaul. Jack'll do that.'

'I wound it up for the sale! I was afraid I might damage it but it was okay.'

'Might have needed oil. They can stand rough handling. He'll love to get his hands on this.' She smiled and I just didn't want to think about Jack. 'I presume your Andy'll pay? Wonder where he picked it up.'

'Don't know,' I said vaguely. 'He'll pay alright. Don't you know him?'

'No.'

'He's a nice guy.'

She wrapped her coat round her.

'He said he'd need an estimate if it was more than £50. Do you think Jack – '

'How can he tell till he gets into it? Good God! I'd have thought that was obvious!' She smiled. 'Don't worry, an overhaul's not expensive. He never charges enough anyway.'

We stood there smiling at each other, quite at ease for a moment, then the shed or whatever it was seemed to get to her again. She gathered the coat round her and hurried away saying she had to be somewhere else.

'She probably thinks I'm ogling the go-go girls,' Jack leered. I smelt beer off him, but he was putting it on a bit for Peter. We were standing in the yard. Peter knew he was the watchmaker. Like everybody in Gledhill he must have looked down at one time or other on the bald head bent over the workbench down there in the basement. 'Great place you've got here,' Jack went on.

He wanted a tour of the workshop and store but I wasn't on for that and walked towards the shed.

'Something wrong with the clock?' Peter asked, coming along too.

'He's going to give it a check-up, Peter.'

Jack put down his tools on the floor beside the clock, humming to himself, rubbing his hands. He'd had a drink, but he was one hundred per cent sharp. 'Where d'you say he got it? That's a damn nice clock.'

'Oh, one of his trips. It came with a lorry load.'

'Down about England, down in England,' Peter said, grinning at Jack. 'It was stood in the office there a long time. Me and him carried it over. I started it for him.'

He looked for an answer, but Jack unrolled his toolkit, stepped in front of the clock and seemed to pull its head off, and Peter stood back with his thumbs hooked in his bib.

'Peter started it no bother.'

'Know your way around them, do you?'

'Aye, had one for years.'

The face and works of the clock atop its long body looked as if he'd gone to take the hat off and the skull had come too. 'Jack, eh,' I said, 'how much will this cost – before you go too far. Roughly I mean? Just an idea, you know.'

'You'll have change out of a thousand pounds easily,' he said, continuing to work.

Peter grunted, 'Eh! I knew from the sound that the gummy grin would be on his face.

'Eh, well, if it's – '

150

'Don't worry! My old Dutch told me. If it's over fifty I've to stop, eh? Don't worry. I'll tell you if I come on anything expensive.'

Peter asked about some difficulty with his clock, peering close to where Jack worked and stabbing with his finger. From there he went on to talk about people I didn't know. Jack could talk while he worked, the two things at once; he would be holding what Peter had said like a piece of jigsaw over his map of Gledhill.

There was no certainty he couldn't do three things at once and watch me as well.

Peter felt guilty about not working and left.

'Peter Calder. He doesn't deserve a man like that,' Jack said.

I hung around and then said stupidly, 'Nobody does.' I went to the bureau and checked there was enough cash to pay him.

But I was thinking of him and her; the casual way together in the house, watching TV and having those arguments. How had it been, when they were younger . . . what did they say, did their eyes shine, did he say things, did she blush?

Old Jack was working at the clock, putting it together now.

'What do you think of her?' I asked.

He removed a screwdriver from his mouth. 'She's alright. What do you think of her, Michael?' He narrowed his eyes and returned to his work, but his look was temporarily there and could return to me in a moment. He was putting a part into the clock, and suddenly facing me without any expression on his face. 'I know what's going on,' he said, and continued working.

Sweat broke out on my neck and prickled under my shirt.

'Uh-hu,' I said.

He reached for a washer and carried it to the bit he was working on, out of my sight. The hand returned, found a brass bolt and took it to the work where his eyes were fixed.

I was cold and damp under my shirt and breathed low in case I caught his attention, but he seemed busy and I picked up an oilcan, clean and small – a cylinder to fit in the toolkit, without drips or leaks. I pressed the lug a couple of times, not thinking. It had a curved metal spout which I'd filled with my two presses, and a drop of clear oil fell from the nozzle. I carried it, because I had to have done this for a purpose, to a

151

desk with a hinged lid and put the can to the hinge, ran it along and worked the lid up and down to let the oil in. And the same with another desk.

'Give us that oilcan a minute.'

I took it to him, and he squirted oil into a part of the works. 'Aye.'

This is it, I thought.

He shook his head, pursed his lips and looked up mildly. 'They say your boss is buying a hell of a furniture? All over the country.'

'In the north of England,' I said in a cramped voice, and added for continuation. 'He'd buy more if we had space.'

'Aah . . . ' Jack said to the bit of clock between his fingers. 'Will he be going to build here, d'you think?'

'Don't know.'

'Bargains to be picked up in the north of England, I suppose.'

'Carlisle.' My neck ached from keeping my head up. It wanted to fall forward, sideways or any way. My body would have liked to slump into a chair. I did not let it start but this slumping was in the background and would creep into the limbs and the neck particularly . . . 'That's right, Carlisle.' I walked to the door and glanced out. 'The auctioneers keep it for him down there, the furniture, and send it up when we've got room.'

'Ooh-ho . . . Eh, it'll need a bit of capital I suppose. Bit of money.' Jack waved his hand at the shed. I kind of nodded. We looked at the naked works of the clock, touched with oil in parts. 'And would he get this down there?'

'Privately.' The word hardly came out.

'Gimme a lift here.'

We took a side each of the top casing and slid it over the clock face. 'There, you beauty.' He sounded angry, opened the glass and wound both parts. 'That's the chime. I'll give it a run and if you don't like it you needn't wind it again.' He looked at his watch and moved the clock hands, opened the case and moved the pendulum and the clock ticked as if it had been doing it silently all the time of the operation. 'Not for sale, I see.'

'He was waiting till you serviced it.'

152

'What will he want for it?'

'You'd need to ask him.'

'No hurry, mind. You can tell him I might be interested. When he makes up his mind. If it wasn't too dear.'

'How much do you think?'

Jack said, 'Oh, I don't know. Let him speak first.' He fitted his tools in their slots in the kit, went down stiffly on one knee and began to roll it up. 'I've a terrible headache.'

'Oh, would you like a cup of tea?'

He rolled, and included a shake of the head. 'I think I've some tablets back at the shop.'

'I'll see if Annie's got aspirin!'

I ran out and across the yard. Having got some pills from her I took back a cup of water as well. He was standing in the doorway, smiling slightly as if it hurt to smile. 'Thanks.'

I grudged him having to say it and hurt his head again. He tipped three aspirins onto his palm, threw them all together into his mouth and gulped some water. 'Thanks.'

I tried to feel the pain in my head to share it, but I was sound as a bell. I had the desk drawer open and some notes visible in my hand. 'How much then, Jack?'

'Ach, don't worry. I'll bill him.'

I carried his roll of tools and he got carefully into the old black car.

The chime made the shed like a church, and I hadn't time for the thinking involved. Should I become a priest? Minister no, definitely, but it sneaked up on me now and then about becoming a priest – not for God or Jesus, but the mystery and secret knowledge, the worming in beside George to discover the secrets. It was too much to think about though. I always put it out of my mind.

That was it, with Jack. We might have become better friends, but he didn't want to go on with it. He talked to Barbara and the kids, at the same time giving me friendly glances of a different grade of friendship. It was up to him.

He made a barrier round his family to keep me out. It re-formed if I had got between two of them – each was wrapped

153

in their own invisible sheet, but nearly visible; it had been there, like mist that's just gone. Barbara broke it away sometimes, but there was another, thinner division between us two. She was extremely nice to me.

I locked the shed and walked to the town centre, if you could call it that, thinking how busy Leeds had been. That excitement had been hellish all the time, but just a bit would have been okay. Here in Gledhill the best way home was the riverside path, the water and the lights shining on it; a different sensation, a different excitement if it could be called that.

A girl had been in sight coming towards me. First a female figure; then by the vigorous walk it could not be old; then it was young, sleek hair and everything, and below the coat legs, the way they, by god, eh!, and I was watching them swinging along, raising my gaze (from deep thought) and wanting a look at the face and etc – to Jill Pellegrini! 'Jill!'

'Michael!' She smiled and kissed me on the cheek; a sign of being left school, or I may have run into her.

Had she met me on purpose, though there was no reason to flatter myself? JP we'd called her at school. She was supposed to choose boys by the length of their willy. It was supposed to be her Italian blood. I'd never been much interested in her and she hadn't been interested in me.

It was great to meet someone you knew. We stood on the path. She might have met me on purpose I reasoned, almost unconsciously, because the riverside path wasn't her kind of place, it was scruffy, junk lying in the bushes, thin mud underfoot, no people – she wouldn't have been seen dead here. It was odd her coming along here and saying to me, 'Leaving your work? Let's go for a drink.'

'Yes,' I said, being turned round, to go back the way I'd come.

We went along arm in arm. It was dark and damply cold. She held my arm lightly and I felt the softness of her coat now and then on the back of my hand. She was asking about the job as we'd already said the general how-are-you-getting-ons.

'I like it okay.'

We were walking in step, Jill giving out a sisterly feeling. I hadn't known her well at school as I said; maybe she too was glad to see someone she knew.

Perhaps she'd picked up this easy way of getting on at university, or perhaps it was her foreign blood.

'Let's go in here,' she said, a place I hadn't been before, an old pub. She got the drinks and brought them to a table away from the bar. We raised the pint and martini.

'Mark told me you'd left uni.'

She wrinkled her nose. 'I dropped out after a year. I work now.'

'You live at home any more?'

'I've a flat in town.' Her eyes had changed more than the rest of her. At school they'd always darted about. I was being drawn, drawn by them, in their new state.

'Where?' I asked. 'I live here, too.'

'Out the moss road direction.'

'Gledhill, eh! What do you think of it?'

A man hobbled from a seat near us to the roasting fire and poked at the coals which fell into a red cavern and blazed up. I was talking too loud.

'I like it fine.' Talking to her at school had been like a game-show chat on TV, she'd always been too damn smart. She had that slight English accent; the family had come from some-where down there in third year. Old man Pellegrini was a kind of industrial chemist and a grim old bird according to Mark who was scared of the whole family. And if I'd got into conversation with Jill then, in those days, I'd never thought of the smart answers till afterwards. Here we were, sitting in silence, and she seemed to be stuck, Jill.

'You've cut your hair,' I said. It was short and shiny.

'Do you like it?' she asked, not necessarily expecting a 'yes' as in the old days. She tossed back the martini.

'Yes. I do. Here, let me get you another.'

When I returned with the drinks I asked where she worked and she named a shoe shop.

'That's near the way I go to work. I haven't seen you. Have you seen me? Is that how you knew where I worked?'

'No. You'll start earlier than me. You'll be past the shop by the time I'm there.'

155

I told her about my work and Andy and the others for something to say and she occasionally looked at the old people who seemed to be regulars, meaning I was too loud. 'What about you?' I asked when I couldn't think of anything more.

'I don't know how to tell you.' She gave me a strange look, and my heart began to thump. Afterwards I couldn't remember the colour of her eyes. I don't think I will.' She began twisting her glass on the table.

'Come on – you must now.'

The dark-red martini and the thick stem of the glass reflected red and white light and the whorls of Jill's fingers magnified, mother-of-pearl. 'I'm having an affair with Andy.'

I must have reacted sharply – freezing. I came to staring at Jill and being openly stared at by two of the old folks. They were going to join in. I huddled forward over the table till our heads were almost touching.

'What?'

'You didn't know?'

'No, I didn't know!'

She shook her head confusedly.

A diabolical liberty, surprising me like this! And in here, where I couldn't do whatever it was I would've done because of these old creeps! She was gazing sadly into her glass, looking sad. 'Can't believe it!' I whispered, 'I mean you and Andy! It's – how did it start?' I crashed all over the place and she stared into the glass. 'Tell me what happened, Jill.'

She looked round and started a low, flat statement as if under duress – but it had been her idea! But I hadn't reacted right – I'd been childish – parentish – disappointed her. 'We met at someone's house, then he asked me out, some time after. We sat in his car at first, we couldn't go anywhere. I was living at home then, after I came back from Edinburgh. You know what all those jerks are like up there and he was such a nice guy, so gentle –' . . . Andy gentle! I couldn't imagine it. Then I thought he's not exactly ungentle, it's just a way I'd never have thought of describing him. I suppose it had been staring me in the face and I hadn't noticed . . . 'He enjoys himself when he can,' she was saying. 'He was bored at home. Then I got the flat and it made everything great.'

I thought of Andy creeping into this room and laughed. Jill

didn't say anything God bless her, she let me laugh, she remembered I used to laugh.

'You really like him?'

'I love him.' Her eyes softened. 'He comes whenever he can. Sometimes every day. It's been easier with the business changing. And I work part-time now.'

Good God, it was Andy being away, that's where he was.

'I'll get them.' She grabbed the empty glasses and went to the bar. The people watched her, because she was a stranger, and because she was good-looking, a natural focus she was. Really classy, Jill, the one you noticed first anywhere. I was proud to be with her. And old Andy? He'd been fooling me. Had he asked her to tell me? Why hadn't he told me himself? I was angry about that, but how could he have told me, why should he have? All the same I had a right to be angry . . . She was turning the other way at the bar, looking at the brands of cigarettes – her side-face – she was out of the ordinary, she had a right to do anything she liked. She looked like that, she could do anything, fair enough. But it was unfair. Something was bloody unfair. Andy! Incredible!

She came back and we lit cigarettes.

'Did he ask you to tell me?'

'Oh, no!' She looked at me as if I was a complete idiot. 'How could he have?' She took rapid puffs and a longer one, letting the smoke out slowly. 'We're perfect for each other.' I looked back into her eyes, the first time for a while. 'I love him, you know. That's all there is to it. I don't know what's going to happen and don't care. Changed my life I can tell you,' she said solemnly like an old person. She took hold of my arm – 'It's the best thing that ever happened to me! I'm so happy, I'm so happy, nearly all the time!' What a look, as if I was the object of it! 'I wanted to know if you knew, and I wanted to tell someone.' She frowned. 'There's been no-one I can talk to. I wanted to tell you.'

'Well here I am!' I laughed nastily. 'It's wonderful! I don't know what to say!' I fancy myself when I start doing this, but it ends up horrible. I'd forgotten where I was, that we were supposed to be keeping our voices down so as not to drop Andy in it. Her too. I was sick of them. 'Tell me about the flat,' I asked in the same horrible voice. I couldn't control my face.

'Relax Michael. No-one's getting at you.'

I didn't look up for a while, and when I did, her sparkling face – was it the drink? – at any rate it washed away my bad feelings.

She'd forgotten the other people or did she want to tell them too? The man in the cap, with the bulge of neck and sprout of grey hair – those were pricked ears, quivering they were; but it was possible that everyone knew, except me.

Her arm was across the back of a chair and the cigarette cocked in her fingers gave a slight twitch. 'Don't worry about them, they're all dodos.' She smiled and recrossed her legs. 'He comes in and takes off his coat, his cap, and his scarf. Hangs them up on the back of the door.'

'He wears that damn great coat all the time. He was different when he was a joiner.'

'He didn't come to my place then. He was glad to get away from that, you know. I hardly knew him then.' She stared at the table for a while and then looked up. 'Oh yes, he comes in and gets himself settled, as if he's home from work. He hasn't touched me and I haven't moved, we play this game every time, see! Sometimes he sits on the floor at the fire. He's got strong arms. Soft here – soft and white like a baby.' She stroked the inside of her elbow. 'I'm not shocking you, am I?' She'd not have seen if she was. As a matter of fact she was. She was silent a long while.

'Sometimes he brings wine or something to eat. He cooks while I lie in bed, or the other way round.'

'Cooks?'

'Yes.'

I shook my head. She was mysterious and Egyptian. I couldn't tell her expression for in the gloom of the pub her eyes had gone completely black. She took a cigarette, frowned at it and lit it. 'Then he goes away – no that's not right. But it happens sooner or later; in the end he gets dressed and goes away.' She blew a cloud of smoke. 'And I stay in, if I haven't to go out.'

There must have been loads of times he'd come into the shed straight from her; and the strangeness of my not knowing. I could have detected something in his look, on his breath, a vague scent off him, but seemed to have been deliberately

158

ignoring it. What surprised me was the sadness. It made her sad.

'Do you go out together?'

'Walk about holding hands? You're joking!'

'I don't know.'

'Once. To Carlisle. Oh no, not for a night! An afternoon, a meal.' She drew back into herself, her eyes black holes and a cloud of smoke in front of her face – it might have been a sunny afternoon that she remembered, the only one. She blew out another plume. 'Still – we had lunch in a place where we didn't know anyone. Like another country. Like a holiday. We had Italian food – Andy had calzone, a great big covered over pizza – and fantastic ice-creams filled with fruit and liqueurs and chocolate chips. We sat over it for hours . . . then we hadn't much time. Looked round the shops. It's a good place. It was warm and sunny and the people were friendly. I'm going to buy him some shirts . . . but I didn't want to waste time going into shops, we just strolled around.' (Hand in hand, arm in arm, their reflections smiling back from the plate glass and in the shop, through the glass, Gledhill eyes. People went there.)

'What are you thinking?'

'Nothing. Well, I was wondering when he'd wear the shirts.'

'On our real holiday!' She leant forward. That was what she desired with all her force, a holiday with him. Andy's wife, and what he'd say to her, were washed away, ignored altogether. They'd just go, she wanted it so much. I didn't know this Andy – it was unreal being so passionate about him, Andy. 'He often talks about places down there, is it Cumbria? I think that's where we'll go,' she said.

'Where he goes fishing.'

'He's going to teach me.'

'Me too!'

'Some other time!' She laughed. 'But no, he likes you, you know.'

'I'm standing in for his son, I think.'

'That would be odd!' She screwed up her face, laughed again and touched my hand. 'No, I think he sees you as a partner.'

'Like you!'

'Look, I'll have to be going. I'm glad I met you. I really

wanted to tell you.' She touched my hand again and took a notepad from her bag and wrote her address. 'That's where I am, if you want to contact me. Someone else might answer if you phone.'

'The owners?'

'No, they don't live there. Three blokes, in the other rooms.' (I got it now, there was Andy, yes, meeting one of these young blokes on the dole, at the Tech or first job, more or less, like me, on his way to her room, nodding hullo, making out this was normal, making out by his way of walking that he was her father or something.) She'd finished her drink. 'Don't hurry,' she said, looking at my half-finished pint.

'Hey, Jill – have you told me? Am I supposed to know, when I see Andy?'

'He doesn't know anything about this.' She nodded very seriously and went out.

There was open interest from the old people, and I kept hunched into myself.

It was a fine, frosty night and I became light-headed and laughed. I killed myself laughing. What a crazy arrangement!

Andy asked if I'd have a meal with them at home. It must have been fixed up by his wife. He'd waited telling me till that very evening and I had no time to go home.

At six o'clock there were not many people about in Gledhill – no-one that night, in our road. A breeze snuffled the dust against closed doors and hardly a light showed in their little panes, or at the chinks of windows. Everyone was through the back having tea.

The headache would have gone away in one of those warm kitchens. Maybe steak pie and cups of tea, the thick kind, not too hot, thick creamy brown, a magic potion soothing the limbs and above all head; flowing into the dry head cavities like soothing mud. Meanwhile pie and beans filling and seeping and glowing warmly in the body cavity. Oh-ho.

Andy's house was newish, I'd heard; probably he'd built it himself – i.e. Crawfords had. Doors, cupboards and shelves probably of an African hardwood from the rack in the store –

Idigbo sounded good; fitted and finished to a tee. And the lounge, a bulging three-piece suite, woolly rugs of pale colours on the thick, pale carpet – a feeling of being trapped by the feet in the carpet, definitely, unable to get out, and hemmed in again by glinting thick-glass bottles of strong spirits.

The air was clearing my head and the thought of tea had softened those dry-edged holes in the skull. I asked Matt in Mailers for a pint and rested one leg at the bar. I was nearly like everyone else; nearly a qualified, time-served regular. I nodded to an old fellow and he replied with one of his own though I don't think he knew me – a hard thing to judge when you were new in Gledhill – far more people knew you than you knew; they knew who you were and made up your past history if they didn't know it too.

My pocket swagged with change but I threw a note on the bar for Matt. Counting out coins looks mean and I'm fairly mean.

Matt knew everyone. Hullo Michael, he said with a friendly nod. He was always friendly to me and I didn't like this friendliness based on nothing. It seemed I mightn't have noticed a rite we'd passed through, which was the reason for his particular friendly look, something sly in it to my way of thinking. I'd rather have started from scratch, from selling and buying drinks, to see if we wanted to be friends. It was unlikely because there was nothing I liked about Matt. He was old and baggy. His appearance spoilt Bridie's. Anyway I said hullo to him too, and he got busy with other people.

I bought Andy one when he came, and we sat down. I was thinking of Jill, couldn't help it although it would have been better not to, and there was the smell that I'd noticed before, her smell, her perfume or shampoo or very skin; and hiding the knowledge, I kept up my part of the chat, sick with disgust, being disgusted with the rottenness that was hanging about. There was nothing disgusting about Jill, or Andy, but it was somewhere – I couldn't look at him straight.

At last he went to the bar. He bought one for Matt too, I heard him offer . . . it was something aggressive in him – a threat of war offering Matt a drink, an offer of combat. Matt wasn't to refuse or it would be an insult. Andy sometimes got like this – something had annoyed him and he got annoyed with everything else. He was like a keen little guy at school with a bunchy face and glistening eyes who used to always shoot his arm in the air to be first to answer – a little guy – he was nodding and hotching from one foot to the other there at the bar, worse than usual in the rotten atmosphere. Had Jill told him she'd told me, and he'd just come from her? He'd be wanting to destroy me for knowing, and taking it out on Matt. I saw Matt's face, listening, watching, frowning, a sudden movement – Andy had knocked something over on the bar and it was being wiped up. Then Matt went back to his work, filling glasses from the gantry.

Andy had bought whiskies. We usually drank beer and the whisky made us different, we talked differently because we were going to his house, as if we were going to a funeral or a wedding for instance.

When he looked toward the bar. I asked, 'Like another?'

'We better be going.'

He leant over in the car to get the pan drops from the glove pocket and a double waft came as his stubby fingers fumbled in there, the one I'd smelt before and that of his shirt and skin.

'Put your seat belt on.' He started the engine and warm air smelling of pipes came from the heater and rose to join a cool blast from the dashboard – the car going to school, scrambling to get the front seat before Helen! Cold knees and the schoolbag scratching them as we crammed our legs – both in the front seat – into the rubbery cave beside the gearstick, the air drying your eyes and the inside of your nose, but warming your knees! I'd been expecting him to speak about Jill in the dark in the car, but I was thinking of those early days in the other car with Helen, and when we stopped he hadn't said it. We'd been through a narrow road overhung with black hedges, and a white gate.

He stretched, and raised his arms; the light from the front porch shone on his legs. The other windows were curtained. His arms slowly dropped. I felt an almost chemical change in him. I saw the different way he stood.

'Come on in, then.' His voice was deeper than usual, and his face seemed to have dropped; it was loose and calm as if he was asleep, or dead – or at home.

Shoes and wellingtons lined the red porch floor. There were

plants in holders on the wall and a brass barometer. Andy called into the house, 'We're home dear!', he hung his cap on a hook without looking and held out his hand for my anorak.

Mrs Crawford appeared in an apron and he motioned us together like two boxers. 'This is Michael. My wife.'

'Phyllis.' She put out a small, hard, gardening hand, with short nails and big knuckles, no rings, and gave a firm grasp. I'd forgotten her deep voice. She wore a blue glittery dress, the brown skin of her neck and tufty grey hair making her look healthy. I liked her, I certainly did.

In the comfortable, shabby room I was on a couch in front of a wide stone fireplace. Andy had put a glass of whisky in my hand. This wasn't the place I'd expected. I had a job adapting him to this one, how could he not want to be here, how could he prefer the bed-sit, or Jill? He was in place here.

He was blethering about the house and I caught up where he was saying, 'This is the original cottage. Two rooms, this is them knocked into one. I'll show you the rest' – meaning later.

Phyllis came from the kitchen, opened the glass-paned door of a cupboard in the angle of the wall and poured herself a glass of something. 'It'll be a minute. Cheers. Nice to see you, Michael.'

We chatted the pointless way that's okay if you're sitting at a fire with a drink. It seemed she hadn't told him she'd been to the shed and we silently agreed not to mention it.

'You don't get that everywhere.' Andy nodded at the glass of whisky. 'Black Label.'

'He likes his whisky,' Phyllis said. They smiled at each other, and there was something behind these old smiles.

'That's Alastair and Sue,' she said. She'd seen me looking at the photos above the fire while they were smiling. The guy I was understudying was in university gear holding the roll of paper, and looked sly or clever or thick. He could have been all three. He was a shock. 'That's his graduation,' she went on. 'We went up for it. A wonderful day for them, wasn't it Andy – and now he's on a special business management course.'

'Electrical engineering. He's clever,' Andy said. 'He was a lazy devil at school! No trouble with his work, not ever though. It was easy for him.'

'He lives somewhere in Glasgow now, with his girl friend' –

Phyllis said it as two words with the accent on the second – 'I can't keep up with his address. He's always moving.' She seemed to like his moving or something, her mouth widened in a smile.

'What's he doing now?' I remembered quite well.

'Business management.'

'Fitting him up for a job with a big national company,' Andy said.

'He's pretty well got the job. It only depends on passing the course, doesn't it?'

'Oh, God knows!' Andy grunted. He was pleased as punch.

'What age is he?'

'Just gone twenty-three,' Phyllis said. I'd been feeling jealous as hell, but the fact of him being older made it better. 'And you?'

I told her. Then we looked at the photo of the girl, hair blowing in the wind, an outdoor type. 'What about her?'

'Sue'll be ages with your sister, I think.'

'Oh! Do you know her?'

Phyllis nodded. 'Not really, but I see your mother at the Trust. I've heard about you both.'

'Oh!'

'Nothing too bad! But I haven't seen Marjorie in a while. I seem to remember Helen was going to Art School in Edinburgh, is that right?'

'She's there now, she's doing her first year!'

'She'll know Susie!' Andy exclaimed.

'Och Andy, it's a big place, Edinburgh. They make their own friends.'

'Two Gledhill lasses! Did you not give her Susie's address woman?'

'They'll be busy with their own affairs,' Phyllis said placidly.

Great to be talking about Helen and Mum – but being back in all that again! That family stuff and all the other families and the connections so that everyone knew everyone and you could never do anything without it being heard of. And you would know that people you hardly knew were talking it over in their houses, nice comfortable houses like this one, what you'd done and worse, your prospects, the prospect of

164

everyone's life, spread out, aerial-photo-like – disappear, rub oneself out, hide under a cloud – where's Michael? he's under a cloud – but when they looked he'd be gone. A piece of mud had come out of the tread of my shoe and squashed on the carpet. I tried to scrape it up to throw in the fire.

'Never mind it,' she said. 'Didn't Marjorie tell me that you used to work with George Lamb, at the gardens?'

'That's right. I'd meant to again, but you know he died.'

'She was very good to him.'

That again. I nodded and looked at the ceiling as if I hadn't heard. 'Lot to be said for the city. You can do what you like. Nobody knows what you're doing,' I said.

'Oh!' Phyllis said, 'I have to agree with that – when you're young. I did my training in Glasgow. I'm a nurse.' She'd clasped her hands round her knees. 'In those days we all lived in the hostel. Hard work my goodness, but there were always parties. It seems all parties looking back on it.' She sighed and straightened her legs, pointing her toes. 'Yes, those were the days.'

'You were a wild lot!' Andy laughed heavily. 'Too much for us country boys! Going up, coming back, early hours of the morning, I, huh . . . ' He took my glass and his and refilled, poked the fire and stood with his back to it.

Phyllis leant back and crossed her legs, one shoe dangling from her toe. 'It's a great thing for you young chaps to get away from home and see the world and sow your wild oats,' she said. 'It's not so easy in a place like this where everybody knows what's going on.'

The Black Label went down like a ball of fire. There were difficulties I couldn't work out after this strong whisky. Did she know about Jill? If she didn't, should I tell her? I'd never done anything like this.

'Don't suppose you know where that expression comes from?' Andy had gone to the fire, restless as hell, and was fishing behind his back for the mantelpiece to lean on – 'Farming! The wild oats are the bad ones. You see them sticking up above the rest in summer, waving in the breeze. Bad news. Very bad news for farmers. If you don't pull 'em out you get the whole field full next year. We used to get paid for pulling them when I was a boy.' He scratched his neck.

'Shilling an afternoon, rogueing they called it. Walking through up to your chest, pulling them up and putting them in a bag. Then they were burnt – green as they were, they were burnt . . . nowadays they use chemical sprays.'

'I didn't know.' I was looking at the glowing arrangement of the criss-cross red logs in the fire and imagining walking on those flaming ledges.

'Come through and eat,' Phyllis said.

I followed her to the kitchen and Andy was piling logs on the fire.

'Make yourself at home,' she said, as if we'd switched off the lives in the other room. 'Pop your drink down. You're sitting here. The bathroom's through there if you want it.'

She was putting out plates of soup at the end of a long wooden table. In front of hers and his were white napkins in silver rings; at mine a folded one at the side; in the middle of the table, silver salts and peppers. The bare kitchen table and the silver. I had a second helping of the thick, milky, old-person's soup.

'I wouldn't have come so dirty if I'd known about your nice house,' I said, seeing the clean napkin on my old jeans. It sounded as if I was getting at Andy. To make up for it I started on a long thing not mentioning that he went to Mailers after work; going out of my way not to mention it. Of course she would know.

Andy got grumpy and carved a chicken brutally.

'You'll be learning a lot about furniture down there,' said Phyllis – the devil!

'Learning every day!'

'Really! I'm on the look-out for something good. That's one of the benefits I'm hoping for from this business. I'd like something in Dutch marquetry – a bureau, say. Be sure and keep your eye out for anything in that line.'

'I will!' (what was it?). This was completely pointless of course. I mean I enjoyed talking to her but because he was there we had to do it this stupid way. I couldn't talk to both and she was the best. She'd be communicating with Andy while talking to me, and maybe that was her main point, getting at him, bypassing him, her old bed-mate (more possible than Jill, these two old wooden creatures clutching each other).

166

He smiled and chewed, as if he liked being silent and listening to her. It was only when he spoke that things went haywire, maybe because I was there. 'I don't know what I'm going to do with my life,' I said to break their silent communication.

Andy looked over his glasses, tucking in his chin, eyes twinkling, taking a relaxed view from a full stomach – and he'd been through to refill his glass, and I'd refused one –' Is my job not up to scratch then?'

'It's fine.'

'Is that so?'

'What would you really like to do?' Phyllis asked.

'I dunno.'

'Stay here then,' Andy said. 'Good wage.'

'Yes. I'll probably be here all my life!' I laughed.

'Heavens, you're only nineteen! Some time you should go abroad. He may give you time off!' Phyllis laughed too.

'What's the point of going abroad?' Andy said. 'I never went abroad, never did me any harm – I'm not a case of arrested development. Well maybe I can't speak Spanish but I get by, communicate with them, get by – dos cognac, eh? But I bloody had to get down to work when I was young. None of this –'

'No dear, just that Michael here might be better to see the world . . . and find out what he wants to do.'

'Oh aye,' Andy grunted.

The ginger cat growled over an enamel plate on the floor, shaking its head as it devoured chicken skin, spraying drops of milk. My fingernails were terribly dirty.

'By the way,' Phyllis said, 'talking of Spanish, I must show you our holiday photos. Marjorie said you were going too.'

'Not me.'

'I'll show you, and you can tell her. I s'pose you've got lots of other friends who go to Majorca, but still – it's lovely.' What would be the relationship between them at the Trust, grey-haired women who hadn't known each other before – while they loaded the tea trolley, between dishing out stuff from it; in between taking patients for walks in the grounds; unlocking their cars? Both crammed with the secrets of their families and wanting to let them out but not wanting; cautious and intimate; the harmless secrets, teeth, exams, size of feet. And

167

the harmful ones. They'd share some of these, and still be strangers, in a way different from men. I know it's different but I don't know what it is. Like trying to imagine what Hindus think. 'Everyone goes there. It's very popular.'

'That's why I'm not going.'

She gave me a fraction of a second of shrivelling contact of her grey eyes. 'Come on, we'll have coffee.' I was going to say I shouldn't be late, to miss the photos, but she went on, 'You go through with Andy, I'll join you in a minute.' The old routine.

'Can I help you here?'

'No, on you go through. There's nothing to do.' It wasn't even to be considered my helping with the dishes because Andy would be left 'through' on his own. More unthinkable for him to stay here while she made coffee! – or he made coffee, while she did the dishes or whatever? No, no! It was the way of these people, and my dinosauric parents – when they were at this caper there was nothing you could do but beat it or switch off, in fact switching off was the key to survival. It would have been no use if I'd asked: why must I go with him, and he put wood on the fire, and you stay here; great wee Phyllis would not have known it was a question even; she'd have thought I was being rude on purpose or something.

'Are you sure?' I tried, spying pots to be washed.

'No, leave them to soak.'

I went with Andy, who'd been pursing his mouth, and carried the whisky glasses to the cupboard. I was powerless to refuse. I didn't want any more yet the thought of that smooth glowing amber slug, slugging the base of my skull not long after it had slithered down my throat . . .

'Throw some wood on the fire.'

In the wicker basket beside his chair were off-cuts and various bits of wood from the workshop, blocks and slabs and spars cut to length. I built them onto the grey and red in the grate and they burst into flame – dry, seasoned wood. I left a heavy block, 6"x 4"x 4" roughly. Something could be carved out of it, but no doubt it would be thrown on later and burnt by him who didn't work there any more; free firing shouldn't be his perk now.

From the kitchen came the quick sharp rattle of an electric

grinder, the sloshing of water and the water-tempered clash of pans.

The whisky went smoothly down my throat. The need for conversation, music. But Andy was not musical, neither was I, neither of us touched the records neatly stacked under a turn-table. Being 'through' was a silent time. Andy seemed to be thinking. We were trapped by the same thing, whatever it was. Under its cloud we could only drink. Drink was like time, not optional; there was so much of it to get through. Still the need for talking though, anything. We could have smoked.

'That's a fine ginger cat you've got.'

'Eh? Tibs! He's a character. Parading on the window ledge every morning, with his big fluffy tail sticking up! Ravenous! I let him in and he'll scoff half a pint of milk and a tin of food. He's neutered, of course. Doesn't roam far. He sleeps in the woodshed.'

I shook my head at Tibs' habits. I hadn't liked the look he'd given me, nor his thin pink lips. Specially not his fatness – cats slid through fences, padded their path through George's cab-bages, carefully over the withered leaves on the soil, alert for a crust, a mouse, a flying stone, a bullet. Their thin striped faces. The body of one at the roadside, its face expressionless. They should be thin.

'Tibs!' I thought they'd chosen the name as a joke and said it in an amused way.

'They've all been Tibs, every cat we've had. It seemed easier, huh, I don't know why. Hey, Phyl!' he called out just as she came in, 'remember our first Tibs? I've been telling him about the cats.'

'First Tibs was a little grey cat,' she said as if she'd been in with us all the time, and putting a tray of coffee on one of the round tables that were so popular, the kind he'd bought at Paisley. 'She was lovely, wee Tibs, mind you that was long ago. She got run over. It was unlucky, then. Unusual. But we lived in the town in those days. But this daft idea of his of calling them all the same, I didn't know what to think of it!' She laughed. 'Here,' she said, sitting beside me, 'I won't keep you long with these, I know other people's are boring.' She'd plugged in the old-fashioned jug and it made a steady blip and a good smell. It was great sitting there passing photos.

169

Not that they were rivetting. Andy and another couple in and out of a villa. Phyllis was the photographer and I couldn't imagine her in holiday clothes till there she was in a one-piece swimsuit at the sea's edge, a neat little dog. Ma-yorka, she told me, but they all looked the same these places down there, Crete and Spain and Greece, that people went to and showed pictures of, in advert-colours. Could they be real – the blue, the white house? . . . Arran for me, the tent in the sheep-shit and bracken-scented field, but I wouldn't mind a look at the Med, or missed not telling people, that's us at the marina, us at the winery – unrecognisable us – this little place is unique, but soon to be spoilt of course, and this is Pedro's, ah yes! Here it is! Andy has his arm round Pedro, they're grinning like clowns – not a once-in-a-lifetime thrill for Pedro but he's giving his best and flashing his gold tooth. A close-up at the villa, on the verandah: Andy in shorts. A terrible picture of him, taken from ground level looking up apparently. She could have been gunning for him. 'Those are the expensive clothes he bought himself.' She smiled at him. I saw him choosing the clothes with Jill. It was amazing how soon the connection had become part of him. Then I remembered she hadn't known him that long ago.

'Glad I got them or I'd have looked like Billy!'

The other man, in trousers and sandals, maybe stayed like that all the time and kept his legs white.

'Was it the beginning of the holiday?' I asked.

'Aye, I got browner – if that's what you mean!' He looked over my shoulder at himself in the shorts and shirt that would have looked better on someone younger, me for instance. He held the photo in the fan of light from the standard lamp Phyllis had set behind the couch. Then hitched up his trouser leg to show his tan.

'Would you go back?'

'Oh yes, it was terrific!'

'All that cheap brandy!' she joked in a way unlike herself – unguarded – he could have been drunk all the time.

'Those were the days,' he said.

Phyllis offered more coffee but I said I'd have a glass of water before I went. At the kitchen sink I was stared at by the cat. They'd only struck a few blows here but they could go on for years. They'd gone twenty, I don't know how many – they were midway in the contest, with strength in reserve for the second half – like the old bare-knuckle boxing, it went on and on. They'd be an ordinary happily-married couple at a social occasion – they probably were! And Jack and Barbara the same. Mum and Dad too though it had been hidden by them or me. Bloody terrifying.

She said I could stay the night. 'The spare bed's made up.'

'No really!' Spare bed. I don't know why I refused. Yes I do, to get out.

'I'll run you back,' said Andy.

'Go on with you, you've had too much.' Her moderation, terrible. 'I'll drive Michael home.'

'Foof!'

'It's dry. I'll walk, I could do with a walk.' The cool night, cold air.

'I'll run you to the road-end,' Andy said.

Phyllis answered him in her level, reasonable tone of many years, steel and granite, 'Huh, poor weak woman that I am. Do you think I can't drive him?'

The light in the hall was a dim forty-watt. All the same it dried my eyeballs during the seconds and minutes of this argument that was starting and could branch out in all directions for hours.

I went to the bathroom, washed my face, drank more water and went back.

They were standing close together, in heavy silence.

I said to Phyllis, 'Thanks for the evening.'

She was saying something about them being two boring old people.

In the car he talked about a sale he said he was going to. I deliberately did not hear the name of the place. To avoid more of his fantasy I said, 'Your clock's serviced. It's running well.'

'I'll see it tomorrow if I'm in.'

He let me out, turned the car in a wheel-skidding circle and drove fast back up the lane.

I forget how many days passed before he appeared. When he did, I asked if he'd contacted that Major about the clock, now

171

it was mended.

'Oh yes. Aye. Old Black. Bearsarse Black. He wanted another job done, that took my mind off it . . . but I was to tell him when the clock was mended. Suppose I should ring the old bugger. How much will we put on it?'

'You said £400. Depends how rich he is.'

'Michael getting smart, eh!'

'Yes!'

'Trouble is,' Andy pulled his lip, 'I don't know for sure. The word is, very rich, but he's a slow payer.'

'Six hundred pounds.'

'Eh! Okay. Put on a sticker in case he comes in.' Andy didn't seem to care much about anything but got angry about some things that weren't displayed; they were together in a cardboard box. 'Can't you do better than this?'

'It's mostly junk.'

'Wasn't when I bought it!'

'Sorry. What prices will I put on, then?'

'That, for instance!' He'd shoved his hand into the box and brought out a cruet set. It was bashed and the blue glass lining for the salt pot was missing. We neither of us knew the value. We knew it was silver, because we'd made that mistake before – 'Put it out!'

'How much on it?'

'Oh . . . 50p. Put it out! Lay it all out! 50p a time. Everyone gets a bargain. Encourages 'em to come back. By the way, there were two pictures' – he made the size with his hands – 'where are they, d'you know?'

'I don't know.'

A while back Major Black had come in and stared at the clock again. I'd been able to watch him, since he assumed I didn't exist. An expert wouldn't just stare like that, I thought . . . but he was strange. He'd moved from the clock to the windowsill where I'd put out the small stuff, and picked up one of the paintings Andy was asking about, a dingy pair for £16 each. He tilted it to the light, licked his finger and rubbed it; studied the back. Then the other one. He'd seemed to know what he was doing this time and had left at a rapid walk, nodding to me as he passed without slackening step or turning more than a millimetre, out, down the steps, shortest distance to the car.

The pictures might be valuable! Not just valuable! You know how it is with pictures, one of these little dingy ones can make millions. They were of a horseman in hills and trees. In the bottom right-hand corner of each a smudged line of Majorical spittle revealed the name, but I couldn't read it, and he probably hadn't – he would have gone to look it up in a book. Wouldn't have gambled £32 that they *might* be Van Gogh. That man wouldn't have gambled a penny on anything . . . I would, though. My instinct told me the ups of consonants and rounds of vowels would be a name that you'd recognise. Almost every week you read of a bloke picking up a little dirty picture for £16 say and finding it's a Something and selling for thousands!

I'd hidden them on the balcony.

'Haven't seen them,' I said to Andy.

'Two sort of brown ones. They were there somewhere. I priced them £16 the pair or each, I don't remember. Someone asked me about them.'

'I'll look for them.'

'Hope there's no-one tarry-fingered around.' After a while he stumped out.

I hadn't done anything yet – they were still up there. If Major Black had come back I'd have said they were sold – Bearsarse sorting through the shed, bored and casual as hell, because it wouldn't do to let even me know they were worth a fortune; and having to ask in the end if I still had a couple of small pictures he seemed to remember – no, I'd say, a chap from London bought them. But he hadn't come back.

At the time I was going through a spell of being fed up with Andy. His interests were not at my heart, he was too stupid to respect. I'd forgotten about us being friends and I was due a perk, many perks. Losing the pictures, valued £16 each, would serve him right for not being there that opening day. You have to keep things balanced, even in a crazy way like curing a headache by cutting your toenails. I feel okay again after sorting an imbalance in my head.

The pictures were there on the balcony – I went up and made sure after he'd gone. I'd never taken them to an art expert or whatever.

173

He could have found them, known that only I could have put them there, and be waiting to see what I'd do. In that case there was nothing for it but to pretend that I'd found them up on the balcony too – how had they got there? – and then he would sell them to Bearsarse for £16 each. I took them home in a black binbag.

I'd heard just a whisper, a wee whisper, half sentences, pauses and wags of heads when I was thought not to be listening and looking; in the street, Mailers, the office, the shed and yard; Annie's phone calls...ending; the way she put down the receiver; Peter's slowness about the yard and the softening of his face as if the warm weather had come, as if . . . he'd relieved a spell of constipation, as if . . . he'd won at the bingo, as if . . . Andy had been nice to him or Norman had talked to him . . .

I was on the edge of the network telling them that Andy was about to conk.

I didn't know as much as other people, or maybe just that they were better at looking as if they knew. We waited for Andy's next move. It was interesting even if your job was on the line.

I went to see Martin Somerville on a Sunday. He was in his greenhouse. The black cast-iron pipes below the benches were cold, but the sun and a paraffin stove warmed the place, mixed with the smells of earth, pots and geraniums.

'You have to be careful not to give them too much.' Martin filled his can from a tank under the bench and steered its long spout between the geraniums to reach the back row next to the glass. The flowers on the U-shaped bench were all geraniums and the smell of their leaves was stronger as the can touched them. 'In winter,' he added, refilling the can, setting it down and closing the door to the house.

I'd seen the figure among the plants as I entered the drive-way and not known it was him. I'd crossed the grass still uncertain, till I recognised his voice asking me to come in. He wore a khaki jersey with elbow and shoulder patches, and military trousers. Without a cap he looked young in spite of greying hairs, his thin, fine hair sticking up. No suit to recognise him by. More like an off-duty soldier, belt and pistol holster missing, I knew them from TV and he was undressed without them – but he was also a family man with his plants, and children's voices coming through the door he'd shut. He could have been Martin's brother.

'Michael,' he said with his strange, calm Englishness. He'd seen me approach of course, and he was so calm, me coming to his house on a Sunday morning.

I stated at once that I'd heard rumours and come to him for a straight answer because I thought he'd know the truth, couldn't ask Andy, wanted to know my position, and hoped he didn't mind.

'I don't, except I wouldn't like you to think I was going behind Andy's back. You'll be thinking this is a wee bit odd.' He said this in his English voice, this was his style and felt by people to be condescending, not to say creepy. The slimy bugger! An unjustified thought, but there it was. He lifted himself neatly onto the wooden staging. 'I came up here to work for old Willy Wallace. He sold up sudden. Your chap bought it. I didn't expect this. Well, I could have gone back home and picked up something, but I'm obstinate and I like it here.' A spider with a small yellow body bouncing on the springs of long legs was transferring leg by leg from the staging to his trousers. 'I wouldn't go back, I couldn't have afforded this down there, and I'm settled now. I want to bring up my children here, you know, so we're staying. I'd like to stay on with Wallace. And they'll not shift me easy – but I must say I've had my doubts since starting with Andy.' He swung his legs. 'Don't get me wrong! He's a nice guy. But not living in the real world, you know. He lives in the past in a way, but he won't let me get on with it, like old Willy. He don't know what he's doing, to be honest.' Martin scooped up the spider and moved it to a flower pot. 'So, you want to know what's up? I can see you think I'm a blether telling you this much. But hold on –' He leant on the staging each side of him and fixed my eyes. 'He'll have to sell now, unless he wants bankruptcy, and he doesn't. They won't wear it any longer, they'll take the firm back off him. In that case I should probably run it for them till they find a buyer. That's on the cards, for one.'

It would be the moneylenders Drew had talked about.

'Then I hope to stay on if the new owners want me. It's a

175

good firm, Wallace.' He stretched. 'As for you, over there – I think he'll go back to the joinery. But I don't know about the furniture bit. He's not said anything to you?'

'No. When'll this happen?' I heard myself ask.

'They won't wait past this week. He should tell you, that annoys me. Should have done a while ago, because he'll have to in the end. Otherwise I wouldn't be telling you, you know that.'

'I won't say I've been here.'

'It'll not make much difference now.' He jumped down to the floor. 'As a matter of fact, it's not up to me, as yet, but if I'm still here I could possibly give you a job.' He stood with his legs apart the same way as Andy, but his slippered feet looked sort of calm. 'You'll want to see how it works out, and so will I!'

'What job?'

'I'll need what the Yanks call 'a gofor boy', do anything, learn the job. Any good with computers, are you?'

'I've done a bit.'

'Come inside.' We went into the house, to a back room he'd rigged up as an office. The house was dark and polished, smelling of roasting meat. Through a part-open door, in what seemed a big room, was a plastic football, part of the frame and springs of an animal bouncer with a seat, and a cushion lying on the lino – children's voices, a boy and a girl; Gledhill kids, not like him – and the sound of Mrs Somerville's feet, her voice like his, as she passed, getting the Sunday dinner.

His office had a wide shelf along one side covered with equipment: typewriter, word processor, printer, photocopier. He watched me looking. 'This is how it's going to be. Personally I think it's an improvement on the old days, as far as the office goes. I'm not so sure about the workshop. I'd like to be making our own stuff. This is my own equipment of course. It's always been my hobby, but there's a lot of Wallaces' material in here.'

'I'll need to think it over.'

'Good,' he said. 'It's as well to let you see the way I work. The way I think. Nothing definite of course – but we can talk about it.'

'I didn't come up here for a job.'

'No, no, I know you didn't.'

'Thanks. Er – you think Andy'll say something to us this week?'

'He's got to.'

'I'll need to make up my mind when I hear him . . . '

'Don't pin any hopes on that furniture business. I know you put a lot into it, but it only runs because I sub it.'

We went into the hall and Mrs Somerville rushed from that other door.

'There you are Martin. Dinner's ready. Does he want to stay for his? There's plenty.' She gave me just a glance.

'There's dinner waiting for me, thanks.'

'Sure?' Martin asked kindly, and wasted no time after that hanging about the door.

I was walking to the road; I'd been in the house – really in it, not the greenhouse – for five minutes or ten, had said one sentence to her, hadn't seen the children or the rooms except for a glimpse of a bit of one – not counting the office but that was the word for it, office – but I knew it in my heart; it was so familiar, like a dream you have often, of where you've never been. Why? I don't know, but I felt like crying.

A tree each side of the gate had dropped leaves and the dead mush had been scraped into two heaps, clear of the car tracks. The road of crushed stone, untarred, was overhung on the side without houses by dark green pines, and the others that had lost their needles to make a yellow ground-cover marked by wheel tracks. The house was half way up the road. This was the edge of Gledhill, next to the forest, each house in a square of garden, each different from the rest, some with caravans and boats in the ample space, logstacks for wood-burning stoves, swings, birdtables, the smell of woodsmoke, coalsmoke, oilfume, meat and gravy. A radio playing.

They'd not lived there long – but the house had their voices, laughs, whispers, cries, smells and silences in it, tight as a rabbit burrow. A stranger would have made no difference, but I'd gone, and there were four places at table. Martin cut the meat, spiked onto a metal plate with a channel round to collect the juice. Wisps stood out from her tied-back brown hair. The children eyed the meat slices fall with greed or loathing. The other rooms in their silence.

The gravy beginning to congeal on the plates, the meat

coming hot out of the oven for second helpings. She sighing and leaning, passing a hand over her hair and an eye over the children; the girl's teeth braced, the boy busy with a thought she can't decipher, a finger hovering to pick his nose. Everyone's nearly full, it's Sunday. Ice-cream to follow. She swings her foot and daydreams.

On it went. No stopping it. If it wasn't them there were thousands more, thousands more families, all so bloody complete, all ready to go. Christ it was frightening. Ours had been unique of course, in friends' houses they never got it quite right – and here were more of the not-quite-right but somehow or other just as unique as us . . . thousands thousands in rows. I wanted to blow them all up till there wasn't a house standing and the wolves came slipping through the trees.

Instead I went to another house, where I was late, and a place had been left on the long side between Barbara and William. A chicken was in the oven and I got it out as suggested by Jack and carved off a leg, saliva running at sight and smell of the red juice.

Barbara stuffed these chickens with onion and garlic and various other things, and sprinkled the skin with herbs and salt. I gobbled. I love getting my whole mouth and throat full of food. They were talking about the bypass. It had been on the go for years and everyone knew someone whose front door it would pass or whose back garden it would take. Other kids as well as William and Steph got worked up and wrote letters to the paper, signed by a dozen of them as if they were town councillors. In Steph's view – I saw by her vicious glances – in being silent I was siding with the planners. I chomped the chicken and roast potatoes as if I was gobbling their objections.

I didn't care where the bypass went – that seemed a legitimate opinion. The road would spoil some houses, leave others. It might cut through Martin's garden for all I knew. I didn't know where it was going and it didn't make any difference to me. The rhythm of the conversation: high voices of William and Steph, Jack's drone; I knew before I heard them how they'd sound and what they'd say; the ebb and flow, the wave-like motion of the talk was as like the other Sundays as the Sunday dinner was like its forerunners, the line of chickens that, you caught yourself thinking, enjoyed being part of the Sunday ritual. The line stretched forever onwards too, what a thought – I don't mean for the chickens.

Barbara did not join in about the bypass. She told me about the bulbs she'd planted: covered in the ashpit for after Christmas, out there in the soil for spring, and in bowls in the bedroom cupboard, to flower at Christmas. I was leaning towards her. The currents of warm air from her skin, when she leant forward to lift a dish, from the angle of her neck and shoulder, mingled with the food and now and then her sweat. Her long rhubarb-and-ginger hair now pinned up could be falling over her shoulders, round my face.

After the meal we went up to the cold, damp-smelling spare room. We were reflected in the long mirror on the wardrobe. She opened a cupboard and took out earthenware bowls wrapped in newspaper, which tore as it was unwrapped because it was damp, and left patches on the bowls and the soil and the fat yellow pricks of hyacinths.

She set out all the bowls on the window ledge, apparently deciding which to bring into the light. I stood beside her.

She leant against me and our touching surfaces expressed resignation . . . the damp room, the others in the house, these plants, Sunday. We remained without speaking, cheeks pressed together. From downstairs came the whine of motor racing on TV. William began practising the piano and I knew she was listening to the notes too. He played slowly, pausing and replaying and going on, as if following the track of his thoughts. A tear in the cleft between our cheeks seeped and spread itself. She peeled her face away, brought a handkerchief from her sleeve, wiped her face and gave the hanky to me. She looked satisfied and smiled quietly, a slight smile. We carried the chosen bulbs downstairs as William's tune repeated itself.

Peter's eyes watered in the keen wind, and the thin hairs stood on his arms. He hotched from one foot to the other. Why did he roll up his sleeves as soon as there was a peep of sun in December?

'Keep an eye on things, Peter.'

He wagged his head and bustled away, neck shiny and red above the shiny grey waistcoat, to brush vigorously, hissing through his teeth, in the teeth of the wind. No doubt he thought I was taking the afternoon off for a job interview.

I knew roughly where Axton Road was. I thought of Andy sitting on Jill's floor while the business collapsed, as I looked for his car in the grid of streets round about. What he'd said was, he was making a raid on the east coast. 'Raid' made the thing sound like a lie because it wasn't his kind of word, and perhaps he was at Jill's. But the car was nowhere around so I closed in on Axton Road. Too bad if I surprised him, he'd been deceiving me. I just wanted to see somebody. Its houses were like all the houses in the district, red stone, two-storey terraces, small front gardens and longer back ones with a lane between them. It was like my place on a smaller scale. There were cars parked in the road, not many. The point was I wanted to tell Jill what was going on. I wanted to talk to her. I wanted her to tell me what was going on. From a corner I calculated where number 23 should be, and walked past. I went back the other way, getting used to the house, checking if I'd missed anything.

I did the first run again. The numbers started at over 100 but it was a tight little road and they went down rapidly – each house with two peaks, a window below each. Someone had a coloured-glass parrot hanging there, someone had a budgie cage in the window. Further on, in a downstairs room, a tall dark plant covered a whole wall. Then the house with herbs in the garden and CND sticker in the window. The china cart horse on a table beside a brass bowl was one before the brown-painted gate and neglected garden. The gate was standing off the latch; I pushed it open, went up the tiled path and rang the bell.

I just thought I'd have a chat with whoever was there. I didn't want to break anything up or anything, it just seemed that I belonged with them, the three of us belonged together, specially in this crisis. We weren't talking to each other, terrible. I wasn't talking to anyone.

I'd thought it would be a back room, but it could easily be at the front, on the ground floor right beside me . . . my eye settled on a red flower-shape in the glass above the door. The panes below were opaque but a person approaching inside

180

would show through the glass. Silence. I rang again. A door banged after a few seconds; someone ran downstairs – not Jill's running. The door opened and there was a small fellow in a dirty white tee-shirt.

'I was looking for Jill Pellegrini.'

'She's no in.' We looked at each other. 'She's at her work.'

I wanted to see her room. I couldn't think how to say it.

'Is there a message?' His feet were bare and jeans ragged. He looked as if he'd been asleep.

There were ways of doing this but my head was blank ... 'I'll see her again.'

We looked at each other. Who was he? He closed the door.

Silly to be trembling. Silly to tremble. Concentrate on the movement of one leg, forward on the pavement, the other, regular as pendulums, driving jellyness from the knees by steady movement, pumping up out of Axton Road, turning centrewards without a backward look.

In no time I was in sight of the shoe shop. The fellow in the digs might have been told she was there, and she'd really have gone with Andy in the car. Then I saw her through the window – smart and official and calm. Why was I bothering? It was nothing to do with me. And I was going away, but I had to go in.

There were two more women and Jill seemed to glide away, so that a bow-legged older one faced me. I said I'd like to speak to Jill for a minute.

She gave me a hard look, turned and beckoned to Jill and I got a whiff of her powerful smell. This was obviously the boss. As a matter of fact there were no customers, and when Jill came forward the other two hung around near the back of the shop. We were beside the row of chairs and there was an old-fashioned stool for your foot when trying on a shoe.

She looked fabulous. How could anything be wrong. But I knew it was. 'Is that your uniform? I like it.' Her white blouse was done up to the neck.

'Yes. A white blouse,' she said.

'I was at your house.'

She was red suddenly, and her face had been so calm. 'The bastard's run out on me!' she muttered. 'He's cried off! We were going next week! He told me a whole lot of stuff. What's

181

that to me. He's going back to his wife.'

I nipped something between my teeth.

'Why did you come?' she asked hopefully.

'He doesn't know I've come.' I jerked my head at the others. A third one had appeared. In the way of Gledhill people they probably knew where I worked, though I'd never seen any of them before. The connection would spring to their minds, or more likely they knew already, all three of them.

'Oh stuff them. Well what? What is it?'

'I wanted to talk to you.'

'I can't talk to you here.'

'Don't you get off for a break?'

She shook her head and kept looking, wanting me to say something. I'd nothing to say. There he was over on the east coast, probably, standing around sucking his pan drops, quite useless. He'd looked pretty happy in the morning and I'd guessed he would see her.

'When?' I asked.

She shrugged. There was a pause. Then she gave one of these female glances, where the head turns in a slant, left to right say, from high left to down over the right shoulder; and the eyes follow pulled by the head's weight, withdrawn and mysterious, downward, from wide open to half closed, religious. No words. The situation, the way they've been treated, the work of a thousand words, all in the look. It's no use explaining or trying anything wild, you just have to get out. I had to do it without leaving her at the mercy of those women at the back; she'd have been quite the madam with them probably, as was her way, and a chance to trample her in the shit, exactly what they wanted. Otherwise, if it hadn't been for this, I'd most likely have said something for Andy. It would have been a mistake in any case. So to throw those old bats off the scent I put on a very breezy manner.

'I had the afternoon off! Just had to see you!'

Some people entered the shop. Jill began to move away, and the women came forward from the back. I didn't get them into focus although I was looking up, so I didn't know if anyone was watching – not that it mattered. I was only writing my phone number, but anything you did in the circumstances, whatever they were, seemed likely to break something. 'Keep in touch,' I said, leaving the shop, after I had put the piece of paper in her hand.

I pulled the binbag out from under the bed and unwrapped its black clinginess from the pictures, and put them side by side. A strong smell of tobacco smoke and dust came off as if they'd been breathing in there. They'd dulled a bit, so it seemed to me, and the mysterious background of browns, and maybe figures or hills, was the best part. However, the value was in the name in the corner. Nails would have to be pulled out and then the various bits would come apart and there might be a name or a date or a message in the artist's pencil, as fresh as the day it was written. I dug at a nail with my knife but nail and wood were hard grown together.

I went down for Jack's pliers. Were the pictures for me or Andy? I had to concentrate like hell to see this thing seriously, as I went slower and slower downstairs. A sum of £10,000 each shaped up in my head. That would be it; I couldn't keep it all, so how would we share it? I'd have to explain I'd stolen them. I was coming to the conclusion that giving Andy the lot was the answer, as I went down. The spicy smell of Christmas tree filled the room.

'Come and take a look at something, Jack.' I'd decided to ask for his help.

He rolled his head on the high padded back of the TV watching chair.

'We'll need your pliers.'

He had gone to the kitchen and came back with a box of tools. Barbara had asked what he was doing; when I heard her talking to someone else in another room it was a punch in the guts. He'd mumbled something, but she'd have heard us going upstairs anyway.

I told him I'd got the pictures at work. 'And I don't want Barbara to know. She might not like it.'

He shrugged, ignoring the pictures. 'She doesn't come up here.'

I coughed and moved away from him, to the bed where they were propped against the wall. 'The first thing's to take them

183

out of the frames I guess. There might be a name we can read somewhere.'

He held one to the room's centre light. 'An Old Master, eh?' He put in his eyepiece and looked at the signature, and I peered over his shoulder.

'Ends in dt,' he said. 'There's a date . . . seventy-seven, looks like.' He scanned back and forward along the name.

'Rembrandt – does it look like? –dt! When did he live?'

'Search me,' Jack mumbled.

'What seventy-seven?'

'Just seventy-seven.' He took out his eyepiece.

'Let's look!' I grabbed it. 'More like tt. Could be ht. We'll take it out of the frame.'

He fished the pliers out of the box. There was hardly room for us to both get round it. A tangle of arms. For all our size the little thing seemed stronger; the nails pulled chunks of wood away with them.

'Bring that bloody light over.' The bedside light hardly helped with us both crouched there; but nails were coming out as he twisted them – a few broke – and when he'd got all of them nothing seemed to hold the picture to the frame. 'God, I hate this fiddly work!' He yawned and swivelled on his bum, stretched his legs straight out on the floor, back on his hands. His slippers fell off.

I was pressing the picture with my thumbs. What was holding it? I pressed harder – with a tearing sound it dropped out of the frame.

'Steady with the Rembrandt!'

Splinters of wood had come with the canvas which was nailed to its subframe with heavy, rusty-headed tacks and the canvas rusted round about them. It was feather-light in my hand, alarming how light it was. And no names or writing .

Jack said: 'I know a fellow. He's the curator up at the art gallery. A painter. A painter himself.'

'Less people know the better.'

He shot me a glance. 'He's alright. Hide them away again for now.'

His heavy steps slid down the steep stairs. I didn't like him saying to hide them, as if he knew where they'd been, and I put them back in a certain position relative to the joins in the

184

floorboards so I'd know if they'd been moved.

A few days later he appeared in the room, where I'd been spending some time, with a bottle. 'This is the stuff he uses. He says we've not to drink it!'

'What do you do with it?'

'I'll show you.' He waited while I got them out; my hand groped in the wrong place at first and I didn't feel the plastic, and he saw I was worried.

'What are we going to do?'

'Take the other out of its frame for a start.'

'What then?' I kept hold of them.

He flicked his eyebrows. 'See this stuff in the bottle? Paint this on to remove the varnish and dirt. Okay? But first we soak them. I told him what they're like, and he said, with the canvas loose like that, you've got to tighten it before you start. He wanted to see them but I said afterwards, when we've made our fortunes!'

I hadn't thought of that, I'd have to cut Jack in too.

'Let's get it out the frame then.' He started pulling the nails and I asked what the painter had said about the signature. 'I didn't tell him, did I?' He pulled and grunted at the nails.

'Maybe we'll see the signature when we put on the water,' I said.

'Do that. Fill the sink and slap it on with that.' He gave me a paintbrush. 'You can dip them in if you like, but it might be better to brush it into the back. Lash it on. Give it plenty.'

I angled the picture so that the water would run back into the sink.

'I think he meant the back. Do it on the back,' Jack said.

The canvas threw off the water in drops; I had to scrub it in. It ran off black with sooty dirt, and then brownish juice out of the canvas. The back of it was like a wet flannel, and the front just as it had been, but that was in order; the front was to be done with the stuff in the bottle.

I did the second picture and propped them on the draining board, then let the black water out of the sink. Jack had been sitting on the bed, rubbing with a rag at the frame on his knee. The gunge had partly come away and rich-coloured wood showed through. 'That's the stuff in the bottle,' he said, 'made all the difference. See – it's dissolved the muck and not

185

damaged the wood.'

'How do you put it on the pictures?'

'Same way, I guess.' He wrapped the rag round a pencil and ran it along a cleft in the wooden frame, the ploughed-up dirt gathering each side of the pencil point. He had more rags bulging out of his pocket.

At first I thought the tap was dripping. Next time it was more like the tooth of a comb pinged, a tick. My back was to that end of the room. I looked at the door. 'What was that?'

'She's gone out with the kids to "Star Wars".'

'That's funny.' The picking, or ticking or whatever it was, went on. A little thing landed without a sound on the floor, seemed to have come off the ceiling, then Jesus – another jumped off the painting! The size of a lentil – more of them on the draining board.

'Jack! Jesus!'

It was the first picture, but the other one began too – cracking.

'We'll dry it!' I shouted as strands of canvas tore round a rusty nail.

'Not to worry, not to worry! Bring 'em with you!' He was running downstairs. I went after him with one in each hand, trying to go smoothly, and caught up with him in the living room with bits of paint all over my legs.

'Set 'em up here, don't panic!' He took the dripping things from my hands and put them against a chair, back from the fire – he'd thought of drying them too.

He ran a hand over his bald head, and we watched them. Perhaps the loose bits had all dropped on the stairs. They didn't look too bad, wet canvas the same colour as the paint, covered with dirt as it was; the cracking looked kind of normal for old paintings. I kept still, wondering what was the best way to collect the bits off my jeans.

'May as well have a beer. There's a Marx Brothers on – "Horse Feathers",' he said when the film came on.

I remembered Barbara sliding from the chair, kneeling in front of that artificial coal and striking a match, those lazy movements. Ahead of us now on its castored stand was the big TV. Left of it, the paintings leaned upright against her chair.

Maybe they hadn't needed cleaning. I stared at them hard,

to see the masterpiece in them, but they were boring the way they were, brown and boring; the faint chance that they were masterpieces was in cleaning away the gunge and getting a new picture underneath. But I looked at them hard, and couldn't see it – it didn't matter, but in accordance with the boring, ploddy side of my nature, I spread newspaper under them to catch the bits that were still falling off, and brushed down my jeans over the same paper.

The old Marx Brothers went on with their capers and I didn't pay much attention to them, I stuck to the slight buzz I was getting from the can of lager and watched Jack for when he finished his, so that as soon as he'd had the last suck and thought about another, I'd be ready to get them.

When I came back from the kitchen the paintings must have got to the right state of dryness. They were exploding in slow motion! They wrinkled and cracked! The flakes hadn't time for the merry jumps of before! They deserted the canvas in droves and fell straight down and built up a ledge like a driftlet of snow at a window.

'Jack!'

If I'd had the fucking channel-changer on the arm of his chair I'd have killed the Brothers dead.

He gave me an evil look. 'There's nothing we can do. We've got the frames.' He sooked from his new can.

I went forward into the light and gave each picture a dunt on the floor. Only a little more fell.

'Collect that into a box, Michael. I'll take it along and show him. He'll do something, for sure. He might well stick it together. He sits in that bloody place doing nothing all day.'

The Major never came back. The pictures had gone up in smoke from the rubbish heap in the corner of Jack's garden. It had drifted through the barren branches and vanished into the mist, leaving a smell of paint and sacking, even though I'd burnt them with old magazines and papers and the ends of sticks left from the last bonfire. The curator had given Jack a fiver for the frames.

I was glad to see Mark in the café, red cheeks, collar turned up over a green scarf brighter than usual. The steam from the coffee machine blew in gusts each time the door opened, across the smiling face of the Italian girl. Christmas chains looped on the wall behind her and thinner chains, orange and green, led to a fat paper bell hanging in the middle of the ceiling. Silver cardboard bells and sprigs of holly were pinned to the wall above us.

Mark had folded his coat on the bench. He brought out a packet and lit himself one. 'Letting it take the strain!' he joked, waving the match to put it out.

'You didn't use to smoke.'

'I don't really. One or two a day, or none.' He drew heavily making the end glow.

In a while I asked for one. He brought the packet out again from his dark-blue suit.

The strong smoke on my tongue and inside of the cheeks, the rod-like effect in the lungs, occupied me. We puffed away under the holly. I told him I was thinking of moving on.

I had meant to tell him about the collapse of the business and Martin's job, and ask his advice – my state of mind was due to Christmas, when I always get wandered and want cigarettes – but part of me knew I wouldn't take the job anyway – even a speech for Martin was ready, so bad I probably wouldn't say it. After long consideration, blah, blah, blah, long term career, etc . . . It seemed necessary to say it like that to escape.

'You should get out before the business goes any further down,' he said.

'How do you mean?' I hadn't told him about that.

'He stravaigs about too much,' Mark said, in a half-hearted way – something he'd heard, the gossip, that kind of thing. It wasn't Mark's usual way of talking though, wasn't like him – he was not saying something. I supposed he thought I didn't know about Jill. He began to go for the cigarettes and then changed his mind, enclosing the ashtray in his hand, turning it slowly.

There was a pause.

'Do you know Martin Somerville?' I asked.

'The chap who runs Wallaces? No, don't know him. I've heard of him.'

'Oh aye. Would you like another tea?'

He shrugged. I went to the counter with the empty cups and watched the Italian girl scooting steam into a teapot from a spout at the side of her Espresso machine, thinking it a poor way to make tea and being content because it was her doing it … a re-inventing tea … but this was passing through my mind lazily and I was watching the instant liquid pouring from the aluminium spout and the fact appeared in my mind, as if I'd always known but had forgotten for a moment, that Mark had been going with Jill before Andy came along – and he was ready to slip into position when Andy left. I knew this in spite of not believing it.

The Italian girl looked indifferently at me as I paid her.

I arrived early at the office for no reason – I'd woken and got up instead of falling asleep again, and walked through the town in the first light, enjoying the grey blackness. The Triumph was in the yard and the office light on.

The warmth of the electric fire contrasted sharply at the door with the outside air. I thought he was dead. In his chair below the clock – 7 a.m .– in his overcoat, lying forward on the desk, head on his arm, grey hair gleaming, cap beside him. But there was the movement of his breathing, when I'd slipped through the counter and gone closer; he was as peaceful as a baby. Not smiling, but the expression of his face contented.

I went out to the shed and lit the paraffin and boiled the new kettle.

The furniture occupied the shed as if it was alive. The legs of Abe's chairs braced themselves. The chests of drawers rested lightly on their round feet, crouched, enclosed in their atmospheres. The grandfather clock and its aura cut a tall block against the back wall; the bureau included me in its comfortable shape; all this because I was going to leave them. It seemed I'd known them all my life and they had a value I hadn't seen before; they had been silent and hidden themselves when looked at; now they showed themselves openly. I saw them now they weren't tangled with money.

Had they changed to tell me I was leaving, or had I known

189

– without saying – and caused them to change? They didn't complain about being sold and treated as merchandise, and they didn't mind my attitude if only I recognised them, as long as I recognised, you're this and you're that – you were jigged out in a factory and afterwards glued; you were handmade by a cabinetmaker, who's now bones, or not bones – a hole, a space, nothing, while your/his dovetails and polished grain are here.

I made myself tea and was drinking it within the iced windows. The car door slammed and I waited for him to drive away – he might or might not have seen the light in the shed – but no engine started. I rubbed at the ice to see out and he was walking across.

In a moment he had come in the door, while I was standing up, going to open it.

'Morning, Michael!' he said, as if it was a fine morning with clear sky and the sun coming up. Actually the sky was the same grey as the frosty windows.

He stamped about and rubbed his hands as if he enjoyed them being cold and giving him a chance to warm them. He punched one hand into the other. 'You're early.'

'So are you.'

'Came in to settle a few things. I've always been an early riser. Early,' he said.

'Yes.'

He stepped about the space at the door, shadow boxing the furniture. 'How's the stuff going, then?' He stopped, facing me. 'Not well. Some bad news I'm afraid. I'm having to wind up Wallaces and this place too.' He gestured, a wide, open gesture like a foreigner, arms out and palms of his hands flat. 'Your job here, well it'll be wound up, it'll be gone, to be frank – but I'll keep you on, of course, at what you originally . . . there in the yard, and maybe it can develop.' He gave me a most friendly look. And smiled, as if it had been good news. He turned solemn: 'You'll have had an inkling of this, of course. Everybody knows before it happens.'

'I had an idea.'

'Of course you did. And you mebbe know that I'm going back to my old trade.' I'd thought he was going to say wife. Did he know I'd talked to Jill? Did he know I'd talked to

190

Martin? Did he know I'd seen him asleep in the office? His face was open and clear like the day I arrived in the yard.

'This was maybe not working,' I said.

'I'm really sorry, Michael, really sorry. But there it is.' He looked solemn for a time, then rubbed his hands again and glanced at the furniture as if checking it was all there and smiled again.

I said it was alright.

'Oh! that's –' He slapped my shoulder, stood back. 'Now look – no hurry, there's no hurry. I've just sprung this on you. Well, that's my way. You'll maybe not want to go on working for me!' He opened his eyes wide as if, you know, this was most unlikely. 'Up to you.' He held up his hand to stop me answering. 'Give it a day or two.'

We'd walked round each other and I was at the door. Out there the greyness had lightened and Annie would soon come.

'Have you told her?'

'I'll away over now. I told the boys yesterday so I doubt she'll know anyway.'

'Will I stay here?'

'Aye, if you don't mind. If anyone comes, sell 'em something! Prices at your discretion! Everything must go!'

He grinned and pushed past. His square back looked tough again and he walked eagerly, swinging his arms.

No-one came to the shed and there'd not been much doing in the yard. They'd transferred the stocks back to us from Wallaces. Martin had come and I'd told him I didn't want his job, but thanks. I said I might stay with Andy and he just smiled.

We'd got back into our old ways. Peter brushing, Annie filling her chair. I at my desk beside/behind her. You could see it had been no use dreaming about them losing their jobs; they were permanent, solid, Andy could do what he liked, it didn't bother them. I forgot that they'd worried about it themselves, and that I'd thought them soft, defenceless and not worth defending, obsolescent – now it looked like masterly inactivity. That was applied to a king or a politician in history – here it was in flesh, especially Annie, how could anyone shift her? It was funny the way she and Peter talked to me – as if I was a full member now after the rough times. What I'd do didn't bother them. They thought I was okay, I think. If I'd gone to work for Martin it would have been what they expected, but since I hadn't, I was okay.

There was something pretty unnerving about taking root in the place. I had to make sense of it so that it wasn't like the Leeds business – I mean, two places where you didn't know what was going on.

Andy asked me to go with him to a job in the country. The trip out did not get away from it. All round about Gledhill was the same.

We drew up at a big country house. There was an open stone porch with pillars that we stood under after he'd rung the bell. 'I did all the work here once. When Stewart had it. This fellow's not much of a fellow,' Andy said. In a while we went round the back. He knocked on a blue, dirty door, scrabbled by dogs' claws.

It was so heavy, being opened by a small, thin woman. She was also respectable, the lady of the house (even though she wore an apron over her skirt). It was the main thing about her, that she was a lady. Her hair and eyes were faded and her voice drawly: 'Hello?'

'Morning Mrs Black. Andy Crawford.'

She didn't know who he was. His eyes twinkled and drew attention to bushy eyebrows and gold rims. He straddled his legs, once more in the boilersuit, and said, 'I've come about your window.'

'Oh! I'm sorry, Mr Crawford. I'll get my husband. He's about somewhere.'

'No need, Mrs Black, just show me the window. I'll measure up. That will be sufficient.'

She hesitated a moment and he smiled at her. She held back the door to let us in, squashing herself against the wall of a dusty, cold-smelling passage, with another smell like withered apples. Then she passed, her head turned away, to go in front, so that she could take us to the window. It was in a bedroom. The smell upstairs was more like something dried, preserved – a bit like a packet of tea when you open it. The fabulous wooden door of the bedroom had opened smoothly; the smell might have been off it. She started an explanation that Andy didn't listen to. He was pressing the rotten wood with his thumb, throwing the window up with a controlled force, to feel the thin panel behind which the sash-weight knocked on the end of its cord. He brought out his steel tape and measured while she went on about the dampness having come from somewhere and it being a mystery. He wrote in his notebook, and looked over his glasses, waiting for her to stop.

'It could be pine or cedar. Cedar's more expensive.'

'Oh, I'll leave that to him.'

Andy looked at her attentively. She appeared to be reassured by him, his solid manner, and she turned quite sparky before him, her face became alive, perhaps thinking of her new window that was being started at last.

'There's another thing I wanted you to look at,' she said, fluttering her hand at the level of her breast, which was quite full, though she'd made it seem she didn't have any when she opened the back door.

Andy's serious attentive look – the same as before when he'd been a joiner – he was calculating how much to put on, I thought, whether this should be a bargain for the customer, or if it would be better to get as much as he could from this one; it wasn't her he was thinking of but the husband – Bearsarse surely though he hadn't said. And there was the other factor to take into account, that he was a slow payer, the Major. Andy snapped out of it and focussed on her.

'Let me see it,' he said briskly.

She took us into an unused front room on the same floor – a bedroom you would have thought but she twittered something about a nice little sitting-room. There was a table and some chairs, a dirty armchair, a worn rug and the rest of the floor covered with newspapers. They were yellow and faded. I stood on *The Times*, Thursday, 7th July and read the headlines, but the small print was scuffed over with dirty footmarks.

'It's this. We think we'd like to open it up.' She pointed to the bricked-up fireplace. Andy was feeling round the inside of his mouth with his tongue and at any moment would pop his finger in with nail extended for the little tendril of breakfast

193

between his teeth; but his frown seemed to mean that he was giving her his attention.

'I know fireplaces are difficult,' she apologised, 'but we've set our hearts on this one.'

'Need to take out some bricks. Take out bricks and have a look.'

'Would you!' (How wonderful!)

He came in, Bearsarse right enough, his head stuck forward as if he'd been following us by scent.

'Crawford,' he said to Andy, who turned his head slightly, didn't move his feet, in brown boots, on the newspapers.

The Major gave me a quick haughty look. I could see it going through his head – the clock and the question of its price and was it for sale and all, and the pictures he might have forgotten till reminded by seeing me . . .

'I'm showing him the fireplace, seeing he's here!'

He gave her a look, and transferred it to Andy. 'Watcha think?'

Andy said, 'I was telling your good lady here, I'll need to take out some bricks to see the state of the chimney.'

'Well?' – a rifle shot.

'Can't do it now. But when the men are at the window – '

The Major covered us all with a steady glance. Then he stumped out of the room and we followed, Mrs Black last.

It was a very grand hall we descended into, with large mirrors and dark pictures in it. The floor was of paving stones, covered by rugs here and there and two blanket boxes or chests against the wall. They weren't pine – dark and carved, probably oak. The stairs opened out into a shape like the widening of a river, and then poured over the bottom step into the calm pool. I ran my hand down the smooth wooden rail that writhed gracefully on top of the wrought-iron banister, and felt the easy shallowness of the steps. Andy went with a jerky, hopping step, holding his cap in his other hand. On reaching the hall he hustled to catch up with the Major, who'd turned on his tracks, almost under the stair, in a passage leading to the back door. Mrs Black had gone, turned off into a kitchen perhaps.

The Major went past the back door into a small room and kicked off his slippers, which landed one on top of the other in

194

the corner, and pulled on wellies. 'Job to do,' he said.

Andy knew how to handle the situation. He let the man stride away out leaving the door open. He calmly looked round the little room. Then he drew the notebook from his pocket, checked the facts, and we also went out.

Bearsarse was going through a wire-netting gate into a henrun and there was a henhouse in the background. We diverted to the van. Andy opened his book on the bonnet and wrote more calculations, or pretended to, then looked calmly in the henrun direction. We strolled across and went in.

I put my hand through the wood-framed space in the gate behind me and fitted the outside wire hook back into its staple. I didn't fancy letting Bearsarse's hens out. Part of the run was enclosed by a wire fence, the rest by a stone wall. There were some trees, some hens, the henhouse and a round, metal bin whose lid the Major had opened.

Andy held the notebook open with his thumb. 'I can do your window for in the region of £140. In cedar it would be £160.'

The Major looked thoughtful, then angry. 'You making that a firm price?'

'The cedar?'

'No!'

'I'll detail it and put it in the post. It won't be more than I quoted.'

The Major's fingers had been working lightly on the rim of the bin. He bent, reached in with a scooping movement as if for ice-cream and brought out a chipped old cooking pot full of grain. 'When can you do it?'

'Next week. My man'll look at the fireplace if you want.'

'Does he know anything about fireplaces? Chimneys?' He scratched the corner of his mouth. 'Who is he?' He took a step while speaking.

'Drew Aitken. He's put in hearths in his time. Did one for –'

'Yes yes.' Bearsarse walked several steps away and stood with his back to us. 'Chook chook chook! Chook chook chook!' The hens ran to the grain he was scattering in handfuls over the grass. More of them appeared one by one from a hole in the manky henhouse, looked around, ran down a little ladder and waddled to the grain.

'Will next week suit?' Andy asked.

195

The Major nodded without looking. Then he shot a glance at Andy as if he was being forced to agree. 'Alright.'

I'd caught the edge of his glance. It seemed as painful from his end as ours and I found I was looking at the enamel pot dangling from his hairy red hand. He had returned his gaze to the hens.

He looked at them with serious attention, his face grim but the anger gone out of it and almost a smile there now; I saw from the movements of his head that he was watching all the hens, each of the twenty or so who were pecking and scratching in the grass so that sometimes you saw their sharp heads, then the flared-out feathers of backside and tail, with a bare bum peeping out of some. The Major shifted his position, not taking his eyes from the hens while he put the pot in the bin and closed the lid. Some of them were leaving the grain with springy deliberate steps, or standing on one leg with the other claw poised as if they couldn't make up their minds. Glossy red-faced ones still darted their heads at the food; and a pale, orange-combed stick-legged creature pecked furtively at the edge where it had scattered thinly. There were two speckled black and white ones.

'A manger, eh!' Andy had walked forward, pointing at a metal tub lying half on its side in the grass. Two hens were sipping water from it. 'A beauty!' Andy went right up and the hens ran a few steps off with little flirty movements. 'That's the real thing! It must be from the stable?' No answer. Andy tapped it with his foot. 'It shouldn't be here,' he said smiling, but giving the Major a telling-off. 'It'll waste. See the rust on it. You should use it!'

'My hens drink out of it.' The Major lowered his voice at the end of this remark.

Andy raised his eyebrows to make a face as if the Major was being deliberately stupid. 'An old tin would do. This is valuable.'

'Do you have a special interest in them?' The Major asked without expression.

'I'll give you a fiver for it,' Andy said.

Our attention was taken by some action at the side. A black dog, probably a Labrador though so black its shape was hidden, pulled itself up on the wall with its front paws, and dropped down with a whump that made the hens skip. It had been let out of the house by Mrs perhaps – one of her tasks, that the dog had to be let out at certain times. It fawned round the Major's legs and then, the tail wagging slowly and secretly, it sniffed the arcs of grain, puh puh puh, blowing out its lips, showing the red pouches inside; it ignored us, and now the man had his back to us too. He spoke to the dog in a different voice, saying its name. A wind sprang up, flapping our trouser legs.

The Major turned to look at us. 'These things are scrap price. Not worth 50p. Thousands of 'em about.' He spoke without expression again. It gave me a shudder.

Andy nodded.

We walked to the gate and then he started the engine and we were tooling down the drive.

He quirked his eyebrows. 'Some fellow,' he remarked, smiling.

I'd been frightened by the guy, I was frightened and angry. 'A pig!'

Andy shrugged. 'Beautiful place that, beautifully kept before he bought it. The stable and all. It's behind the house there.'

'But –'

'We'll just have to see. It's rumoured he's into money. Could be worth battering away at. Otherwise' – he yawned – 'he'll soon sell up. He'll be out.' Andy wasn't bothered at being snubbed.

'What a pig!'

'You get them like that.' He seemed glad to be back at it, in a way, and chuckled. 'Chimney's a mess, anyway.'

'How do you know . . . ?'

'It was me bricked it up for old Stewart. He'd thought of using the fireplace, but realised there was too much work in it. He was a sensible man.'

'Oh.'

I'd been fascinated as well as scunnered by Bearsarse and his hens. There'd be something to be said on his side if you knew it, some crazy rightness he was pursuing. And here was Andy, back in it, where it was all decided in some kind of way like that. It wouldn't do. I'd get out . . .

Andy swung the van round a corner he'd have negotiated thousands of times. 'That manger lying there. It's not right.'

I thought of a van like Norman's full of gardening tools. I'd get away from being the schoolmaster's son – my arms ached to dig, digging was the thing. The inside of the van: wooden frame on both sides, to fit tools in, secure not to fall out on corners; spades and such might be stuck behind the framework – and boxes of nails, nuts and bolts, oil, wood preserver, string, brushes (for Snowcem too), screwdrivers, wrenches, pipegrip, tap washers, jubilee clips, spirit level – the middle for a mower and barrow, but I could have a sleeping bag and mat strapped up below the roof – a camping stove and pan. A van can go anywhere, a week in this town, a week in the next. Bonfires, the frosty air!

'You're probably right.' Andy slowed into the road, bungalows on the left, scabby railway embankment on the right, the black shed looming ahead blocking the middle of the yard, half the Nissen hut visible. He faced round; his face showed that he knew what went through my head. 'Aye, you're better moving on.' He changed gear. 'Not much for you here now.' We passed the shed, slowing again to enter the yard, and saw Annie through the window. 'Stay on till the holiday,' he said.

'I'll go now if it's okay with you.' The few days to Christmas seemed endless.

We got out and stood in the yard.

He screwed up his face. 'Any plans?'

'Maybe.' There was that van, there were other countries and I was smiling broadly – it could be any one of a hundred things.

Andy smiled too and from the other top pocket, not the one the notebook bulged, he brought out a business card. A. Crawford, Joiner. 'If you know anyone wants anything done –' We shook hands and went on smiling.

198